Chattahoochee

Chattahoochee

A Thomas Night Crime Novel
Book V

Paul Casper Scherer

Soul Attitude Press

Chattahoochee

The Thomas Night Crime Novels
    Book I: La Florida
    Book II: Punta Rosa
    Book III: The Oar House
    Book IV: Indian Hollow Road
    Book V: Chattahoochee

Published by Soul Attitude Press
Pinellas Park, Florida
www.soulattitudepress.com

ISBN 978-1-946338-54-9

Printed in the United States of America

Table of Contents

Maps

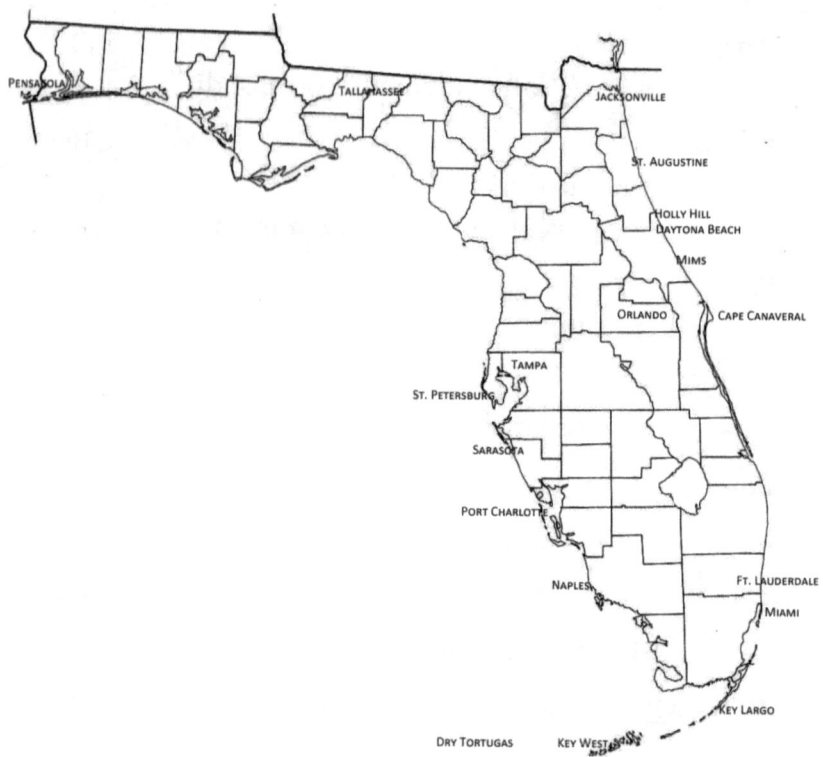

Map of Florida, circa 1990

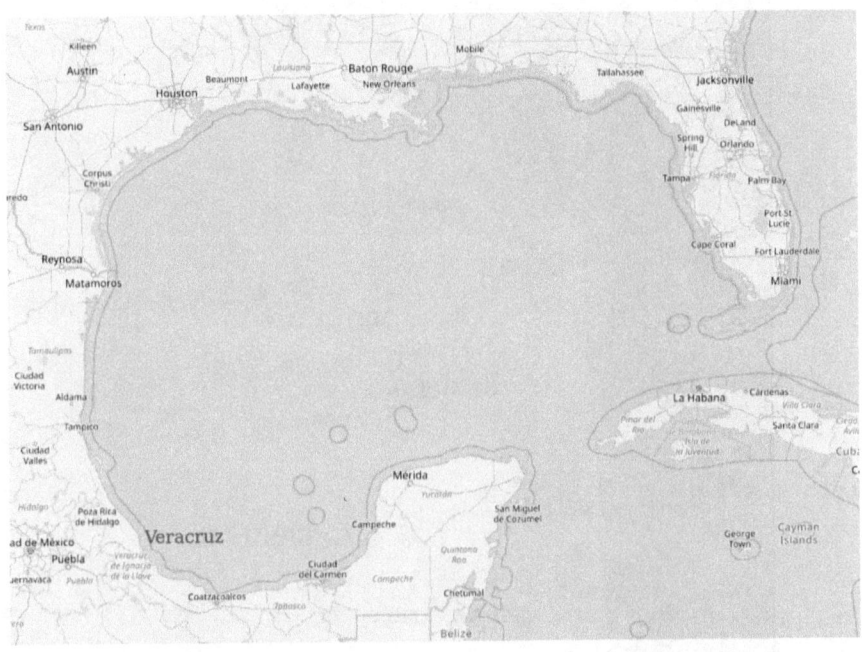

Map of Gulf of Mexico showing Campeche and Vera Cruz

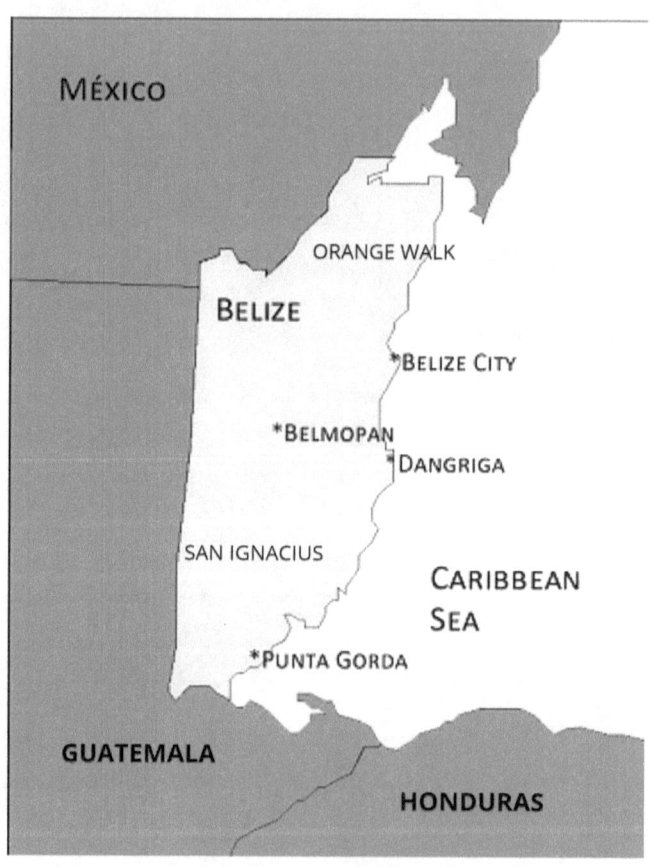

Map of Belize showing Orange Walk Province
and San Ignacius

List of Characters

Francis Aloysius Barnes

"The Senator"- retired State Senator-his family owned Plantation #7 in North Ormond, Florida. The Senator, a widower, organized a company called CCC that owned timberland, saw mills and semi-trucks that delivered lumber to the Northeast US, used to construct housing after WWII.

Francis Aloysius Barnes II

"Frank" –the Senator's son- married to Beatrice "Bea" O'Brien-Barnes. Frank headed CCC, creating the largest privately owned timberland and saw mill operation in the Southeast USA. Frank was the natural father of Jimmy and the adoptive father of Robert, Albert and Jenny Johnson-Barnes. He and Bea lived at the Home-stead which was in Holly Hill. Frank's best friend and attorney is Thomas "Tom" Night. They attended school together at Stetson University in Deland, Florida and they created CCC. Ultimately CCC was sold to JRD, a Fortune 500 Corporation and Frank and Bea formed Homestead Creamery.

Beatrice "Bea" O'Brien Barnes

Bea married Frank when she was 15 and Frank was 17. They had a child, Jimmy, who was born breach. His spine was injured by forceps used in delivery and he suffered severe cerebral palsy as a result of oxygen deprivation during birth. Bea devoted her life to Jimmy and her adopted children, Bob, Little Al/Albert and Jenny. Bea also operated the dairy on the Homestead and developed the dairy into a large milk and cream processing facility that shipped dairy products by rail throughout the USA.

Thomas Night, Esquire

"Tom" was orphaned as a teen. Father, Mother and brother died from pneumonia as a complication of influenza in St. Petersburg, Florida. Tom was raised by two aunts who were professors at Stetson University. Tom met Frank at Stetson. Tom studied law and his first clients were the Barnes Family and their businesses. He began his practice in Daytona Beach and then moved back to St. Petersburg and established a law firm and married Darlene Street.

Marlene James Reynolds

"Marla" grew up in St. Petersburg. She took business and secretarial courses in high school. Her first job was as Tom's legal secretary. Marla was trusted by Tom and Frank and the Senator and she helped Tom and Frank's family and the businesses. For years she was Tom's girlfriend. She married industrialist, James Reynolds.

Jorge Mendez

Crew member on Anthony's dive boat; murdered on orders of Anthony Arnold

Rick Ibn

Pilot and once the owner of an Aero Commander stolen by Anthony Arnold, Winston Grey, David Lucius, and Harish Patel

Anthony Arnold

Owner of the dive boat and treasure; criminal partner with Winston Grey, David Lucius, and Harish Patel

Frederick

Ranch owner and neighbor to Winston Grey and the Grey Ranch

George

Head ranch hand at Frederick's ranch

David Lucius

An appellate court judge, Anthony's alcoholic partner

Andrew Prince, Jr.

Law partner with Tom Night in Belize City

Anna Hernando, M.D.

Doctor in Belize, married to Rick Ibn

John Hale

District attorney in Florida, now deceased, father of Lucy Hale

Winston Grey

Ranch owner in Belize; Anthony's partner; drug runner

Sargeant Major James

Owner of the D-8 Bar

Marie

Sargeant Major's wife

Lucy Hale

Reporter and daughter of John Hale, mother of Lucy Hale, Junior. Lucy Hale and Lucy Hale, Junior worked for the Tampa Bay News Journal newspaper

Darlene Street

Tom's wife and law partner

Adolph Frierman, M.D.

One of Clem's doctors

Portia de Veracruz Botero

Woman in charge of the Botero Cartel

Thomas Bernard

Reporter for Guardiana Newspaper in Veracruz, Mexico

Deacon

Team leader; Rick's friend

Arthur Franklin Thomas

Solicitor General of Belize

Hugo

Albert's assistant manager at lime rock mine

James DeMarco

Working partner at Night, Adams, Street, Alesse and DeMarco, P.A.

Alphonse Alesse

Working partner at Night, Adams, Street, Alesse and DeMarco, P.A.

Jenny Barnes

Mother of three girls; sister of Albert and Bob Barnes; married to James DeMarco

Albert Barnes

Brother to Jenny and Bob Barnes; CEO of Belize Lime Rock, Ltd.

Bob Barnes

Brother to Jenny and Albert; Secretary of Department of Interior; husband to Smiling Waters, step-father to Robert Waters

Harish Patel ... Disbarred Florida lawyer

Karen ... The law firm's bookkeeper and Tom's secretary

Colin Frasier ... The billionaire

Coleen Frasier ... The billionaire's daughter

Bosco ... Colin Frasier's bodyguard

Mike ... Colin Frasier's butler

Mary ... Colin Frasier's cook

A. Hardy ... Colin Frasier's CPA

Patty ... Bartender at the Bell Bar

Eddie ... Pool shark at the Bell Bar

Clem Bondi ... Murderer

Charles Young ... State Attorney

Governor Adams ... Governor of the State of Florida

Greg Teague (GT) ... The Speaker of the Florida House

Herman Moines ... Campaign manager for Bob Barnes' campaign for governor

Smitty ... Bob's bodyguard

Part I

Resurrection of Clemenso Me Bondi

Chapter 1
Florida Hospital for the Criminally Insane

Tom Night had been recently diagnosed with Parkinson's disease. Early on, he had primarily struggled with Apraxia of Speech due to a lesion on the left hemisphere of his brain. Then he began having difficulty with his balance in addition to difficulty in his ability to speak. Then he had a bad fall and broke his right femur in three places.

When Tom had to leave his home after he broke his leg and it healed, he could maneuver short distances with a walker or a cane, but he hit a plateau in his rehab and could not go out of this condo apartment without the assistance of an aide to help him with the wheelchair if he needed to go shopping or to the office. He also needed someone to express his wants and desires if he needed to make a purchase. The doctor had promised that with time he should be up and out of the wheel chair and more mobile, and with more practice he should speak better. But he stuttered.

Tom became depressed. He spent much of his time in an overstuffed chair by the large picture window overlooking Tampa Bay in the condo he shared with his wife. He watched the pleasure craft and the freighters pass in the distance below him maneuvering through the channel heading for the docks.

Tom's wife, Darlene Street, was semi-retired. She still handled pro bono appeals. These were cases no one wanted, involving civil rights issues, death penalty appeals, and convicted criminals who said they were innocent. Pro bono clients were "for free" – non-paying. Tom still maintained a limited practice for old clients. He expected payment for his work.

Tom also followed one old case carefully. That was the case against Clemenso Me Bondi (aka "Clem Bondi") for the murder of Tom's investigator, Anthony Stewart.

Tom blamed himself for Anthony's death. Tom had assigned Anthony to surveille Clem's house alone late at night. Tom felt Anthony should have had assistance. Anthony was shot dead by Bondi's criminal conspirator, Detective Richard Cook, a St. Petersburg police officer who was now deceased. The shooting of Anthony Stewart was performed on the order of notorious killer, Clem Bondi.

Clem was the primary suspect in five homicides; however, he had never been convicted of the crimes. The number of killings would have reached six were it not for the fact that his last intended victim, Regina Cameron, was able to out run him and he was severely injured in the chase.

Because of injuries Clem Bondi sustained when he rammed his head into the trunk of a mangrove tree when he tried to tackle Regina, Bondi did not appear to understand the nature of the legal process and he was declared mentally incompetent and unfit to proceed to trial on any of the five homicide cases. He was hospitalized.

Two medical experts examined Clem every six months. The standard for a court to find a defendant incompetent to stand trial meant the State psychiatrists had to find that continuously, the prisoner did not understand the charges, the possible penalties, the adversarial nature of the legal process, could not communicate with his attorney, could not act appropriately in court, or testify relevantly. Therefore, because he was determined to be continuously incompetent to stand trial, Clem had never been to trial on the homicide charges and he had remained hospitalized in the Florida Hospital in Chattahoochee, Florida.

Tom followed Clem's case through the system. Tom wrote to the State Attorney at least once a month looking for an update; however, his letters to the State Attorney were late being answered, if they were answered at all. Tom's information about

Clem was delayed coming from the State Attorney and normally a response arrived months after Tom's inquiry.

While convalescing, Tom rarely went in the office. He had a secretary/ legal assistant (Karen) assigned to handle his court filings and correspondence. Darlene had purchased a set of computers, one for Tom and one for Tom's assistant, and the machines were connected through the phone so Tom could communicate with the office by email or use of a phone. Tom was embarrassed using the phone because of his speech defect and the advancements in the computer and e-mail were god-sent. The internet also allowed Tom to communicate from home with Alphonse Alesse, who handled all civil cases in the office, and with James DeMarco and Jenny Barnes, who handled all criminal cases.

A few years back the law office had been renamed, "Night, Adams, Street, Alesse, DeMarco and Barnes, Attorneys at Law". Although the firm had been re-structured, Alesse, DeMarco and Barnes still looked to Tom for advice. Tom would spend time reviewing case files that had been scanned onto discs and delivered to the condo for his review. Then Tom and Darlene would respond to questions from the attorneys who were partners in the firm. Tom and Darlene were listed on the firm letterhead as being: "of counsel" to the firm, meaning they held a special relationship with the firm as senior counsels to the firm and its clients.

Tom and Darlene appeared to be well off, safe and secure. Tom's bank, Century Bank in Tampa always covered the law firm's checks. The firm had a line of credit. The firm deposited their earnings from legal fees with the bank and the bank paid the firm's checks as they were presented. Tom's health issues were unfortunate but they could cope and Tom's condition was expected to improve.

Chapter 2

The History of Forensic Patient Clemenso Me Bondi

Clem was awakening from a dream. He was running on a kickoff; intending to tackle an opponent. But then he awoke and realized that he was trapped in bed and that fact caused Clem Bondi the most agonizing depression a human could experience. Clem was not on a football field. He was in bed in the medical ward at the Florida Hospital for the Insane.

The ward was in a building first erected as a military arsenal by the US Army during the Seminole Wars early in the 1800's. Then the arsenal was captured by the Confederate forces in the Civil War. The brick building was constructed near the river in the small North Florida town of Chattahoochee, which was named after the river. The facility was converted from an arsenal into a medical hospital and then later into a mental hospital for the insane in the 1870's. The hospital also derived the name "Chattahoochee" from the river nearby. In Florida if you were "sent to Chattahoochee" you were dubbed insane.

The ward that housed Clem had large windows with screen mesh embedded in the glass. The steel mesh strengthened the glass to prevent breakouts by the inmates/patients. The patients in Clem's ward were not considered likely to escape as the patients were all bedridden because of infirmity or paralysis. Clem was the worst. He was paralyzed from the neck down and could not or refused to speak or communicate. The doctors thought the inability to communicate was probably a psychological overlay caused by his paralysis because there did not appear to be any physical impediment preventing Bondi from speaking.

When he awoke each day, Clem saw the windows and realized where he was and tears welled up in his eyes. This was purgatory on earth. It was St. Vitus' Dance of the brain. It was horror and hot, inflamed. He tried to wish himself dead. He prayed to God for a friend like the one he was for Detective Richard Cook, someone who would end it, someone who would kill him like he killed Detective Cook—a mercy killing.

It was rare that anyone spoke to Inmate Bondi. He was a forensic patient being held by order of a trial court pending a trial on the homicide charge for the death of Anthony Stewart. Because he was a forensic inmate, at least once every six months two medical doctors visited him to conduct an examination to determine whether his mental status had improved and he was mentally competent to proceed to trial.

This examination was required by Florida Statute 916.12 titled: Mental Competence to Proceed. Another statute (916.145) stated the charges should be dismissed without prejudice if Clem was found to be continuously incompetent to proceed to trial for a period of five years. It was rare that an inmate would remain continuously incompetent and unable to stand trial for five years but anything can and will happen. For proof, just read a newspaper.

The specific reason that Clem had been determined to be incompetent to aid his attorney in his defense was because he could not communicate (verbally or in any way) with his counsel. The doctors were of the opinion that he was not malingering or faking a mental illness. He was either suffering a defect of the brain due to the impact of his head with the tree trunk or he suffered a psychological overlay from the physical injury and paralysis. In either case he could not communicate and was incompetent to proceed to trial. The doctors also relied on nuclear testing for their opinion. Regular MRI (Magnetic Resonate Imaging) and CT Scans (Computed Topography) showed there was an infarct or bruise to the brain stem in the area of the stem cell barrier. The CT and MRI depicted severe degeneration and herniation of the spine of the discs at C-2/3 in his neck. These defects of the spine could cause paralysis and therefore there was objective evidence for the paralysis. The paralysis was real according to the doctors.

The doctors were required to treat Clem with psychotropic medication ("any drug or compound used to treat mental or emotional disorders affecting the mind, behavior, intellectual function, perception, mood, or emotion and include any anti-psychotic, anti-depressant, animatic, and anti-anxiety drugs." FS Section 916.12.4c). The hope was that some drug would cure his mental incompetency or disease or defect and he could stand trial for murder, be convicted, be sentenced to death, and executed.

It was ironic that this extreme effort was expended by the state in order to then kill him in the electric chair. However the law required that Clem understand why he was being executed. Therefore he had to be cured so he could comprehend why he was being executed if he was convicted and sentenced to suffer the death penalty.

The doctors used every modern modality to treat Bondi's brain and even reached back to the psychiatric Stone Age and employed shock therapy. The doctors even suggested a lobotomy. Clem's attorney objected and the judge agreed the operation allowing a metal probe to be inserted into Clem's frontal lobe to scramble his brain was not medically reasonable. A member of the Board of the American Psychiatric Association testified and objected arguing that any psychiatrist who performed the lobotomy would violate the Hippocratic Oath which states the physician treating a patient was first to do no harm. A lobotomy would more likely do harm, the expert testified, and no good.

Of the two primary treating doctors, psychiatrist Adolph Frierman, M.D., was the most liberal. He argued lobotomy and chemical and electric shock were appropriate treatments that could somehow jar Clem out of his psychotic state. He argued vigorously for the lobotomy procedure. The other psychiatrist, Gene Chertoff, MD, thought the only appropriate treatment was palliative care. The idea was to make the patient comfortable and ease his mania and depression using the newest and most effective drugs available. Nature would run its course and Clem would be cured mentally and be executed or eventually die of sepsis from his bed sores. A slow death from infection was horrible enough. Certainly, Dr. Gene Chertoff argued, it was at least as horrible as death in the oak arms of "Old Sparky" (the name given Florida's electric chair in Raiford Prison). Of course, the doctors were unaware if the drugs themselves were causing Bondi to be incommunicative.

Dr. Chertoff also pointed out that Clemenso Me Bondi was presumed innocent and had never been convicted of a crime. Therefore he was reluctant to perform any experiments on Bondi. Florida Statute 916 provided procedures for individuals like Bondi and he was to be released from Chattahoochee if he remained incompetent for five years. The charges against him would be dismissed without prejudice and he would be transferred to a facility where he would remain bedridden and eventually die of natural causes.

* * *

Then, just before the five year statutory period had expired, Bondi was dropped by two orderly's who were transferring him by stretcher to the baths for treatment of his decubitus ulcers. When he fell he hit his skull on the tile floor. He bled profusely but remained silent, expressing no alarm or concern.

Clem was transferred from Chattahoochee to Shands Hospital in Gainesville, Florida for orthopedic treatment. The emergency room doctor was accustomed to treatment of inmates and prisoners and patients in Florida's correction facilities and mental wards. Normally the injuries were from inmates on inmates ... attacks, rapes, assaults, etc. This case was much more interesting to the ER physician.

The history showed the patient to be paralyzed from the neck down and uncommunicative. However the ER physician was able to elicit movement in Clem's toes and his fingers. He also was able to elicit a response (a grunt) when he asked Clem his name. The doctor noticed a glint in Clem's dark murky eyes.

Clem was transferred from the ER to the orthopedic ward with orders for surgery to the neck to relieve the pressure on the spinal column and nerves at the level of the disc at C 2-3 and for intensive physical therapy and deep tissue massage to coax life back into his nervous system.

Later, the Florida Prison Board investigating the snafu at the hospital would ask why the ER room would transfer an inmate who came from the hospital for the insane, who was the suspect in five homicides, to the orthopedic department for surgery and treatment without contacting the mental hospital to obtain permission. The ER department said they were not told Clem could be dangerous. The orderlies who delivered Clem from the hospital for the insane to Shands were ordered to deliver the patient for treatment and they were to return to their duties at the hospital in Chattahoochee. The orderlies did as they were told and when they signed the Consent for Treatment form they signed Clem in for an examination and treatment. The finding at the inquiry was that the treatment Bondi received at Shands was ordered by the mental hospital through their orderlies acting as Chattahoochee's agents, and that the ER doctor at Shands had violated no procedures.

While Bondi was in Shands being treated, the five year limitation period of Florida Statute 916 expired and Clem was eligible for release. An efficient clerk presented the court with an order dismissing all five homicide charges. The judge who signed the order did so without reading the text of the form order and without speaking to Drs. Frierman or Chertoff. The judge had been presented with a stack of orders. He signed the orders. With the order signed, Bondi was a free man. The cases were dismissed.

The short story was that Clemenso Me Bondi received exceptional treatment at Shands in the orthopedic department from the best surgeons, therapists and physicians in the Southeast USA and he was released from care wearing shoes and socks, a pair of pants, a shirt and a dark wool overcoat. He was rehabilitated and let go – walking and talking – onto the streets of Gainesville, Florida.

It took two months for the various hospitals, agencies and bureaucrats to understand that Clem was gone. By that time, his trail was pretty cold. Investigators from State Attorney Young's office were able to determine that Clem was first on the streets of Gainesville, then Jacksonville and then Atlanta and Savannah. He was living with the homeless.

After Savannah, Clem became a ghost.

Chapter 3
On the Road

After Clem went missing, Tom Night was irate. He was now personally in contact with Charles Young, the State Attorney (SA). Tom insisted he receive regular reports from SA Young about the status of Clem's escape and his possible whereabouts. Tom wanted Clem to stand trial and face his fate.

Others shared that desire. The reporter, Lucy Hale, had an interest in the case through the State Attorney's office because her father, John Hale, had been the SA for decades. John Hale was the State Attorney who held office at the time Clem Bondi went on his killing spree. Being the chief prosecutorial officer in a circuit was a difficult job. Being an honest SA was even harder. There was no evidence that John Hale was ever dishonest or that he used his office for personal gain or aggrandizement although he held power for over forty years. Lucy Hale hoped Bondi would be electrocuted. Clem's punishment would be a testament to her father's tireless work for the victims of crime.

When Clem went free, and especially when it took months to realize he was not in custody and had escaped, and then when he was sighted three times but not caught, the newspaper had a field day with Prosecutor Young, both in the news and on the editorial page. One of the milder comments printed in the newspaper was that SA Young was a "buffoon".

When Clem went free it was cold and winter. Clem's cover while he was on the lamb was that he was homeless. It was an effective disguise. The bums he hung with were wrapped tight in rags and heavy coats and hats and scarves due to the weather. It wasn't easy to pick out a particular individual from a person dressed as a bum who was bundled up. The hoboes all looked alike. The police had printed posters of Clem and placed them in hobo camps and in bus and railroad stations and other similar locations where Clem was expected to have hung out.

Seeing the posters was a sure indication to Clem that he was in an area of danger of capture. If he saw a poster, Clem took greater precautions or he fled. Within the year after he escaped, Clem had traveled hundreds of miles and worked as a migrant laborer and cotton picker in the South and then in New York harvesting grapes, then out West and through the orchards and the vegetable farms and back to Florida picking fruit. He even tried his hand at cutting cane in Okeechobee but that work was too hard. The Federal Government allowed cutters from Jamaica into Florida with temporary work permits to harvest cane. But even if he was working in a cane field, eventually a wanted poster would catch up with Clem and he had to move on.

* * *

The last year had been hard on Clem. He was gaunt and tough as leather. He was never handsome but now he was ugly, a rough, roust-about brute. He still had a great anger in his heart and he would sometimes explode violently and fight ferociously. His opponent normally also desired the release obtained by combat. He and his opponent fought and then parted ways. Each had ground the other down. Surprisingly, there was no permanent harm from these encounters. Neither of the men called the cops or made a formal complaint. Had the police become involved both of the men knew they would have been arrested.

As often as Clem might have come to the attention of the police and been arrested for fighting he could more easily have been pinched for dishonesty. Since his escape from Shands Hospital, he couldn't keep his hands off other people's property. He had a bad reputation among the pickers and hoboes and he wasn't welcome in camps after he showed his true self with his fighting and thievery. Bondi became an outcast among his fellow travelers, he was a thief. Clem was oblivious and selfish. He had no conscience and felt no guilt for the harm he caused. He didn't care what others felt about him. He was going to go his own way.

* * *

Lucy Hale kept a journal and a calendar. In February she noted on her calendar that it had been one year since Clem Bondi had escaped. She decided to do an in-depth report on the man and the murders he committed (ignoring the fact that he had never been tried or convicted for any crime).

Lucy worked for the Tampa Bay News Journal which alleged it was the "Best Newspaper in the Land". Her office was in St. Petersburg in the Times Building.

The expose' regarding Clemenso Me Bondi was pure yellow journalism. Lucy took advantage of the First Amendment of the US Constitution. Clemenso Me Bondi and Charles Young were public figures and Lucy slandered them viciously in her page one story. Clem was cited for his mean, murderous nature and Young was called negligent and stupid. If Lucy had been found dead the day after the story had appeared in the News Journal either Young or Bondi would have been prime suspects in as much as each of them had a motive for her murder the way she described the men in the press.

Young ignored the story.

Clem saw the newspaper in Naples, Florida about a month after the story had been published. Clem was stuffing paper in-between his undershirt and his jacket for warmth when he recognized his photograph. He read the story and he reasoned that it was publicity like this that was causing the police and civic groups to print and post the wanted posters containing his picture. The continued publicity caused Clem to move on and hide.

Clem decided he would do something about it. He would take action.

The next day Clem awoke and headed north from Naples on US 301. He hopped a freight train transporting new automobiles from the shipyards in Miami up to Tampa and through the South. The train rode through Hillsborough County. At about midnight, Clem was awakened by a blast of cold air and the train whistle. He looked to the west and saw the Sideshow Bar in Gypsonton, Florida. That establishment brought him nothing but bad memories. Clem ground his teeth in anger.

The train slowed near the Port of Tampa and Clem disembarked and rolled out on the gravel surface of the rail yard as the train slowly rumbled away. Clem knew there was a hobo camp nearby and he spent the night. He was not known there. He was given coffee laced with gin. He slept till 10:00 am and then headed into Ybor City for day work. He asked the labor chiefs for work in Pinellas County and was able to find a manual labor job in Largo. Pinellas County was pouring concrete at the new Criminal Justice Center in the Gateway area. Clem would be right at home. He would be hiding in plain sight – a criminal fugitive working among the criminals at the courthouse who were being tried and adjudicated for their crimes.

As soon as the truck brought the laborers across the Howard Frankland Bridge a few of the men, including Clem, jumped and then ran from the truck in order to escape the hard labor. Their intent all along was only to get over to Pinellas County. They had no intention of working. They wanted a free ride across the miles long bridge.

A cop saw the men sneak into the woods and began to chase them. The men ducked through a bramble patch. The officer followed until he realized he was trapped in the briars and he was being cut to pieces by the thorns. The men continued on. The heavy coats and wool pants worn by the bums protected them from the brambles. They were laughing as they broke out of the forest of Honduran pine and Brazilian pepper trees on Fourth Street and Gandy Boulevard.

Clem left the men and hoofed it south on Fourth Street. He figured it would take him about two hours to get to The Times Building. As he walked, he fingered the Derringer pistol in his pocket. The handgun was another product of his thefts. He had flinched the pistol from a bum in Miami.

Clem did not fit in on the street in St. Petersburg. It was obvious that Clem was up to no good, but he was committing no crime. As he walked south on the sidewalk next to 4th Street he was passed by a number of policemen. He looked suspicious but there was no reason to stop Clem. The fact that he appeared to be insane and out of place in the area was not a basis for a stop and frisk. Ronald Reagan had released all the patients from the insane asylums, at least those who had not killed someone. And if Clem was stopped the cop knew he would have to deal with the smell of the man. Looking at him you could see he was crusty. He had not washed in weeks.

But there was no basis for a reasonable suspicion that could be formed by looking at Clem as he walked on the sidewalk that he intended to shoot and kill Lucy Hale imminently.

So Clem was given a free pass.

Clem would be aided in his search for Lucy Hale. The offending newspaper story in The News Journal had a full column photograph of Lucy Hale. Clem had kept the newspaper with the story to refer to the picture so he could identify her.

* * *

When Clem arrived at The Times Building on the southwest corner of Fourth Street and First Avenue South he found a perfect scene for the assassination. There was a small park with benches occupied by 40 or so visitors. There was a bus stop with large vehicles and noise and smoke exhaust. There was some frenetic activity with children chasing their siblings and being scolded by their parents. Visitors to The Times Building entered and left the business through a large door that emptied into the park.

It was dusk, cold, Winter, about five pm, and in 15 minutes it would be dark. The park was lit with old fashioned lights that offered poor, dim lighting. Clem's idea was to wait and see if the Tampa Bay writer and Pulitzer Prize winning author would exit the newspaper's offices at closing time and cross the park and head into the Traymor Cafeteria or if she would cross 2nd Avenue to the employee's parking lot.

Clem Bondi sat on a bench. He smelled badly. The occupants of the bench moved away and Clem snuggled in the corner and waited with his hand in his pocket fingering the gun.

As though scripted, Lucy Hale exited the large doors of The Times Building and began to cross the small park. Clem did not see her at first. He was re-reading the story and studying the picture of the writer. The closer he brought the paper to his eyes the more the pixels separated and the more difficult it was to see the image of his prey. Then Clem heard the sound of a high heel striking the granite walkway. It was like the sound of steel on a flint rock. Sparks flew. His eyes were drawn to the sound and the sight. It was pure happenstance. There she was. Clem arose from his seat and pulled the two shot .44 Caliber Derringer from his coat pocket, then aimed and fired both bullets as he stepped toward his target.

POP. POP.

A woman fell dead.

Clem ran.

There was panic and confusion. Some ran from the scene because they were wanted by the police. Some ran to protect themselves from the gunfire. Some ran to protect their children. Some stood in place not knowing what to do or why everyone was running away.

It was dumb luck. Lucy was dead and Clem got away. Scot free. No one who was interviewed by the police could identify the shooter, not even to say if the shooter was a man or a woman. Lucy was assassinated by a ghost. The police were at a loss.

* * *

A team of newspaper reporters was assigned to the story. The city editor wanted coverage of the incident from the perspective of the witnesses but there were none. They were all distracted. Her family (they were all deceased except her mother, who refused to speak to the press). The authorities (they had nothing). So, the reporters were left to interview each other.

Because of the awards Lucy had won, including a Pulitzer Prize, The New York Times sent a staff writer to cover the story. The NY Times argued she was a martyr. They believed that since there was no obvious motivation for the killing (a jealous husband for example) the reason for the death was connected to her employment – someone she had made very angry through the art of journalism had pronounced the ultimate criticism of Lucy Hale's work.

After a couple of days and coverage at the funeral and there was no arrest, the newspapers had nothing to print and the story went quiet in the press.

* * *

After the murder, Clem headed out west of town to a one acre wood in an industrial area. Clem knew there was a tramp camp there behind The Oar House night club that he had managed when all his criminal problems began. Clem hung out there in the woods after the Hale killing, cussing and drinking and fighting, trying to think of what to do next to show the world that he still existed.

Clem wanted to reload but could find only one bullet for his Derringer pistol. He felt sure he had more than one bullet and he repeatedly rummaged through his meager belongings like a senile old lady searching her purse for a penny. He removed the two spent shells from the gun and replaced the one shell with a live cartridge. Since he was injured hitting the tree trunk with his head, he felt he needed to rely on aids – guns and knives – besides his hands to kill. Finally, his search for the last shell was successful. It was in the recess of his inner coat pocket. His weapon was now fully loaded.

It didn't matter though whether Clem killed with his hands or a weapon, he was efficient. Lucy Hale was dead. The first shot hit her in the temple and the second bullet hit her in something vital in the neck. Clem liked to relive the scene of the death of Lucy Hale in the park. There was a lot of blood. It had been so simple. Clem saw Lucy Hale. She was with a friend. They were talking excitedly. The friend was laughing. Clem got up from the bench and approached the pair of women. He was hunched over. The cuff of his large coat covered his right hand. The hand held the Derringer. He lifted the weapon to her head and fired twice. He lowered the gun to his side and walked away through the screaming witnesses who were running in terror from the horror.

Lucy Hale died before she hit the ground. She fell awkwardly. The placement of her head, legs, arms and hands on the pavement all signaled she was dead. Her head lay in a halo of blood.

It had been so easy, thought Clem. He felt he could kill with impunity with the Derringer. He continued to search through his clothes for more bullets. He may need the Derringer again.

The editors of the Tampa Bay News Journal were astonished that their reporter was lost. They had no inkling that their reporter was vulnerable. Following the killing the newspaper implemented security measures, including a metal detector, to protect their employees, and assigned guards at their building and at the cafeteria and the parking lot.

Chapter 4
The Wood Near the Oar House -A Long Memory

The hobo camp in the one acre wood behind The Oar House exotic dance club was a city of garbage and cardboard hovels. There were refrigerator boxes that were fortified with wooden sticks and the exteriors of the boxes were covered with canvas to keep out the wet and wind. Most of the people living there were middle-aged men, but there were a couple of families and a few couples. The single men were drinkers and dopers, mostly. They worked if they could find a job, but there was another economic downturn. But really, the folks in shanty town were always in recession.

The police rarely came to the camp. The residents were left to fend for themselves and they meted out justice on an individual and personal basis. Everyone knew it was wrong to rape or steal from or assault another member of the camp but they didn't have jails or courts. If a crime was committed the offender was ostracized and shunned, or thrown out of the camp. For some crimes, beatings were administered. Pay-back was a remedy. A long memory was a necessity.

One man at the camp carried a grudge for a wound that was inflicted by an outsider. The thumb on his right hand had been chopped off with a knife. The wound was cruel because the recipient could no longer grasp with his right hand. The hand was useless for any task involving a firm grip.

Clem did not advertise the fact, but he was the one who had inflicted the wound to the man's hand after the man stole liquor from The Oar House when Clem managed the business. Clem's purpose in amputating the thumb was to cause the thief to remember the punishment so that he would not repeat his crime.

When Clem saw the man's face he remembered him and the circumstances that lead to Clem chopping off the thumb. With that gruesome memory came a flood of data. Clem now remembered his entire history at the club. After his pro football career failed he worked for a number of strip joints, first in Jacksonville and then in St. Petersburg. He fell in love and then killed the woman, and he was intending to obtain revenge from Derek Kline, the man who caused him to kill his lover.

A long complicated series of events led Clem to kill his lover and then Anthony Stewart (Tom's investigator), then Derek, then a police detective, and finally Paul, the bartender in Gypsonton. Before all this mayhem, Clem had been assaulted by a hobo who stole liquor from The Oar House. Clem retaliated by chopping off the bum's thumb. When Clem saw the man again after he shot and killed Lucy Hale, he could not ignore the man with no thumb, because Clem knew that when the man realized he was the one who had punished him, there would be a fight. This was no time for Bondi to suffer a debilitating injury. It's hard to be on the run with a sprained leg or any serious injury.

Clem decided it would be safer if he removed the threat. Clem clubbed the man and choked him until his tongue protruded grotesquely from his mouth and turned blue and then black. His victim's eyes began to pop out of his head as he fought for breath. Even Clem was grossed out by the sight.

* * *

Clem Bondi stayed at the camp for two days after the murder. The body was at the north edge of the woods. When Clem saw the circle of turkey vultures in the sky to the north, he knew someone would be suspicious and look for a body. He packed his gear and headed east on foot to his old house near the Quick Mart.

* * *

Tom wrote an email to James DeMarco with an urgent request. Tom wanted to use Jim Faircloth, the firm's investigator, to help locate Bondi. Tom knew in his gut that Clem was the one who assassinated Lucy Hale. That seemed to be confirmed when Tom saw a small story in the paper about the corpse of a man found in the woods near The Oar House. The man had been strangled. They identified the dead man from his fingerprints. A visual ID was impossible because the turkey vultures had made quick work of the man's face and there was nothing left to look at but a bare skull.

The deceased was a small time thief. He was a shoplifter. He had been arrested many times and he was remembered by the police for the fact he was missing his thumb. Tom's brain flashed past details about Clem's life. Tom remembered that a man had accused Clem when he was the manager of The Oar House of committing the amputation, but there was no corroborating evidence except the testimony of a drunk. Because of the man's missing thumb, the fingerprint technician didn't have to go far to find his fingerprint card and make a match.

Tom's guess was that Clem had returned to the area of The Oar House thinking he could hide there after killing Lucy Hale. Somehow he was found out by the man with one thumb and the witness was eliminated. Tom felt positive Clem killed Lucy Hale and then the man with no thumb and he was still in the vicinity. Tom wanted to send Faircloth out to Clem's old house near the Quick Shop convenience store. Faircloth could look in the window of Clem's house for signs of any recent activity. Tom would have done the investigation himself, but he was still having difficulty walking on uneven ground.

James DeMarco agreed the trip was worth the expense, but he did not want Faircloth to go alone and he wanted Faircloth to be armed just in case he ran into Clem.

"Good idea." Tom emailed back and he added that he wanted to go, too.

"Okay." DeMarco wrote. "Pick you up at 10 a.m. tomorrow."

Faircloth had to search to find his .38 Caliber Police Special that had been issued to him by the St. Petersburg Police Department. Since working for the law firm he did not carry a weapon. But today, he felt more comfortable with the gun. He didn't want to run up on Clem Bondi again without it.

* * *

Two days earlier, after Clem had quit the wood, he walked to his old house near the Quick Mart store. It was evening. There were no lights on at the house that his employer, Harry Heade, had provided him as a perk when he managed The Oar House. Clem went to the side door to the garage and found the key to the back door that he hid under a rock. There was just enough light in the garage for Clem to see that his old 1956 Chevy Bel-Air was parked where it should be. It was like he never left; a time warp. He took the key to the back door of the house and opened the door. Inside the kitchen on the hook over the stove he found the ignition key to his car. He put the key in the pocket of his gray coat.

His old "Strato" lounger was in the living room. The living room rug was gone. The bullet holes were still visible in the wall of the room. The wing back chair Lori was sitting in when Clem shot her was the only thing besides the rug that was missing from the room. Clem had hauled the wing back chair from the house because it was smeared with Lori's blood. He had thrown the chair onto the interstate and it was destroyed when it was hit by a truck the night he killed Lori, wrapped her body in an Oriental rug, and hid the evidence in a cypress tree swamp. Clem had no idea why the house and its contents were still intact. It probably involved a civil suit and an insurance dispute. Insurance companies never pay claims until they are forced to. (Deny, Deflect, Delay)

Now that he was home, Clem relaxed and stretched out in the recliner. He slept soundly until he was awakened in the morning by a knock on the door. It was the lady next door.

It's that witch, thought Clem.

"Who are you?" the lady asked the bum. "What are you doing here?"

"I'm Clem's friend. Clem gave me a key. I'm going to clean up and be on my way."

"The police are looking for Clem."

"What's new, lady?" Clem reached in his pocket and pulled the contents of the front pocket out of his trousers. The lady saw the Derringer and she stepped back.

"No worry," said Clem as he replaced the gun in his pocket. "This here key was given to me by Clem. I didn't break in. Here, try the key in the door, yourself."

The lady took the key and used it in the lock of the front door. The key worked easily in the lock. The lady was satisfied the story was true.

"So, you're leaving today?"

"Yes," Clem said as the lady turned and left the house. "Thank you for waking me up."

The lady ignored Clem's sarcastic comment and returned to her house and spoke to her husband.

"Don't you think we should call the cops?" The wife insisted. "I think that's Clem."

"Mind your business," said the husband. "If it is Clem, he'll cause us problems if we call the cops. The cops can't control him."

* * *

Two days later the lady saw three men at Clem's house. Faircloth could see the woman in the window of her house next door and he went to the door of her house.

"Ma'am, we are trying to find out if anyone has been in Clemenso Bondi's house recently."

"I haven't seen anyone there in a while." (What is "a while"? She wasn't really lying, she thought.)

"How long ago?" He insisted she answer the question.

"Maybe two or three days ago."

"That's pretty recent, don't you think?"

"My husband said I should mind my own business." The lady moved closer to Faircloth and spoke quietly. "Are you the cops? The man who was here two days ago had a small gun. It almost looked like a toy."

"I used to be the police," admitted Faircloth. "Did he threaten you with the gun?"

"He made sure I saw it. I would say yes, I was being threatened ... intimidated, so to speak."

"Did you recognize the man?"

"It was Clem Bondi." She seemed reluctant to say it. "I haven't seen him in years but I could see his black, dead eyes. It was Clem."

"When exactly did you last see him at the house this week?"

"It's been three days. I think he left the same day I saw him. That was three days ago."

"Is there anything else I should know?" asked Faircloth.

The lady looked at Faircloth and asked, "Had you ever seen him?"

"Yes, I saw him once. He shot at me once and tried to drive over the top of me. I saw the gun in his hand more than his face," admitted Faircloth.

"Well he's thin now," said the lady. "He looks like he had been real sick. And he looks and smells like a dirty bum who lives on the streets. He was wearing an old gray wool coat. It looks like he never took it off. He has a bushy beard with a lot of gray in it."

"He looked like no one you would invite to dinner, I guess?" Faircloth chuckled.

"No, not hardly." The woman laughed, but she was nervous. "You won't tell Clem I talked to you. Do you promise?"

Faircloth nodded to the woman and went over and spoke to DeMarco. DeMarco had been in the garage. It was empty.

"Go ask the lady if there was a car in the garage."

DeMarco and Tom waited for the answer to the question.

"The lady says there was a car in the garage that was about 20 years old but in real good shape. It had been in a wreck and the insurance company had it repaired. It was painted crème over brown. She says she thinks it was an old Chevy. She says the insurance company is suing Clem for the car to pay restitution for some claim or another."

Faircloth continued, "I remember that car. It was the car Clem drove into the front door of Derek Kline's house during the shootout in Tampa." That was the worst day of my life, thought Faircloth. That was the day his partner, Detective Randell, was shot and died later in surgery.

Faircloth, DeMarco and Tom reviewed what they found. They began to work on the assumption that Bondi looked like a bum with a beard and he was driving the 1956 Chevy. They also knew he had at least a two day head start. He could be in Canada or Mexico if he drove straight through.

Chapter 5
Charles Young, State Attorney

Prosecutor Charles Young had been the State Attorney for seven years. The office of the State Attorney was an elected office and he had won the election for the first time a year ago. Prior to that time, he had been appointed by the Governor to fill the term of John Hale.

John Hale had been the State Attorney for 40 years before he put the barrel of a gun in his mouth and fired the weapon, blowing a wad of skull from the back of his head. He left a short suicide note saying he was sorry for the way he had treated his three ex-wives and his daughter, Lucy Hale, the award winning news reporter. At the time of his death, he was the duly elected State Attorney and Lucy was still alive. The note had a pen and ink drawing of a most beautiful swan. Hale used his right hand to draw the picture of the majestic bird and then he took a gun in that same hand and in desperation killed himself.

Although Tom Night hated John Hale, he respected Lucy. Tom felt she had deserved the awards she won even though she was sometimes over the top when she wrote a news story—not enough fact, a lot of opinion and supposition.

Charles Young was the opposite of Prosecutor Hale. He was open in his dealings with the defense and negotiated plea bargains if they were warranted. If a case was a dog he dropped the matter quickly, but explained in the court file in the text of the Nol Pros the reason he was dismissing the charges.

Tom had even contributed money to Young's campaign. Tom trusted Young to do what he said he would do. However with all his faith and his honesty, Tom thought Young was in over his head dealing with Clem. You had to be as mean as Clem to defeat him.

Tom felt there was a connection between Lucy's death and Clemenso Me Bondi even though Bondi was not connected to the homicide by any tangible evidence or witness identification. The details of the murder in the park in front of The Times Building had all the hallmarks of an act of hate. Hate was typical of Clem Bondi. Tom had a strong, nagging hunch that Bondi was back in town. He also felt that there was a connection between the deaths of the man with one thumb and Lucy Hale. Tom could see a trail from the murder at The Times Building and the death of the man who was missing his right thumb that occurred in the woods near The Oar House. It was like there were bread crumbs leading from one crime scene to another.

Tom knew the police did not see the two cases as being connected. He felt the cases should be investigated together. Tom's hunch compelled him to return and re-investigate the scene of the murder of his investigator's death in a van parked next to Clem Bondi's house. He felt that if Bondi killed Lucy Hale and the bum with no thumb that he would re-visit his old house. He and Faircloth and DeMarco hit pay dirt when the lady next door told Faircloth that Clem had been in the neighborhood three days before.

Once Tom had solid evidence from the neighbor, he called Charles Young and told him what he had. In addition to the ID, Tom had also had Faircloth ask the lady if she would help an artist draw a picture of Clem as he presently appeared. The witness agreed; Tom hired a sketch artist, and the picture was drawn and given to Young.

Tom also suggested to Prosecutor Young that since Clem had a car he could now head across the border. Young said he would give that information and a copy of the picture to US Customs and the authorities in México and Canada. Tom also offered a $5,000 reward of his own money for Bondi's capture.

All of these costs ... the reward, the fee for the artist, the cost of the investigator's time ... were paid by Tom through the credit arrangement – the line of credit – that Tom and Darlene had with Century Bank.

* * *

Tom put his bet on Bondi heading for México. In the 1960's Clem had been a pro football player and he had played a lot of ball in New Orleans, Houston and Dallas. It was likely he had visited México, and he would see that as friendly territory if he had any money.

Tom contacted The Tampa Bay News Journal and gave the newspaper the exclusive story of the information that he had discovered; however, he left out the part about the identification of Clem Bondi by the lady who lived in the house next door to Clem's old house. Tom was afraid the lady would be in danger. The newspaper ran a front page story with Clem's recent picture by the sketch artist. The story related that Clem may be driving a cream over brown colored 1956 Chevrolet sedan and that he was armed with a Derringer pistol and that he was the suspect in the deaths of seven people. The story also mentioned the $5,000 reward. Charles Young felt the reward would stir the pot and put pressure on Clem. Newspapers in the southern USA picked up the story and were running it on the front page.

Now they had to wait and react. Tom felt that Clem would make the next move.

Chapter 6
Stash of Cash

Detective Richard Cook and Clemenso Me Bondi had grown up together in Daytona Beach, on the East Coast of Florida. They were both wild kids. Cook went to college and became a cop and was promoted to the rank of detective on the force in St. Petersburg on the West Coast of Florida. Clem played football in college and then played in the professional leagues for the Bears in Chicago and then the Sharks in Jacksonville. He was injured and dropped from the team and he took a job as a bouncer at a topless night club in Jacksonville. Ultimately, Clem was promoted to manage The Oar House in St. Petersburg. Cook and Bondi re-connected and became the same bad pair they had been as kids. Only now that they were fully grown they had the power to inflict real harm on folks. Both men were big and strong and had been trained to hurt their fellow human beings. They were both gladiators.

The Oar House was connected to organized crime. The syndicate supplied Cook and Bondi with the opportunity for side work, mostly collections where they were hired as the enforcer of last resort to extract debts from people who owed organized crime. Cook and Bondi were collecting blood from a stone. They were normally paid a percentage of what they could force from the debtor. The pair would split the fee 50/50.

After working for a couple of years as enforcers each of them had put aside over $32,000. Both of the men had squirreled the money away in the walls of their homes, waiting for the day when they really needed the money. Cook never was able to use his stash. He had a stroke, died, and the money was found in his house and it became part of his estate on his death. It was devised to his mother, who still lived in Daytona Beach. Cook's mother gifted the cash to the Catholic Church, suspecting the money was ill-gotten gains, and she wanted nothing to do with it.

Bondi had his money wrapped in a brown paper bag hidden in a heater duct in the attic of his house near the Quick Stop shop. He never retrieved the cash before he was injured and admitted to the hospital in Chattahoochee. When he returned to his home and retrieved his car he grabbed the packet of cash. He drove his Chevy north on Interstate Highway 75 until he was out of Florida. Then, in Tifton, Georgia, he sold the car to an antiques dealer for $3,500. It was a great deal. He had only paid $800.00 for the car when he first bought it used. Now the car was considered a classic and had greatly appreciated in value.

Clem got back on the road. He didn't have to walk anymore; he was flush, he could ride the bus. He took a circuitous route through the USA like he was riding a pancetta, the wooden play piece on a Ouija board. He didn't know where he was going. He rode into a town on a bus and then stayed a day in a flop house and then he was gone on another bus.

On a whim he headed northwest. When he arrived in Wichita, Kansas, Clem saw the newspaper with the article about him and the police sketch. He read the story. He knew the snitch had to be the lady who lived next door to his house in St. Pete. It drove him crazy. He wanted to return to St. Petersburg immediately and poke out her eyes, but he was able to stifle the urge. If he went back to St. Petersburg, he would be caught by the police. He took a room in the Wichita Inn and Motel and bought a razor and soaped up in the shower and shaved off all his body hair. He looked like a hairless cat. He was nothing but skin, muscle and sinew. But though he looked weird he no longer looked like the artist rendering in the newspaper. He even bought new clothes in a thrift store. He found old army boots, 'hippy' bell bottoms, a silk 'Nik Nik' shirt and a heavy sweater. Again, he looked weird and flamboyant. He tossed the old, smelly, gray jacket.

He got back to the Trailways' Bus Station and laid $100 on the counter and said, "Take me south, as far as I can go on this bill."

The manager gave Clem a ticket.

Clem climbed in the bus and fell asleep.

* * *

It was a Mexican policeman who jostled Clem awake. The bus was in the City of Matamoros, Tamaulipas Province, the sister city of Brownsville, Texas. Brownsville is the southern-most city in Texas. The ticket taker at the Trailways' Bus station in Wichita took Clem literally when he asked to be driven as far south as you go in Texas.

Bondi was rousted out of the bus and into the station in Matamoros. He went to a tamale vendor in la tacqueria and gave her a ten dollar bill. She loaded him up with tamales and handed him a bottle of Pecos Pete hot sauce and a brown bottle of 'Dos XX' beer.

Clem sat down on a bench and a local Mexican police officer came over to him and put a picture of a man with a beard next to his face to compare him with the image. Clem pulled the officer's hand around so he could see the picture the officer was comparing him to.

Clem laughed and he said, "No, no, that's not me." and he laughed some more. Clem recognized the picture was one of him taken some years back when he had hair on his head and his face.

The officer went over to another man and compared the sketch to the face of the other man sitting on the bench. The policeman checked every male in the taqueria/bus station. No luck. The officer would not win a kewpie doll. Clem guessed the officer would have been paid a handsome reward if he had recognized and been able to arrest Clemenso Me Bondi.

The policeman went outside to wait for the next bus. Clem decided he best get out of this city and head farther south into Mexico.

Clem was balancing his box of tamales when he went to the ticket kiosk in the center of the room and pointed at the map of

Mexico, and said, "Veracruz, por favor," in his best Tex/Mex accent. The station master began to speak very quickly. Clem ignored him and repeated, "Veracruz, por favor."

The station master continued to speak quickly in Spanish and finally became exasperated and said, "Vamoose, Senor." Clem could not understand why the bus agent was so rude. Clem became angry. It was times like this that he would explode violently. If he did so he would be noticed and arrested.

A woman in a shawl came over and stood beside Clem and took his arm and began to speak to Clem politely in Spanish and she addressed the ticket taker as though both understood her and each other. She reached into Clem's pocket and removed a Ben Franklin and paid for two tickets to Veracruz and then gave Clem one ticket and the change. The woman continued to jabber at Clem and placed the other ticket in her purse. He did not understand a word of it. She directed Clem to a table and sat with him as he finished his beer and tamales.

When the bus to Veracruz arrived for boarding they both entered the vehicle with the woman continuing to speak non-stop in Spanish and she sat next to Clem until the bus left the station. Then she took her bag and moved to a seat with another woman in the back of the bus and Clem fell asleep as the bus headed south.

* * *

When the bus was within an hour of the City of Tampico, Tamaulipas Province, Mexico, the woman in the shawl returned to the seat next to Clem and she began speaking to him in Spanish. She was telling him the passengers would have to board another bus in Tampico for the final leg of the trip along the coast and the Bay of Campeche to Veracruz.

Clem did not understand a word of what she said at first, but then he picked up a word here and there. He did not understand the words, could not translate the words, but the words themselves were familiar. Picking fruit had introduced Clem to

Hispanics. He never learned to speak Spanish but he listened to them speak and understood a word or phrase. Clem began to get a sense of meaning from the flow of words from the woman sitting beside him and he began to nod appropriately as the words gushed from the woman.

Then Clem began to recognize there were some English words being spoken by the woman. "We are 20 minutes from Tampico. We need to stay together there. The police are a swarm of bees when a bus arrives. They are always alert, looking for someone to arrest. You are the same height as my brother and you are bald like him. You will be my brother. Here is his wallet. You must have identity papers or they will arrest you."

Clem nodded. He understood.

She handed him an old black piece of leather containing official identification papers and small denomination Mexican currency. The wallet was held together with a thick rubber band. She continued, "My brother's name is Pedro Botero. Let me speak if the police approach us. I will tell the officer that you are dumb and cannot speak. I will tell them I am taking you to the doctor in Veracruz."

Clem looked at the woman and said nothing. He understood the role he needed to play to avoid arrest.

From that point of the trip until they reached Tampico the woman sat next to Clem and made comments such as, "Who choses your clothes? We need to get you dressed more like the locals."

Clem nodded appropriately.

The bus followed the Panuco River into Tampico, a business and industrial center of 200,000 people. There was a large plaza downtown with many people milling about. It was very festive and there was a dais set up in the corner of the plaza and there was a man speaking into a microphone.

"They are having elections," explained the woman. "They are giving speeches."

Clem nodded.

The amplifier was very loud and the speaker system crackled as the candidates spoke. The crowd, maybe 500 strong, seemed attentive and Clem noticed they were laughing. The crowd was in on the joke.

The bus swung into the parking lane in the bus station just outside the plaza. Together the pair exited the vehicle and lined up to retrieve the woman's baggage. The woman was returning from a trip to the USA and she had bought many products and items of clothing to resell to pay for the expense of the trip.

The pair stood in line. The woman grabbed her baggage and enlisted Clem to help move the luggage to the new bus. The police were there as she had forewarned. They swarmed around and isolated a man with a beard who was about 50 years old and Clem's height and weight. The police began to question the individual vigorously. The woman stayed close to Clem and if a policeman began to come their way she intervened and told the officer they were on the way to Veracruz to see the doctor.

When the officer began to question Clem, the woman interrupted.

"My brother cannot speak," she explained. "His name is Pedro."

Clem smiled appropriately and nodded.

She produced their bus tickets and she gave the police the old wallet and their identification papers. Then the woman began to prattle on incessantly. The police abandoned the pair and let them go on to the next bus for the last leg of the trip to Veracruz.

* * *

Veracruz ('The True Cross'), Mexico's largest port city, was the site of Hernan Cortes' landing in Mexico on the Gulf of Mexico. Cortez established a settlement and port to use for his conquest of the Aztecs and the theft of the natives' gold in the early 1500's. Present day it was an energy center and had a nuclear power plant, and was the base for the country's oil industry.

The city was very large. It was modern but polluted with brown/ yellow air. It had an historic plaza, and hotels designed in a mode thought and intended to emulate Spanish construction and design.

During the trip from Tampico to Veracruz, the woman explained to Clem that her name was Portia Botero de Veracruz. Her family had lived in Veracruz province west of the city of Veracruz on the trail of the march Cortes, the conqueror, took to Mexico City. The Botero family was poor and had lived for 300 years on the same 500 hectares of land, growing agave and sugar cane and manufacturing tequila and rum. They were poor businessmen and had turned to smuggling to make their way. Her brother was a drug smuggler. The brother who owned the wallet they used to disguise Clem's identity from the police in Tampico was in jail. Portia needed to replace Pedro in the family business.

It was a point of pride when Portia Botero de Veracruz described the family enterprise to Clem. She said that in the past her family had smuggled rum into the US to the Port of Tampa during Prohibition.

She continued, "We need help in our enterprise in Central America. In Belize particularly, we have no one to act as an enforcer for our operations. I know your story. You are on the run. I read about you in the newspaper in Houston. You have special talents. We could hide you and in return you could work for us."

Clem looked at Portia Botero de Veracruz with his liquid black, murky eyes. Why should I trust her to do as she says, he thought. She will turn me in to the police. Better I should kill her if she knows me.

Portia Botero de Veracruz anticipated Clem's reluctance and the danger she was in and said, "You can trust me."

"Maybe I will for a while." He nodded his assent to her proposal.

Chapter 7
The Ghost

Like a spirit, once he entered Mexico Clemenso Me Bondi bled into the background. There was no trace of him in the United States. Tom's hunch that he would leave the country was substantiated by a report from the police in Tampico, Mexico, that he had been sighted there in the local bus station near the Plaza de Armas. The confusing aspect of the report was the fact that Clem was with a Mexican woman. The woman was properly dressed and was in her early 40s. 'Matronly' was the word used to describe her. A matron was hardly thought to be the type of woman Clem would travel with.

Tom sent Jim Faircloth on Air Mexicana to speak to the policeman in Tampico who claimed he saw Clem. Faircloth had copies of various photographs, pictures and sketches of Clem. He flew into Veracruz and then drove north to Tampico on the super highway that the federal Mexican authorities were building through the State of Veracruz with much of their oil money. The corporation, Pemex, was headquartered in Mexico City, up the Cortez Highway from Veracruz.

Faircloth spoke to the officer in the presence of the Chief of Police, who acted as translator.

"Can you describe the man?"

"He was taller than me and I am six foot two. He weighed 210 pounds or so. He was bald and shaven. He had black, dead eyes. His face looked pasty, like he had been sick at some point in his life."

"Did he have any difficulty walking?"

"No."

"Anything else?"

"He wore strange clothes, like a hippie from the 1960s."

"Have you seen him since?"

"No. I don't think he is still here in Tampico. We have been looking for him. We are aware there is a $5,000 reward for his capture."

"Tell me about the woman."

"She was middle-aged. She looked like a Senora, married, but not to the suspect. She was very normal ... plain. I remember she said the man was her brother and she showed me an old leather wallet. She called him 'Pedro' and said he could not speak. They were going to visit the doctor in Veracruz."

"Had you seen her before?"

"I think so. I think she re-sells clothing she buys in Texas. She is like a mule. I have seen her in the past but I never spoke to her before. She may travel through the area and I have seen her in the bus station. She is harmless to our knowledge."

The officer was lying. He knew the woman to be involved in the Botero Cartel. The police collected payoffs from the cartel. The relationship between the police and the cartel had existed for decades.

Faircloth took out the sketches and photographs. The police officer identified the photograph taken of Clem in Florida Hospital for the Criminally Insane as being the man with the woman in the bus station. Faircloth then asked the chief if he would call the Chief in Veracruz. Faircloth wanted to meet with the chief there. The accommodation was made. Veracruz was on the road on his way back to the airport for his flight back to Tampa.

* * *

The Police Chief in Veracruz made copies of the photographs. Faircloth had also had 500 copies of wanted posters with Clem's picture that could be circulated around the city. The posters advertised the $5,000 reward for Clem's capture. The Police Chief required a service fee of $500 to have his men post the notices. Faircloth agreed but thought, all these nickels and dimes, how is Tom going to pay for all this expense? The chief took Faircloth's personal check. Faircloth would be reimbursed by Tom personally, at least that is the way things always seemed to work out.

During the conversation with the chief Faircloth asked about the woman who was reportedly with Clem. Just as with the authorities in Tampico, the Police Chief agreed that the woman was not known to the police except as an honest business woman. The police did not mention the Botaro Cartel.

While Faircloth was meeting with the Chief in Veracruz there was another man present in the chief's office who was identified to Faircloth as a detective. When Faircloth finished his business the detective volunteered to drive Faircloth to the airport. The detective spoke English fluently. When they arrived at the airport, Faircloth invited the man to stay and have a drink. The detective suggested a Tequila Sunrise.

"Interesting that we should be drinking tequila," said the detective as he lifted his glass.

"Why is that?"

"There is a drug cartel here in Veracruz on the Cortez trail that uses its tequila factory as a front for its drug activities. The cartel is run by a woman named Portia Botero. She has a brother named Pedro, who is in prison."

Faircloth wondered why the chief did not mention that fact if it was so well known.

"Did you ever visit the factory?" asked Faircloth.

"No, not if I wanted to remain alive. The Botero clan would know I am the police. The woman who runs the cartel knows the police and the police know her and they accommodate each other."

"I see." Faircloth pulled on the lobe of his ear. "So, I have been made a fool?"

"It is lucky you are not dead. The cartel is very violent. They get their way by killing and torturing their enemies."

"Why don't the authorities take action and arrest the members of the cartel?"

"The cartels are stronger than the local police or even the Federal Authorities. I am sorry to admit to you that the cartels control the police."

"How would you investigate the Botero Cartel to see if this man, Clem, is working with the Botero Cartel?"

"A reporter for the newspaper may talk to you and share information. The press is the only entity that has the cajones to cross the cartels."

"Can you help me with a name?"

"Speak to Thomas Bernard at the Guardiana Newspaper. But please do not use my name."

"I won't," said Faircloth. "I will do as you ask."

* * *

Faircloth called Tom and updated him before he boarded the Mexicana Airlines flight for Tampa. After hearing the information Faircloth had gathered, Tom asked if he wanted to stay overnight in Veracruz and speak to the reporter the next day. Tom said he would contact the editor of the newspaper and see if the reporter would speak to him. Faircloth agreed that made sense and he took a room at the hotel in the airport.

* * *

The bidet in the bathroom at the hotel was intriguing to Faircloth. He turned the handle and leaned over the fountain of water and felt its warmth on his hands. The Airport Hotel at the international airport at Veracruz had a four star rating. The hotel restaurant shared the same rating. The eye to detail and the attention the staff paid to the guests and the care taken with the facility made the difference between this hotel and a good hotel in the States. There were flowers from the jungles, bromeliads and orchids, rare and exotic, that adorned the main guest areas and hallways. The hotel had a staff botanist to care for the flora. The botanist had his headquarters in a green house on the roof of the hotel. Guests did not miss the opportunity to tour the garden. The botanist was always devising new colors and varieties of native plants. Faircloth took the tour of the greenhouse and had dinner. When he returned to his room he was tired but he had a message from the office.

With the grace period he got for the earlier time zone Faircloth was able to call back to the office before 5 pm EST. Karen, Tom's secretary, had word that Tom had spoken to the Editor of Guardiana (The Guardian), a Veracruz newspaper. The investigative reporter, Thomas Bernard would speak to Faircloth at the office in the evening tomorrow. Karen had also made return plane reservations.

* * *

Faircloth had a wife and two teenagers. He really did not want to be away for three nights. He called home. The news was the same; boring and yet wonderful. The kids were doing homework. They had reluctantly done their chores. Nothing had broken in the house that needed an immediate fix. Faircloth was the handyman around the house.

Faircloth's wife Jane suggested he could go shopping for her birthday while he waited for his appointment with the reporter the next evening. He said he would ask the concierge where to shop. The street the hotel was on seemed to have very expensive stores. Faircloth kidded his wife that he would ask for the nearest J.M. Fields or Montgomery Ward. Typical, thought Jane. Faircloth described the fountain in the bathroom to this wife. She explained the use of the bidet and explained twice that the stream of water was not to be used for drinking.

* * *

Faircloth slept in. He had a continental breakfast in the hotel dining room and spoke to the concierge about where he could find a gift for his wife that would be very nice, but in his price range. He was directed to a department store that specialized in consumer goods from the region. There was pottery and weavings, clothing, shoes and handbags. Faircloth thought the leather goods were the best deal and he relied on a sales woman to choose a handbag. His purchase was wrapped. They would deliver the gift to his hotel and it would be waiting for him, wrapped and ready to present to his wife.

Faircloth had spent $200 US for the gift. Exorbitant, he thought, but his wife deserved something special.

Faircloth had the rest of the morning and the afternoon to kill so he spoke to the concierge, who suggested he hire a cab and take a trip to sightsee through the city. He was told the drivers all spoke English.

Faircloth was interested in seeing the antiquities in the city and they drove past a couple of archeological sites, but then the driver was hesitant to leave the city. As they reached the outskirts of the city, the driver said he would not go any further. He said he was embarrassed to explain that the drug cartels controlled the road from that point west. It was too dangerous to proceed further. The driver went on to say that the cartels were in a war outside city limits and civilians were in the crossfire.

Faircloth agreed to limit their trip, but asked where they could have a good local meal. The driver took Faircloth to a tacoria restaurant. The eatery was full of locals, and Faircloth tasted the language and the food. The driver ordered for both of them. There was a mariachi band outside and good Mexican fare: beef, chicken, rice, corn, potatoes, beans and squash.

Faircloth needed a nap ... too much good food. He asked the driver to return to the hotel. As they drove back, the driver mentioned that they had company. There was an old car, a VW Beetle that was following them back into the city.

Faircloth's driver became nervous. At a traffic circle that diverted traffic from the circle throughout the city the vehicles, mostly VW Beetles, bunched up and the car following the cab was able to move closer and came to the side of the taxi. Faircloth looked to his right and he was able to see the driver of the VW that was in pursuit.

The driver was a large bald man who snarled at Faircloth. The man's body was so large that he occupied the entire front of the Beetle automobile. The man was hairless. He was very animated. He was bouncing in the seat and causing the small car to bounce too. Faircloth could see the man was yelling at him; cursing him.

The man was pointing the index finger of his right hand at the cab driver and motioning him to pull over. The driver shook his head and was able to pull away from the VW and make his turn away from the traffic circle so he could head back to the hotel. The driver took a pair of rosary beads that were hanging from the rear view mirror and he began to finger the cross and mumble a prayer. The driver was sweating.

Faircloth did not understand the danger he had just faced and from which he was lucky enough to escape.

At the hotel, the cab driver spoke to the concierge and explained the incident at the traffic circle. The driver felt the man in the VW intended to kidnap Faircloth.

The concierge explained to Faircloth what the driver was saying and he carefully stated that he needed to be more careful where he traveled. He explained that there was a reason that there was a fence that surrounded the hotel; there were armed guards within the enclosure. He was advised to stay within the confines of the fence. Faircloth said he understood.

"This area is guarded for your protection." The concierge pointed out that there were armed guards surrounding the hotel. "It is very expensive to protect our guests. Please do not make it harder by allowing our security to be tested against the wolves who are at the door."

Faircloth again apologized to the concierge.

Before he was driven to the La Guardiana newspaper to meet with the reporter, Thomas Bernard, Faircloth called and spoke to Tom and told him what had occurred at the traffic circle. Tom listened very carefully.

"Did you recognize the driver of the VW Beetle?" Tom asked.

"No."

"Was it Clem?"

Faircloth considered the possibility.

"Maybe ... probably. I do not know. I had the feeling I had seen him before, but this man was very large. He was bigger than I remember Clem to be. Also, he was bald and he had no facial hair. He did not even have eyebrows." Faircloth paused. "I wish I could have seen his eyes. I would have been able to recognize him from his eyes. My memory is that his eyes were dark black pools."

"If it was Clem then we have to assume you are in danger and the incident was not a random attack. I want you to come back home now," said Tom.

"I think that is rash. I can be attacked just as easily by Clem in the States as here in Mexico."

Tom paused. "We have to assume we are in jeopardy of Clem so long as he is out of jail."

"But how can you trust the authorities can keep him in prison?" asked Faircloth.

"I do not know. We have to trust something in the system. If we can get Clem to the United States and if he is held on death row, the prison system should be able to hold him."

"I am going to stay here and meet with the reporter." Faircloth decided. "I will be extra careful and I will be home soon."

Chapter 8
The Guardiana

The city room of The Guardiana (The Guardian) Newspaper was noisy with reporters punching away at the keys of old mechanical typewriters. The telephones were ringing and there were reporters in "the pit", an area of desks in the center of the room. Some writers were talking, but actually it was a picture of concentration. The City Editor oversaw the activity from the front of the room where he sat at a desk pointed in the direction of his writers.

Surrounding the room of desks and workers were offices with glass windows so the occupant could see the center of the room full of reporters at their desks, but could hide from the noise and concentrate by shutting the door. Faircloth was directed to the City Editor, who then walked him through the pit to the office of the columnist, Thomas Bernard.

Faircloth had been briefed by Tom's secretary, Karen, that Thomas Bernard was a respected journalist. He was often described as courageous. He faced down the criminal element in the Yucatan Peninsula and Central America with his pen. Other columnists had occupied his office and some had retired because they were threatened and some had been killed for what they said in print. They were punished for reporting the truth.

Bernard was short and stocky and he had a bushy mustache, and he was bald on the top of his head with hair and a bald spot like a medieval monk. Faircloth thought that when the reporter smiled he resembled a comedian he saw in the movies. He was easy to talk to. Faircloth explained that the law firm he worked for was searching for Clemenso Me Bondi, a man who had ordered the homicide of Anthony Stewart, one of their employees. Bernard had some familiarity with the story. He had received photos of Clem by Telex from Tom Night's secretary in St. Petersburg together with news reports from The New York Times about his escape from the hospital and the death of Lucy Hale and the murder of the man who was missing his thumb.

Bernard wanted to know something about Faircloth, the man he was talking to. Bernard was friendly but he was also cautious. Who was Faircloth?

Faircloth told a little of his history – a wife and two children. He served in the US Army, then he was a detective with the St. Petersburg Police Department and then a private investigator for the law firm of Night, Adams, Street, Alesse, DeMarco and Barnes.

"Does your law firm also have offices in Belize City?"

"Yes, attorney Tom Night represents the Barnes Family. They have an interest in Belize Resources, Ltd. and Belize Lime Rock, Ltd. which have operations in the south of Belize. The family found it convenient for Tom to open an office in Belize City."

"Have you ever been to Belize?"

"No. I hear the country is beautiful in spots."

"Are you aware Clemenso Bondi may be working for a cartel that has operations in Belize? He may be in Belize in Orange Walk."

"No. We were not aware of that."

"You say you were with the police force in St. Petersburg?"

"Yes."

"Did you ever have any experience with police corruption?"

"Yes, this case involving Mr. Bondi involves police corruption," said Faircloth. "Bondi was involved in organized crime and he had a partnership with a compromised detective."

"Is corruption pervasive in this police department?"

"I would say the answer is no. More like bad apples in a barrel of good, ripe fruit. It is sometimes worse than other times. But I do not believe the corruption is pervasive."

"Has corruption ever invaded every part of your society? The politicians? The military? The press? The clergy? The schools?" asked the reporter.

"No. I would know if it did. It has never been that bad. It is a case of a rotten apple here and there. Those rotten apples infect some of the other apples, but not the whole barrel."

"You need to understand that systemic corruption is what the Yucatan and other parts of Mexico suffer from. The corruption controls whole areas of the country. It is so bad that the people have lost confidence in every institution in the country. They can rely on nothing. They are concerned for their families and themselves. They are in a war."

Faircloth did not want to interrupt. He sat quietly listening to Mr. Bernard. He had heard Tom's stories about Central America. Tom hated to go there anymore. The only place he would go was to Belize. Tom still felt safe there.

Thomas Bernard could see he was losing his audience. To say that you have lost control of your country seems like an exaggeration to an American who can openly criticize the government without fear of reprisal. Bernard noticed that Faircloth was looking at the photograph on the wall behind him.

"I don't understand that photograph," said Faircloth. "What is it?"

"It's my predecessor. It shows how he looked when he was found. He was chopped up and boiled. That's his remains in a barrel."

Faircloth tried to look away but he had to see what was there in the mass of red, black and white. He saw the orbit of an eye in a skull and he then could see the bones and muscle mass and liquid, and his mind's eye could see it was a corpse. Faircloth felt woozy.

"Let's get some air." Bernard went and spoke to the City Editor and then came back with another man who was big and strong. "He will walk with us."

The trio went out the door and downstairs and passed through the metal detector that Faircloth had gone through on his way into the building. They went onto the street and over to a vendor in a small park who was selling icy, fruit flavored cones. Faircloth and the guard ordered grape. Bernard ordered cherry.

Bernard and Faircloth sat together and the guard sat on another bench and ate the cold treat.

"I am sorry about your co-worker."

"I think he went quickly. The cartel wanted us to see the body. The method of the murder was a threat to the living." Bernard paused. "This man, Bondi, I have heard of him. I believe he is with the Botero Cartel. He was working out of the Botero Tequila Factory. But now we think he is in Belize. He operates a way station for the drug trade. The facility is located between Orange Walk and Veracruz."

"Are the Mexican police aware of where he is?" asked Faircloth. "There is an extradition warrant out for his arrest in Florida."

Mr. Bernard seemed to ignore the question and asked, "Does Florida still execute prisoners?"

"Yes, it has the death penalty. The state executes prisoners. Why do you ask?"

"The court in Mexico will not extradite a person who is wanted in the US if the prisoner could be executed. In short, the Mexican Police won't waste their time arresting Bondi if the Mexican court system will release him. The police have only been interested in him to this time because of the $5,000 reward. However I do not think the Mexican court will extradite him if the police make an arrest. The courts will let him go."

"Would they extradite him to the US if they were assured he would not be executed?"

"I will find out," said the writer. "It would be better if you could arrest him in Belize. You might have more of a chance to send him back to the courts in the United States if you could take him in the country of Belize." He paused, and continued with a smile, "Also, you could execute him."

Faircloth ignored the reporters statement regarding the imposition of the death penalty. "How do you know Clem Bondi is with the Botero Cartel?"

"The federal police have very good sources in the cartel and they have good intelligence, but they cannot act on the information because the local police are corrupt and refuse to do their job or follow orders that will interfere with the operations of the cartel."

"Do you think you could supply us with information that will prove Clem Bondi is with the cartel and tell us where he is located?" asked Faircloth. "If we had proof we may be able to obtain assistance from the DEA and the CIA to arrest him."

"What type proof do you need?"

"A serum sample from him would be the best evidence for our federal authorities."

"You could run a DNA test for a match?"

"Yes. He was in the hospital and his DNA was coded."

"I will see what I can do."

The men finished their snow cones and said good bye. Faircloth took a cab to the airport.

* * *

While in the plane flying back home, Faircloth made careful notes of the events of his trip and he gave his opinions. First, since speaking to Mr. Bernard, Faircloth had become convinced that the driver of the VW "Beetle" was Clemenso Bondi. Second, Bondi had access to an intelligence network that was strong enough to know Faircloth was in Mexico and what he was doing for the firm.

Third, Bondi was working in Orange Walk, in Belize, a country where Tom had some influence. Fourth, Bondi was committed to the destruction of anyone who was a perceived threat. Ergo, the law firm and anyone connected to it were at risk from the man.

Chapter 9
The Plan to Capture Clem Bondi

"Look at that picture, you idiot. What do you see?"

James DeMarco looked at the picture.

It showed a soldier in his early twenties. Gaunt and muscular, the soldier held the strap of a grenade sack in his right hand. His trousers' legs were tucked into his boots and his boots were laced to his calves. In his other hand he held an M-16 rifle. He wore a floppy green canvas hat and a camouflage jacket. His face was smeared with black grease paint.

DeMarco could see a facial resemblance in the man seated across the desk, but otherwise the man in the photo was young and the man sitting in front of him was in his forties and well worn.

"What do you want me to see in this photo, Mr. Jones, if that is your name?"

"I want you to see a man who walked through the jungles of Panama for fifteen days chasing guerrillas who were going to do harm to this country.

"How old is this photo?"

"I admit I was younger then, but I can still fight. I am fit."

DeMarco had been given the job of reviewing the resumes of the qualifications of candidates for a paramilitary expedition to snatch Clem Bondi from the operations center of the Botero Cartel airport and way station in Orange Walk, Belize, Central America. Essentially, DeMarco was assuring himself that the recruits could speak and understand English.

DeMarco thought this was the dumbest idea ever. He did not know anything about military matters, other than what he had seen in a John Wayne movie. Once he completed the interview with Mr. Jones, James DeMarco gathered his papers and nodded to the team leader who sat with him.

"I need to report to Tom," said DeMarco.

The team leader, a young 50-something named Deacon, said he would be at the motel's pool.

"I'm going to work on my tan."

The recruits were housed together on the first floor of a small motel on Fourth Avenue North about three blocks from Tom's law office. Deacon had taken charge. The men sat around the pool and lied to each other about their exploits in the military. The only member of the law firm with any military experience was the investigator, Jim Faircloth. His experience was in Viet Nam as a foot soldier.

The team leader had been highly recommended to Tom by an old friend as someone who could get things done in Central America. The old friend, Rick Ibn, had been Tom's pilot in the 1960's and 1970's when he was first opening his law office in Central America. Tom still did some business with Rick Ibn, whose wife, Anna Hernando, MD, operated a hospital and surgery center in Belize City and a medical clinic in Big Creek at the Belize Lime Rock Ltd. mine that was operated by Albert Barnes. They were all clients and friends.

* * *

The team leader's idea for assembling a squad of men for an unsanctioned military operation was to place a want ad in the back pages of "Soldier of Fortune Magazine" and interview the men who responded. There were a hundred or so mercenaries who were looking for work who responded in reference to the advertisement. The team leader culled through the applications and he came down to ten men to be interviewed. From those ten, six men and a team leader would be hired for the job, if Tom went through with this idea.

At the firm meeting when the plan was hatched, Alphonse Alesse's comment was, "Isn't it illegal to snatch a man out of a country against his will? It is kidnapping." Alphonse always pointed out the obvious truth and therefore he was immediately ignored. He was a spoiler.

Tom replied, "The government of Belize will be working with us. They will coordinate the operation. We have only agreed to provide assistance. We will operate as a combination posse and bounty hunter. These activities are legal in the US, particularly since our actions will be sanctioned by the government of Belize."

Darlene was so upset with Tom for proposing the idea that he would subsidize the Country of Belize with men and money in its attempt to arrest Clem Bondi and return him to the United States for trial that she refused to talk to him.

DeMarco's wife, Jenny, who worked for the firm for over 10 years, argued against the idea on behalf of herself and Darlene:. "Clem Bondi is the most dangerous man alive in the world in my opinion. He lives when another would die. He escapes death and he kills for pleasure or just to be able to eliminate his enemies. The authorities in Belize have been unable to root him out of his hideout in Orange Walk. The CIA and DEA have refused to help the Belize Government; the US military refuses to get involved. What makes you think you can arrest him and bring him back to this country to stand trial?"

All Tom could say was, "Someone has to do something. If we don't go to Belize and capture him, he will come here and kill us."

DeMarco and Faircloth understood this argument, but were afraid they were taking on a task they could not complete or it was one that would backfire. The downside risk was like a fall from Mount Everest. Someone would get killed.

Alesse added: "Everyone who opposes Bondi ends up dead. Bondi has the advantage over us. He has been operating out of Mexico and Belize for about two years now. The Botero Cartel has become very strong with his help. Even the reporter Thomas Bernard was killed and the Mexican Police have done nothing."

Jim Faircloth had stayed in contact with Bernard through Telex after they met in Veracruz, Mexico. Bernard had been able to obtain filters from cigarettes Clem had used and discarded to conduct a DNA analysis. The lab at the FBI had been able to obtain sufficient DNA samples from the filters to be able to make a comparison between the sample from the cigarette filter and a known sample of Clem's DNA taken from him at his time in the Florida Hospital for the Insane. There was a match. The man working for the Botero Cartel in Orange Walk, Belize, was Clemenso Me Bondi.

After Thomas Bernard provided the cigarette filters to Faircloth, Bernard was killed in the same manner as his predecessor; he was chopped into little pieces and boiled. No subsequent reporter was hired by the editor of La Guardiana to fill Mr. Bernard's position. The editor had lost his nerve.

In the year since Portia Botero de Veracruz had moved Clem from the Botero Cartel's operations in Veracruz State, Mexico to Orange Walk, Belize, Clem Bondi had reinvigorated the cartel's business in Belize. The drug smuggling operation was conducted on what was once the cattle ranch of a Bahamian ex-patriot named Winston Grey. Grey was believed to have died in a fire in the mountains of Northwest Mexico. In addition to ranching, Winston had operated a way station for planes hauling cocaine, marijuana, and heroin from Columbia, Peru, and Ecuador, to Florida. Winston Grey offered the smugglers a safe haven where they could refuel and repair their planes. Grey had a 2,500 foot long lime rock runway on his property, and he had old, wood-drying barns where a plane or drug cargo could be hidden so it could not be seen by a passing airplane or a surveillance satellite.

When Winston Grey was killed, the Botero Family claimed Winston owed their tequila factory money and the family foreclosed and was awarded the ranch in payment for the debt. Portia Botero was now in charge of the ranch. However, the Botero Cartel could never gain control of the Belizean workers at the ranch until she brought Clem on board as the overseer.

Clem was particularly cruel. He gained a worker's attention by grabbing him by the ears. If the worker complained to a government bureaucrat Clem grabbed the bureaucrat by the nose and pulled harder. The police did not have enough deputies to mount a counter offensive. No one had the guts to take Clem to court. Clem would threaten a worker that he would kill his mother if he continued to cause him trouble. When anyone died violently in the city of Orange Walk it was felt Clem had a hand in the death no matter what the obvious cause.

As a result of his reputation the Botero operations in Belize ran smoothly and were very profitable.

Chapter 10
Freedom through Truth

The only entrée Tom Night had to the US Government was Bob Barnes. Bob had resolved an environmental problem for his company, CCC, Inc. That success led to his appointment as Secretary of the Department of the Interior. So far as the timber industry was concerned, he came to be looked upon as a guru in the field of ecology. His boss had mentioned his name to his boss, who was dinning with the President of the US. It was a working lunch and Bob's name was mentioned as a possible candidate to be the secretary of the Department of the Interior. By a fluke he was put in a pool of ten or so names up for consideration.

Bob went to Tom for advice regarding the vetting process for the office. Tom counseled Bob to reveal every sin from his past for the US Senate committee so that there would be no fact in his background that was not known.

"The truth shall set you free," Tom advised. "If you hide anything they will more than likely find out about it and you will be held up to the world as a liar. Better to reveal the truth no matter how embarrassing it might be, then be shown to be a prevaricator. Otherwise, if you cannot stand to reveal the truth, withdraw your name from consideration for the post."

Bob Barnes had a long and bumpy road leading to his confirmation hearing, but Tom's advice was sound and Bob ultimately won confirmation as Secretary of the Department of the Interior. That post had nothing to do with the CIA and the DEA (Drug Enforcement Administration), but Bob was a full cabinet member. When Tom asked Bob if he could arrange a meeting for him with the CIA and the DEA regarding Clem Bondi, Bob made a call to the Attorney General about the problem with the Botero drug cartel operating in the Yucatan, and Bob got Tom a meeting with two undersecretaries of the Justice Department and one from the CIA.

Unfortunately, getting a meeting and getting action were two different things. The undersecretaries were swamped with investigations in the continental US and did not see how they could fight the drug war in the US by attacking the Botero cartel in the middle of Central America. The officials in Belize and Mexico complicated the situation. They would not open their borders to an American law enforcement operation. It was a political problem; these governments would be seen to be forfeiting their control of law enforcement to a foreign power.

The failed meeting with the CIA and DEA led Tom to the idea of working directly with the Solicitor General of Belize.

The Solicitor, Arthur Franklin Thomas, was a Cambridge-trained lawyer who was born in the south of Belize in Stan Creek. His family had lived on the coast harvesting fish, and farming papaya, mango, avocado, and other tropical fruits from a 50 acre orchard. The foodstuffs were loaded on a boat and shipped north to Belize City and sold to restaurants at the hotels in the city. Solicitor Thomas' father saw a better life for his son if he was sent to school, and he encouraged his son to study to gain a scholarship. Mr. Thomas did work hard and won a scholarship, and passed his boards for the practice of law, and was eligible to work as a solicitor. Mr. Thomas was hired by Tom's Belize law firm when he first began to practice and later he worked for Herbert Johns, Esq., in Belize City and was groomed for a political career. He was elected as a Member of Parliament and when his party won the majority of seats in Parliament and formed the government he was appointed Solicitor General.

Arthur Franklin Thomas and Tom's Belizean law partner, Andrew Prince Jr., were good friends. It was Tom's thought that eventually the two lawyers would take over Tom's firm in Belize

City and Tom and Darlene would retire from the firm. So Tom had good connections with the Government of Belize and Bondi would force Tom to action to solicit aid from the government.

The Letter

Tom visited Belize City for meetings concerning Clem Bondi in late September. After the first meeting there was more planning and preparation in Florida. Between the dates of the meetings in Belize and Florida, Tom received a letter from Clem threatening Tom and his firm that if they came after Clem in Belize or further threatened him in any way that the members of the law firm and their families would be killed.

Obviously, Clem had a mole somewhere providing him with information that Tom was a threat.

Tom circulated the letter among the partners of the firm. The letter strengthened the resolve of Tom, DeMarco, Alphonse and Faircloth to act, but scared Darlene and Jenny.

Darlene was fearful foremost because somehow Clem knew what the firm was planning. Did they have to worry about the secretaries and clerks in the office having loose lips?

Tom knew the leak was in Belize ... not in St. Petersburg. He had to be careful who he talked to when he visited Central America.

In his letter, Clem reminded Tom that Tom had disrespected Clem at the Oar House and that was one of the reasons he had killed his girlfriend, Lori. That event had occurred at least ten years prior, but Clem acted like it was yesterday. Clem stated in the letter that if he had to come to Florida to remove Tom as a threat he would also use the opportunity to seek revenge. He would take particular pleasure in killing Tom's wife, Darlene Street.

When Jenny became aware of the threats, she took a copy of the letter to the police. The police, and later the State Attorney, said they could not do anything about the letter. The threat was not a crime. It was not an assault. Clem was in Belize and Darlene was in St. Petersburg. Clem had no present, apparent ability to carry out the threat.

"Besides," said the State Attorney, "how can we be expected to provide around the clock protection to the members of the law firm?"

* * *

In late October, Tom advised his firm in St. Petersburg that he would return to Belize with the idea of firming up a plan to kidnap Clem and return him to the court system in Florida.

"The meeting in Belize is for planning purposes only," Tom assured each of his partners.

Tom said if the plan was implemented, the date for the capture would be at the end of the year in December. Tom was still having difficulty walking and so he was accompanied on the October trip to Belize by Jim Faircloth, who had become the coordinator of the military operation. Deacon was still the team leader who would execute the actual attack.

However, Tom had lied to his partners. The real reason for the October trip to Belize was to actually execute the attack and kidnap Clem. To do that Tom had to obtain final approval for the operation from the government of Belize for immunity for the kinapping. Tom had aged. He was no longer spry. He took shortcuts to obtain approval for what he needed. One shortcut was to lie. Tom was not called out for his lies. Most were white and harmless in any event. But this lie about the assault in Belize using mercenaries was hugely important if the plan failed. No one in the law firm but Tom knew what was planned nor did they approve the action – which was what Tom intended. This lie was a good lie. It gave the firm deniability.

As cover for the true purpose of the October trip, Albert Barnes met Tom and Faircloth at the airport. Albert still owned the 1949 Piper Cub Special and he flew in from Monkey River Town near the mine at Big Creek. He and his assistant, Hugo, met Tom at the Fort George Hotel. The cover for the meeting was an alleged crisis at the mine.

There was always a problem at the lime rock mine that needed Tom's attention. The business produced the largest number of jobs of any business in the country. The government was under pressure for the mine to remain in operation although it produced little or no profit. The Barnes Family, through Barnes Lime Rock Inc., had owned 35% of the mine at Big Creek. The balance of the business was owned by a group of Belizeans who purchased the 65% interest from the Thompson Timber Fund's (TTF's) bankruptcy trustee after Thomas N. Thompson had been sentenced to jail for securities fraud.

Tom represented the Barnes Family interests in Belize. Albert Barnes was the chief operating officer for the mine. When Tom had any questions about operations he had a meeting with Albert. Albert loved his work and everyone agreed that no one but Albert could make the mine run successfully.

Following the business meeting, Albert, Hugo, Faircloth and Tom had dinner at the hotel. One topic of conversation was the shock of seeing a decapitated body lying on the road as they rode in the taxi into the city from the airport. There was an ambulance at the scene and the taxi driver was able to get his passengers by the official vehicles, but he was not able to prevent the trio from seeing the grim scene in the road.

The taxi driver had commented that encounters like this were disturbing. "I will move to Miami soon," he said.

When he heard what the driver had said, Albert's reaction was to say: "The drug gangs will follow you to Miami." Albert was matter of fact. He was making Tom's point for the necessity to take action against Clem and the cartels in Belize, and the sooner the better.

"Do you have these problems in the south in Big Creek?" asked Faircloth.

"No, we have a civil defense society. We take care of the ones who cause these problems."

"Do you mean a vigilante society?" asked Tom.

"Yes, it is the only thing that works. The drug dealers corrupt the police and the judiciary eventually, unless they are killed."

* * *

Tom, Albert, Hugo and Faircloth were back at the hotel. Albert was playing with his drink. They were at the Fort George waiting to be served their meal and they had their drinks. Albert always avoided the ice to avoid an amoeba and dysentery, so he was drinking his Cola neat. Tom stuck to a chilled bottle of pasteurized seltzer water and a wedge of lime.

Albert continued the conversation. "What have George and Frederick told you?"

"You mean my spies?" asked Tom.

"Yes, your spies." Albert smiled.

George and Frederick were the closest neighbors to the Winston Grey Ranch, and they were friends with Clem's assistant manager at the cartel's operations. Clem's assistant liked peppermint schnapps and he would talk and tell his neighbor George the cartel's secrets when George got him drunk. He told George the inner workings of the Grey Ranch. The assistant explained that when a customer (drug dealer) landed his plane, Clem always met the plane. That way, Clem could collect the cartel's fees for services from the pilot. Clem always took a cut of the payment made by the drug pilot. It was Clem's share. The other members of the cartel were upset because Clem did not share with them. That was only one of their gripes. George was told all the cartel's secrets.

George was so trusted by the members of the cartel that he and Frederick had even been invited to the property and had done maintenance work for the cartel; repairing fences, mowing the pastures, and filling pot holes in the runway. During those visits they learned how much Clem was hated by the members of the cartel and that there would be no objection if Clem were gone. In fact, Clem's demise was a subject of the workers' prayers.

"My spies say we can kidnap Clem anytime we want," said Tom. "My spies assure me that the members of the cartel will not interfere with his capture."

"Do you believe them?" asked Albert, always the skeptic.

"Yes. George and Frederick hate Clem. We can use that hate to our advantage."

Everyone acknowledged this was the most positive aspect to the plan to capture Clem. Tom had known George and Frederick for as long as he had come to Belize. They had been Winston Grey's friends and they did not feel Grey's nephew was treated fairly when the cartel made the false claim for Grey's ranch when Grey died. The nephew was cut out of the estate and the nephew was now living in Sarasota, Florida with the Mennonites. Tom could trust George and Frederick.

The meal was quiet. The red snapper was very tasty, cooked in a white paper bag ("a la papilla"). The food was always superb at the hotel. Albert spent the night. It was not safe to be on the road to the airport after dark. Albert would take a cab back to his plane and fly to the mine the next morning while Tom finalized plans with the government.

Another of Tom's jobs when he came to Belize was to see that Albert was in touch with reality and that his schizophrenia was under control. In Tom's opinion, Albert was in good mental condition. He would report that fact to Albert's mother, Bea Barnes.

When Tom and Faircloth had left his law office in St. Petesrburg they planned to be gone for three days. The main reason Tom had told the office he was to make the trip to Belize was to meet with Hubert Johns and that was not a lie.

* * *

The next day, late in the morning after Albert flew back to the mine, Tom and Faircloth were driven to Hubert Johns' office across from the mud flats. These flats were home to millions of black crabs with a single red claw. The crabs were in attack mode and charged at Tom and Faircloth as they walked across the yard. The law office was built up on stilts in defense of a storm surge from the next hurricane and the crabs swarmed under the building.

Once let inside the locked door of the office, the men were led by the receptionist into the back room that was part of Mr. Johns' living area. There was a picture window that looked over the sea and the mangroves lining the shore. Andrew Prince, Jr. and Arthur Franklin Thomas had already arrived, and they were sipping hot tea. The receptionist took Tom and Faircloth's order for tea, with sugar and milk, and left the room.

As they waited for their tea Tom kidded Hubert about the encroachment of the sea over his property and that he would have to leave his office soon. Hubert said he did not believe in climate change.

The receptionist brought the tea and the meeting began with Tom giving a recitation of his knowledge of the evil Clemenso Me Bondi. Tom described Bondi's work for organized crime as an enforcer and his killing spree, where five persons lost their lives before Bondi was incarcerated in the hospital for the insane. He also related the facts of the killings after he escaped, and the killings in Mexico and Belize since he became a member of the Botero Cartel.

Tom explained that the Florida state courts would prosecute Clem to the full extent of the law if he was returned to the jurisdiction of the court in Florida. Clem would not buy his way out of the justice system. There were seven warrants out for his arrest for First Degree Murder. The charges carried the death penalty.

Mr. Johns wanted to know why Belize would want to take the chance of losing any of its law enforcement officers in an attempt to arrest the man. Mr. Johns pointed out that Clem was not wanted by the authorities in Belize.

Tom recited the opinion of the CIA and DEA, that unless action was taken, Belize would lose the northwest portion of the country, the Orange Walk District, to the cartel. Eventually, the entire country would come under the control of the cartel. Tom said he was willing to help with six soldiers who would assist in the capture of Clem Bondi. Tom explained that Clem was like the head of the snake. Cut off the head and the snake will die.

"Why would you do this?" asked Mr. Johns.

"I do not want to give Bondi the chance to come to Florida and kill us all."

"When would your team be able to attack?"

"Soon. It will be before the end of the year. We are assembling a team of soldiers and planning an assault to capture Bondi."

"What participation would Belize need to make?"

"We need nothing, except to ensure us that we can leave the country with Bondi without the intervention of the Belize Defense Force. If we are able to capture the man, we intend to fly him to Florida as soon as we have him. The plan will not work if Clem becomes involved in the courts in Belize."

"What if there are collateral victims of the operation?"

"You have that already. Who was the man who was decapitated on the road last night?" asked Tom. "I have been coming here to Belize City for years and I have watched it deteriorate. Do I speak the truth?"

"Yes," admitted Mr. Johns.

"Our country, the United States of America, is also being corrupted," said Tom. "Our countries have a symbiotic relationship; we are the buyers and you are the suppliers of drugs. Before it was cannabis, then cocaine, and now it is heroin. It is a corrupt relationship. We are killing each other. We have to do something to stop this."

"We understand," said Mr. Johns. "The Belize Defense Forces (BDF) know about the illegal drug operation in Orange Walk and that there is a warrant for Clemenso Bondi's arrest and our government has reminded the BDF of their responsibility, but the BDF will take no action. They fear the cartel. We cannot help you capture this criminal."

"We do not need manpower," said Tom. "Will you ensure me that if we capture Bondi on Belize soil the Belize government will not interfere and will allow us to remove him to the US? Assure me that Bondi will not be taken before a judge in the country of Belize after we capture him."

"There is an exception in the law that would allow a bounty hunter to remove a fugitive to the United States. To avail yourself of that law you will need to file certified copies of the arrest warrants from Florida with the Solicitor General. This is the normal procedure for extradiction," said Johns. "If you do that, I will assure you that Belize will not interfere and the Belize court system will not become involved with your rendition of Mr. Bondi to the authorities in Florida. Also, we will take no action against you or your men for kidnapping Mr. Bondi."

"I brought certified copies." Tom handed copies of the seven homicide warrants to Mr. Johns. Tom smiled broadly as the attorney reviewed the warrants and found them to be sufficient.

* * *

Faircloth did not realize why Tom was so happy with the result of the meeting. The fact that the government of Belize would not interfere with the capture of Clem Bondi was not the positive result Faircloth expected. He was hoping for an army of Belize officers who would storm the ranch where the Botero Cartel conducted its business and overpower Bondi and his men. He expected Belize and the BDF would participate in the attack and then turn Bondi over to the Americans. Faircloth would discuss this change of plan with Darlene when they returned.

* * *

Hubert Johns, Esq. was the chairman of the People's United Party (PUP), which was in power, and he could speak for the government. He was also the Chief Counsel to the Solicitor General, Arthur Franklin Thomas. The Solicitor General relied on his advice to the exclusion of all other members of the government.

Mr. Johns offered all that he could offer to aid Tom in returning Bondi to the court system in the US. By allowing Tom to bypass the Belize Court System and the BDF, Johns had helped Tom avoid Clemenso Bondi's best chance to escape jail after his capture. Clem's best chance to avoid rendition to Florida was by paying off officials in Belize.

Chapter 11
Execution of the Plan

Faircloth awoke before dawn the following morning after the meeting with Herbert Johns. Tom was not in his bed. Faircloth figured he was at breakfast. He showered and dressed. The domestic (TAN Airlines) plane did not leave that morning for Tampa until 7:00 a.m., so there was plenty of time to eat and arrive at the airport.

When Faircloth sat at his table in the dining room he was approached by the hotel manager. The manager gave Faircloth his plane ticket and a note from Tom saying he should go without him back to Tampa. Tom's note said he had to help Albert and it was a confidential matter. Tom wrote that he would see him in the office tomorrow. Tom had underlined the words: GO HOME.

The manager had no other information except he had seen Tom leave in a taxi very early in the morning, but Tom did not say where he was going.

There was a bellman in the lobby and he said he had not seen Tom leave.

Faircloth decided he should do what his boss had ordered him to do. He went in and ate breakfast and left the hotel in plenty of time to make the flight to Florida.

* * *

Three hours earlier, at 4:00 a.m., Tom took a taxi from the hotel to Anna Hernando's Hospital and surgery center downtown. Tom was let out of the cab and he managed the stairs with his cane. He had taken a double dose of Carb/Levo and the tremor in his left hand was under control. He used his cane for balance and he could move at a quick walk when he had the cane, but he could not run. No one who saw Tom would think Tom was beginning a war.

Anna met Tom at the door of the clinic. It was 4:15 a.m. The doctor had a medical field kit prepared in a metal box that was painted olive green. The doctor shoved it out the door. In three steps she and her husband, Rick, managed to carry the box of medicine and field dressings and the stretcher down the stairs of the clinic to the ambulance which was parked in the rear of the hospital.

Anna had the hospital fully staffed as a MASH unit with a nurse/ physician's assistant in each of the five treatment rooms of the facility. The surgery center had been scrubbed and dis-infected. The post op room had four gurneys lined against the walls, with IV's prepared for each gurney. Anna had flown an ER/ trauma nurse in from Jackson Memorial Hospital in Miami to act as triage coordinator. The reception room of the clinic became the triage center.

Once the ambulance, a white 1977 Pontiac which could hold two patients, was loaded with field supplies, they were prepared for a military engagement that no one wanted to happen. Tom and Anna were seated in the front passenger seat and the rear jump seat, respectively.

As Rick drove from the hospital in downtown Belize City to the International airport it was 4:30 a.m.

* * *

The ambulance lumbered onto the airfield behind the Central Hanger at the Belize City International Airport. Rick's DC-3 was on the fight deck at the airport, fueled and prepared to leave.

Rick left the ambulance and inspected the plane and began his pre-flight as Tom and Anna drove away from the airport and entered the Western Highway and headed to the D-8 Bar located at the intersection of the Western Highway and the Northern

Highway. It was about a 45 minute drive to the D-8 from the airport.

After the ambulance departed the airport, a small plane, a 1949 Piper Cub Special owned by Albert Barnes, landed and parked on the flight deck next to the DC-3. Albert had a passenger, a tall (6'-5"), large (250 pound), muscular man named Hugo, who was Albert's assistant at the lime rock mine. Albert and Rick inspected the Piper airplane and finalized preparations for their flight to the Grey Ranch. Albert and Rick had rehearsed the tactical landing maneuver they would be required to perform in the assault on the Grey Ranch for the last four weeks at the airport at Monkey River Town near Big Creek.

The pilots were prepared.

The weather had been a question that could nix the operation. But, the weather was perfect. The weather at dawn would be clear and bright with ground fog.

* * *

At 5:15 a.m. Tom was greeted at the D-8 Bar by the owners, Sargent Major James and his wife Marie. The couple had known Tom for many years. The couple owned the bar and a large barn and a residence on the road from the airport to the capitol, Belmopan. Whenever Tom made that trip along the Western Highway he stopped and talked. It was there that Tom was introduced to the sport of pig hunting. Sargent Major had a large flat-bed truck that was used for pig hunts.

The flat-bed could be needed in the capture of Clem Bondi. Sergeant Major and Marie agreed that they would help. The flat-bed had a dog carrier that was jerry-rigged to carry extra equipment. It could be used as a personnel carrier if the ambulance or one of the planes used in the operation were destroyed. The two friends of Winston Grey, George and Frederick, would ride with Sergeant Major in the truck and provide back-up if the raid on the ranch went sour. Marie would coordinate by satellite phone from the D-8 Bar. The D-8 also had a land line that connected the pay phone in the bar to Belmopan and Belize City. The satellite phone and the hard line at the D-8 Bar provided communications for the operation connecting the airplanes, the vehicles and the clinic in Belize City.

Deacon and the men who had made the cut for the mission had been flown in to the Belize City airport over the last several days. Marie had transported the men to the D-8, where they bivouacked behind the bar in the barn. They spent their time shooting their guns and blowing things up with stun grenades as they practiced for the mission to capture Clemenso Bondi at the Grey Ranch. The bar patrons watched the exercise. Tom had told Marie not to worry if the customers overheard the military teams' orders. The customers were oblivious. No one would believe what was playing out before them. Marie touted the activity as the first British Military Olympics to be held in the country. The locals brought their kids and kept their distance during the events. The bar drew quite a crowd, especially for night maneuvers. Earlier in the morning of the actual attack the team had been driven from the D-8 Bar to the airport to board the DC-3 for the airborne assault.

Deacon and the other mercenary soldiers would fly to the Grey Ranch in the DC-3 and rendezvous with Albert and Hugo in the Piper Special for the attempt to capture Bondi.

* * *

It was 5:30 a.m. when the flat-bed was loaded with the extra medical supplies that Anna hoped would not be needed for the engagement. Marie rushed around and secured the flatbed on the truck and made her husband, Sergeant Major, show her he had his shotgun. Marie called Rick on the satellite phone and told him to get into the air with Deacon and the five soldiers.

Albert was to be called to take off once the flat-bed truck had reached the gates of the Winston Grey Ranch. The flat-bed truck had to be at the gate of the Botero Cartel/Grey Ranch no later than 6:00 a.m.

The entire plan was predicated on the fact that George and Frederick had permission to enter the Grey Ranch from Clem Bondi's chief assistant the day of the planned attack. The cover story was that George and Frederick were hired to bring a crew in to eliminate the feral pigs and razorback boars from the property. The pigs had become a danger to operations at the ranch because they grazed on the runway and threatened aircraft when they were landing or taking off.

The gate tender at the Grey Ranch was aware the men would be there before 6 a.m. and waved the flat-bed through the gate to the ranch house at 5:45 a.m.

Simultaneously, Rick lifted off in the DC-3 with his passengers, the assault team.

Simultaneously, at 5:45 a.m., Albert was airborne with Hugo.

* * *

Tom was driving the ambulance. A mile before the gate at the Winston Grey Ranch, he pulled off the road. Tom parked the ambulance a short distance away from the gate as planned. He was concealed behind dense, tropical bushes so the vehicle could not be seen from the road or the main entrance gate.

Then Anna called Rick by satellite phone.

Rick verified he was in the air, 10,000 feet above the air strip on the ranch.

Meanwhile, Albert, who was flying the Piper, pretending to be a drug trafficker, had radioed the ranch. Albert reported he had an emergency, that he was leaking fuel from a fuel bladder in his plane that was hauling cocaine to Florida.

Clemenso Bondi was at his post in the radio shack at the Grey Ranch and he heard the distress call. As was his routine, Clem said he would handle the emergency call and he went outside to await the plane. Clem would collect the fees from the pilot. The runway had been constructed in an east/west direction. The plane would land from the east. Clem looked to the east but he could not see the plane because the sun was just breaking over the horizon. It was 6 a.m. In addition to the sun, the conditions offered low visibility with ground fog, which was typical for late fall. There was no wind.

Rick had made a wide turn so that he was prepared to land from the east behind Albert's plane, which also arrived from the east.

Albert landed first. He was hot, very fast. Albert and Hugo saw Clem standing on the flight pad. This was perfect. They would not have to chase after him. He was a sitting duck.

Rick landed just behind Albert's Piper in the DC-3. Rick jammed on the brakes immediately on touch down and feathered his engines. Albert had landed his plane and rolled past the flight deck. The DC-3 was to the right of Albert's plane.

When the Piper stopped, Albert's passenger, Hugo, jumped out of the Piper Special and ran back to the DC-3 as it came to a stop. Rick brought the DC-3 to a halt at the flight deck that extended off to the side of the ranch house and he gunned both engines. Clem watched the action, oblivious to the danger he was in. Clem was confused. Why were there two planes? He thought.

Then Hugo tackled Clem from his blind side. Bondi did not anticipate he would be wrapped up by Hugo. Clem had covered his face with his hands to avoid the dirt, dust and debris kicked up by the propellers of the DC-3 and the Piper aircraft and did not see he was going to be tackled.

Deacon opened the cargo door to the DC-3. The men in the DC-3 jumped out of the cargo door and leaped to the ground and grabbed a hold of Clem like dogs attacking a pig. He was quickly trussed up in a duffle bag and thrown in a cargo bin on the floor of the DC-3 airplane.

Albert pulled his plane forward to the west end of the airstrip and waited as Rick turned the DC-3 for takeoff. Then Albert waited. As soon as Rick was in the air, Albert gunned the engine on his small plane and took off. Once Albert was in the air he headed to the International Airport in Belize City.

When Rick's plane reached 5,000 feet he called and reported the operation to capture Clem was a success so far. Rick reported he was heading NNE. Now Anna and Tom and Sargent Major, and George and Frederick, still had to get away.

As they had waited for Clem's capture to be completed by the team, Sargent Major had looked off the ranch road for a stretch of pasture that was drivable. Once the DC-3 and the Piper Cub Special took off, Sargent Major drove across the pasture to the fence line. George jumped out and cut the barb wire and they were free. They drove the flat-bed on to the road and waited for the ambulance to catch up. Then the vehicles were driven back to the hospital in Belize City.

It was 6:15 a.m.

* * *

Tom was dropped at the hotel at 7:15. Tom showered and shaved. He hired a cab and drove to Hubert Johns' office. The receptionist said Mr. Johns wanted Tom to join him for tea. It was 8:00 a.m.

After they were settled and had their tea, Tom reported that about two hours past, Clemenso Me Bondi had been arrested for seven homicides and that he was out of Belize and the country's air space and he was on his way to the State of Florida.

"Were there any casualties?" Mr. Johns was concerned.

"No, not a single shot was fired. As a matter of fact, our men reported heavy cheering from the ranch house when Clem was taken aboard the plane and trussed up in the duffel bag."

Tom was smiling. "Apparently, Clem yelled to his fellow drug traffickers for assistance and none of his friends came to his aid." Tom had been sweating it. "That was as we anticipated, but we were not sure it would go that way."

Chapter 12
Aftermath

After visiting with Hubert Johns at his office and speaking by phone with Solicitor General Thomas, Tom took a taxi to the clinic.

The facility was crowded with civilians who were sweating profusely and feeling the rush of combat, and were elated that they had beaten death and suffered no casualties. Tom, Albert, Hugo, Sargent Major, George and Frederick, together with the medical personnel, congratulated each other for a plan that was well thought out, simple and well executed.

Tom had made three trips to Belize to coordinate Clem's capture. In the first trip in September he became convinced that the manpower needed to capture Clem Bondi, in addition to the mercenaries, would best come from the citizens of Belize ... they had skin in the game.

Rick Ibn and Anna Hernando owned businesses, were married, owned a home and had three daughters in the country.

George and Frederick lived on a ranch next to the Botero Cartel operations at the Grey Ranch. They were angry that the Grey Ranch had been stolen by the cartel. They were regularly threatened by Clem Bondi.

Albert and Hugo managed Belize Lime Rock, an honest business that paid its taxes and took care of its workers.

Sergeant Major and his wife had lived in Belize for over 30 years. They owned the D-8 Bar and a ranch and a home. They refused to be run out of their house, home and investment by a group of criminals.

*** *** ***

Tom threw water on the celebration. "We still need to see that Rick and the team have made it to Miami to deliver Clem to the authorities. Then, if that works out, we need to get each of the members of the team back to Belize when they return from Miami. Then there is a plane to Tampa that leaves tonight at midnight. The team should be back by then and they fly to Tampa."

Anna had called the airline. There were seats for six men on the midnight flight. Tom reminded her that he had a ticket and they could transfer it to Deacon.

"All of the men need to go back to the USA together. We need to get their property together. Do not let them take any weapons. The weapons need to remain here in Belize. You may need them in the future."

*** *** ***

Tom then took George into Dr. Hernando's office to use her private phone. George regularly spoke to the drug traffickers at the Grey Ranch. They were his neighbors. George had tipped the workers at Grey Ranch that Clem would be kidnapped. George just did not say when, where, or how. George did say that as long as the Botero Cartel workers did not interfere they would not be hurt. The cartel members at Grey Ranch did not disagree with Bondi's capture. They hated Clem.

"George, I need you to call the ranch and see what is going on there."

"What do I say?"

Tom told George to ask for Clem.

George dialed the number.

"Who is this?" George asked and nodded. He recognized the man who answered the phone.

"Look, this is George. Is Clem there?" George covered the phone with his hand and said to Tom, "The man asked why we want to know."

"Ask him what happened there this morning."

"We were out there this morning to catch your wild hogs and all hell broke loose. We thought there was a raid by BDF and we cut the fence to escape and came to town to call you."

George looked at the phone. He was listening, then said, "New management, eh. Well, do you want us to come out and get the hogs or no?" George ended saying, "Yeah, I know. Clem was bad for business."

George hung up. "They want us to get the hogs next week."

"I understood what he was saying," said Tom. "You and Frederick need to keep your heads low."

"It will be bad for a while, but Clem didn't give us any choice," said George. "Clem would have killed us eventually."

* * *

At 3 p.m. Tom and Anna began to get nervous. That was the time Rick was supposed to call them from Miami after they turned Clem over to the US Marshals office at the airport. They were also to deliver certified copies of the seven arrest warrants for the US Marshals naming Clem as being wanted for murder in the first degree in the State of Florida. They wanted there to be no question that Clem was a wanted man and needed to be taken into custody. What if they had gone through this exercise and the customs agents in Miami refused to arrest Clem?

The call from Miami finally came at 4 p.m. Rick said they were delayed by weather, but otherwise they were alright and would be back in the air in a short while. Rick said they had one incident with Clem. He tried to wriggle free from the duffle bag but the team had been watching and when they saw his fingers coming out of the bag, they attacked. They then nailed a top on the cargo bin and Clem was in a cage the rest of the trip.

Rick said Deacon, Hugo and the other five members of the team should be back in Belize City by 10 p.m., in time for the midnight flight back to Florida.

* * *

When the DC-3 landed at 10:30 p.m. they were met by the rest of the group who had remained behind. Tom explained to Deacon that they would return to Tampa that night at midnight.

"What am I supposed to say to Faircloth and DeMarco and the members of the law firm?"

"I have been trying to figure out what is best to say to Faircloth. Probably, he needs to know what happened. Tell him everything about the operation but tell him that you and I had agreed that he was not to have gone to the Grey Ranch. Tell him that we thought it would be too dangerous. That he had a wife and two kids ... "

"I'll tell him. What are you going to do?"

"I will call Darlene, Alphonse and DeMarco. I will tell them what happened. Otherwise, I want to wait here and see if there is any blow back from the cartel. I will come back tomorrow in the afternoon."

"Do you want me to stay?"

"No." Tom went in his pocket and removed $35,000 in cash. He counted out five piles containing $5,000 each and one pile with $10,000. Tom gave Deacon the pile with ten thousand dollars and asked Deacon to pay the other members of the team five thousand dollars each.

"Thanks, boss."

Tom smiled. He thought how lucky he was to have the firm's line of credit at Century Bank. Without the loan, the capture of Clem would not have been possible. Tom had paid for the food, transportation, lodging and weapons on credit from the bank. Governments borrow to prosecute wars, why not me? he thought. Without the line of credit, Tom was dead broke.

* * *

Tom returned to the Fort George Hotel with Albert and Hugo. The three had dinner and sat in the bar watching a pirated movie on TV. The movie was playing on a VCR. The VCR technology was new to the country of Belize.

"Still not drinking?" asked Albert.

"Yeah, I think I have quit for good," said Tom. "But who knows?"

The movie wasn't that interesting. It was a Miami Vice type shoot 'em up. Later, there was a football game from Jacksonville. The Florida/Georgia SEC Championship Game was tied. It was while they were waiting for their food that Albert explained that he had asked Hugo to go with him on the operation because he was a ball player. He had been an All-American tackle.

"Good choice." said Tom.

* * *

The next day the three men went to the airport. Tom left at 3:00 pm on a Delta flight heading back to a meeting with Darlene. Albert and Hugo flew south in the Piper Cub Special to Monkey River Town.

* * *

Portia Botero de Veracruz had been in hiding for three months. Clem Bondi had threatened to kill her the last time he was at the Botero cartel's headquarters in Mexico on the trail to Mexico City from Veracruz. Clem made Portia's brother, Pedro Botero, a noted killer, look like a priest by comparison. Since Portia's brother was in prison she had no family to protect her from a man like Bondi.

Portia Botero had tried to rein in Bondi, restricting his authority at the Grey Ranch. She knew Bondi was skimming from the receipts because the operations were reporting less and less in gross income since Bondi had begun to run the operation. Anyone Portia sent to the Grey Ranch to control Bondi ended up disappeared if he failed to follow Bondi's orders.

Further, there was disruption among the other workers who were subject to his random acts of violence.

When the assistant manager at the ranch reported that Clem had been snatched, Portia was silently grateful and crossed herself that her prayers had been answered. However, Portia did not lose the opportunity of Clem's disappearance to chide the workers at the ranch to be on guard for other attacks. Further, she demanded that the assistant manager investigate to determine who had conducted the kidnapping, and to determine if the intent was to steal the business. However within a week Portia had forgotten about Clem and she did not press her demand for information. Portia had other problems.

Other cartels had seen the weakness of the Botero Cartel without Clemenso Bondi and within a month of Clem's capture the obituary of Portia Botero de Veracruz was printed in the front section of Guardiana Newspaper. There was an allegation in the story that Senora Botero was the leader of the Botero Cartel and that she had ordered the murders of two of the Guadiana's courageous investigative reporters, the last being Thomas Bernard.

When the Botero Cartel crumbled in Veracruz, the criminal operation in Orange Walk, Belize, was mortally wounded and the Belize Defense Force (BDF) felt it was vulnerable. The BDF launched a military assault in December 1989. There was much bloodshed. The BDF lost three men and two were severely wounded. All 13 members of the old Botero Cartel who were at the Grey Ranch were killed. Some relatives of members of the cartel alleged the action by the BDF was murder; an execution. The buildings comprising the Grey Ranch were burned to the ground purposely with the men inside, they said.

Arthur Franklin Thomas, the Solicitor General, defended the action by the government of Belize and asserted that the allegations by the relatives of the dead drug dealers were political propaganda and they were lies.

What the Solicitor General learned was that his country could not allow a criminal enterprise to establish a foothold. Belize was too small to defend itself once a criminal cartel became established. They had to be vigilant and use all means to protect the country from organized crime.

Chapter 13
Maya Riviera

In March, the weather in the Yucatan is the best for the beach. It is mild and dry. The resort at Cancun is taken over by the Spring Break holiday market and children 15 to 20 years of age chance fate by drinking to excess for the monetary benefit of the hotel owners on the Caribbean beaches. Over the years, Cancun's hotels had stolen the market for teenage hedonism from Daytona Beach and Ft. Lauderdale, Florida.

The older crowd who wanted to enjoy the beach and the weather and avoid the crowds of youngsters would go south of Cancun to the Mayan Riviera north of Tulum and relax on the sugar sand beaches of Playa del Carmen.

* * *

It took Darlene a while before she forgave Tom for participating in the military operation that resulted in the capture of Clem Bondi. She had refused to talk to him before he left for Belize. When Tom returned, Darlene suggested he move out of the condo. This had never happened before. Since their marriage they had never separated.

Tom moved into Jim DeMarco's house with his wife, Jenny Barnes, and their three children. Tom had never had children, and he grew up as the only child under the care of two unmarried aunts who taught Humanities at Stetson University in Deland, Florida. He enjoyed the DeMarco-Barnes kids, but hated the noise. The three girls were always looking for attention, sometimes deserved. Tom wanted a place to hide and so he spent a good deal of time in the office, to the consternation of the primary working partners, DeMarco and Alesse.

* * *

Jenny and Darlene were best friends. Darlene confided that she was concerned the next thing Tom got involved with would get him killed. She couldn't take the anxiety in his life. She wanted Tom to retire. He was 70 years old. It was 1990. Enough is enough. Let Alphonse and DeMarco take over the firm in St. Petersburg completely and the same with Andrew Prince and Arthur Thomas in Belize.

The Barnes Family was happy with Alphonse's representation of their corporate interests in Belize Lime Rock Ltd. and Belize Resources Ltd. and Barnes Lime Rock. Marla and James Reynolds had relied on Alphonse's legal advice since they purchased Plantation #7. Bob Barnes had a political career that didn't require Tom's advice. Albert relied on Andrew Prince Jr. in Belize for legal representation. As far as criminal cases were concerned, there was always some crazy attorney who wanted to beat his head against a stone wall representing murderers and rapists. DeMarco had a good reputation and he could draw cases from throughout the state.

"Give them their chance" Darlene pronounced. "Tom, you should retire."

Tom was reluctant to tell Darlene that he was broke. He could not afford to retire.

Jenny suggested Tom and Darlene take a vacation. That way they could discuss the matter. She volunteered to make the suggestion to Tom at dinner. Darlene agreed.

When Jenny reported back she said that Tom wanted to go to Cancun.

Darlene was suspicious. "Tom wants to see if Harish Patel is still there running the bar on the beach in Tulum," retorted Darlene.

"Who is Harish Patel?"

"He was one of the men involved in Tom's first misadventure in Central America. Tom is convinced Patel was the lone survivor of four Americans who organized a criminal enterprise to sell Mayan gold and jade, and in the process stole Tom's pilot's plane. The police reported that all four men died but Tom is convinced he saw one of the men, named Harish Patel, in Tulum. Tom has wanted to go back and talk to the man."

"Would it hurt if that was Tom's ulterior motive for the trip?" Jenny tried to mediate.

"No, it wouldn't matter. But I hate to give in."

"Do you know you can take a cruise from Tampa to Grand Cayman Island and then over to Cozumel and the ship then makes a stop at the Maya Riviera. You could go shopping and Tom could go down to Tulum. Tulum is a day trip just 30 miles south of there."

"Have you been there?"

"We went last year for our anniversary. It was very safe. They even have a Walmart. They have a ton of Mexican pottery. You can even buy Mexican roofing tiles." Mexican tiles were "in".

* * *

Carnival Cruises operated a large ocean liner into the Caribbean Sea out of the Port of Tampa. The ship made a short run for a four day cruise that included stops at the Caymans, Cozumel and Maya Riviera.

Tom should have come clean and told Darlene he intended to take the day trip to Tulum, but he knew she would know he wanted to see if Harish Patel still existed.

* * *

When they got to Playa del Carmen, Darlene said she wanted to stay in the boat in the casino and play the card game called Hearts.

"Why don't you take a ride to Tulum and see if that man is still there?" suggested Darlene with a smile.

"I would like that." Tom was amazed, but then his wife was amazing.

I might as well let him get the itch out of his system, thought Darlene. He even danced with her.

* * *

Once Tom was on shore he walked up the brick street to the bus stop on the escarpment. He was relying more on his cane now. Even after he took double the medication the doctor ordered, he was not steady on his feet.

The main street in Playa del Carmen was festive and had many shops to tempt the Yankee out of his dollar. Tom walked with his head down, watching his feet. He was afraid he would trip on the uneven bricks or be knocked down by a tourist chasing a bargain. He did not want to suffer a broken bone in his leg, particularly if he had to seek medical care in the Yucatan.

At the top of the hill, Tom looked for a bus to Tulum and he was directed by a young boy in a white shirt and grey pants and an official shiny black cap. "Here, Senor. Here is the bus to Tulum."

Tom tipped him with a few Mexican coins.

"Thank you, Senor."

The bus was air conditioned. It was almost freezing. The passenger seats operated with individual power control switches so each passenger could get a view of the highway and the visage along the road. It was a thirty mile trip. The road was smooth as glass and after they had passed a pantheon of world brand consumer emporiums (Walmart, Costco, CVS, et cetera), the passengers were served drinks and snacks.

Soon, Tom was asleep.

* * *

"Watch your step, Senor, Senora. Please be careful."

Tom was awakened by the young boy who was speaking to the passengers as they disembarked. The passengers formed into lines and in groups, English speakers, Japanese, Spanish and German. Each group was marched off to visit a separate part of the Mayan ruin and they then had an hour of free time, and were then expected to be back at the bus. However, if they missed the bus, they were advised that they should just embark on the next bus. The buses ran every two hours all night long and it would carry them back to Playa del Carmen and they could catch a launch to the ship.

Instead of going to the ruins, Tom got off the bus and into the line of old men headed for the bar. There was a sign that said "Cantina" and "Whiskey" and "Beer" in as many languages as there were lines of men who headed out to the ruins. Tom went to the bar and asked to see the owner.

"Cervices?" asked the bartender. "An ice cold beer would be refreshing?"

"Fine, fine" said Tom as he watched the bartender pour the beer. "Is the owner available?"

"Could I ask why you want to see the owner? Have we displeased you in any way?"

"No, it's not that. I met the owner here about 25 years ago when he was building the cantina. I wanted to say hello."

"Just a minute, then. I will get him for you."

Tom waited. His bus left to return to Maya Riviera and another bus took its place. The frost on the beer had turned to sweat and Tom replaced the full glass of warm beer with a can of soft drink. He did not drink any of the beer or the soda.

Tom was persistent. The second bus left and a third pulled up to the curb. Another group of tourists stepped out and split up, with some going to the ruins and some to the cantina. Tom moved to a table and was bored. He began to read and re-read the menu until it was memorized.

A tall man came over to the table.

"Sorry I took so long, a busy day," said the man.

"Are you the owner?" asked Tom, thinking, this is not Harish Patel. He was too tall and he had a full head of hair. I have looked at a number of pictures of Patel, thought Tom, and I saw him in person. This is not Patel.

"Yes, yes, I am the owner."

"Did you build this cantina?"

"Yes, I built it after the hurricane about 25 years ago."

"Do you know Harish Patel?"

"Yes, he works here." The tall man laughed. "You didn't mistake me for Harish Patel, did you?" The tall man laughed again and shared the joke with the bartender. "He thought I was Harish Patel," and both men laughed.

Tom apologized. He said he was embarrassed and he was sorry to have bothered the successful businessman.

"No problem, senor," said the man.

Tom asked, "Where are the restrooms?"

The barkeep pointed to the sign marked: "banjos".

Tom took his cane, paid his bill and apologized again, and headed for the bathroom.

"Save the change for Mr. Patel," said the barkeep and he smiled. Tom did not understand.

Tom went down the hall and the hall split to the left and the right for separate rooms for men and women. There was a chair and a small table with a tray containing a few coins and pesos for the attendant in the men's room. Tom tossed in more coins that clinked into the tip tray.

"Gracias, Senor" a voice said from inside a stall in the men's room. The man walked out holding a toilet plunger. He was bald. Tom recognized him as Harish Patel. He took a minute to study him, to make sure.

Patel asked Tom if he was alright. This old man was staring at Patel and it made him nervous.

"A little dizzy," said Tom, leaning on his cane.

"I am like that too. Life is like purgatory. It is my purgatory. I am like that all the time. I am dizzy. Can I tell you about my life? At one time I was a lawyer in America."

"No, I am sorry," said Tom. "I am late for my bus."

"Can I help you to the bus?" asked Patel.

"No, no. Everything is in order."

* * *

A young boy helped Tom back on the bus for the trip back to Maya Riviera. When Tom was back in town he boarded the launch. Tom was the only person on the small boat that shuttled passengers back to the ocean liner.

When Tom entered the door to his berth on the ship, Darlene was dressing for dinner. She wore a powder blue gown.

"Did you see Mr. Patel?"

"Yes"

"Did you speak to him?"

"Yes." Tom explained what Patel was like and where he worked as a bathroom attendant.

"Just desserts," said Darlene. "Tom, get dressed or we will be late for dinner. We have a seat at the Captain's table"

"Okay, okay."

Chapter 14
Clemenso's Trials

After Clemenso Me Bondi was arrested in Belize, the law firm continued to practice criminal and civil law without any particular distinction for a period of four years. Tom got stronger and he could walk with the assistance of his cane alone. He could speak well if he concentrated on what he was saying.

During that time there were numerous trials and appeals of the eight homicides Bondi was accused of committing.

The results of the trials were surprising.

First, the evidence that resulted in Clem's convictions for the deaths of Lori Schaeffer and Detective Richard Cook were the shoe impressions from Bondi's size 14 shoe found on Lori's back and on the piece of dry wall in the detective's home in the Town of Kendal. The death penalty was not imposed on these convictions. The jury failed to reach a majority decision in order to recommend to the judge that the death penalty should be imposed, and the judge did not intervene and impose the death sentence over the recommendation of the jury that Clem should live.

Second, Bondi was found guilty of the crime of manslaughter for the death of Derek Kline on the basis that Clem was acting in some semblance of self-defense when he shot the piece of wood that splintered and hit Kline, causing the rupture of Kline's carotid artery and his death. Tom's analysis of the trial was that Bondi had a good lawyer who confused the jury. The maximum sentence for the crime of manslaughter is 15 years in prison, and Bondi was sentenced to the maximum.

Third, there was insufficient evidence to proceed to trial for the murders of Lucy Hale and the bum with no left thumb. There was no one who could testify to identify the killer, nor was there any physical evidence that Bondi committed those crimes, and Clem did not confess to the homicides.

Fourth, Bondi was convicted of the first degree murder of Phil, the bartender of The Showtime Bar in Gypsonton, Florida, and the death of Det. George Randell in the shootout at Derek Kline's home in Tampa. The jury recommended the imposition of the death penalty for the death of the bartender and Det. Randell; however, these convictions were overturned on appeal. These cases were awaiting a ruling on the motion for a new trial.

Last, the jury convicted Bondi for the death of Anthony Stewart, Tom's investigator, and there was a unanimous recommendation by the jury that the death penalty be imposed and the judge sentenced him to death. The appeal court affirmed the conviction and the imposition of the sentence of death. This is the sentence that was carried out by the state.

Once Clemenso Me Bondi was executed, the defense attorneys for the other cases filed Motions to Dismiss the cases on the basis that Bondi was deceased. These cases were summarily dismissed.

Chapter 15
Old Sparky

Joanne Stewart, Anthony Stewart's widow, received a letter notifying her of the planned execution of Clemenso Me Bondi on February 17, 1992. Mrs. Stewart was 78 years old and had diabetes. She did not feel she was physically able to attend but she wanted the family to have a representative to witness the execution. She asked Tom if he would go.

After Bondi's trial and conviction and the appeals, Joanne Stewart just wanted the matter to be over. Tom knew what she meant. He was over it, too. It seemed like his practice had stalled; he accomplished nothing. He was waiting for Bondi's demise, but the state's view of justice ground ever so slowly.

Clem Bondi's execution had been set more times than Mrs. Stewart cared to remember, and then it would be postponed. The reason for the delays had nothing to do with the question of Bondi's guilt, but the question of the appropriateness of the application of the death penalty. This time it looked like it would go off as planned at 7:00 a.m. Clem had waived all rights to appeal his conviction and sentence, and had fired his lawyers so no one would file any papers on his behalf to extend his life. Clem Bondi had controlled his fate. He knew the manner, time and place of his death. Waiving his right to appeal was another act of bravado on his part.

Tom and Faircloth had to leave St. Petersburg at 1:00 a.m. to make it to Florida State Prison at Starke, Florida, on time for the event.

Although there had been appeals arguing that death by electrocution was cruel and unusual, and Janet Reno, the US Attorney General, opined the death penalty was not a deterrent to murder, "Old Sparky", as the electric chair was called in Florida, was still a constitutionally viable option of capital punishment.

As Tom drove to the prison there were demonstrations for and protests against the death penalty. The demonstrators were in a field across from the prison. The groups respected each other's space and were mostly quiet. The groups could be heard but the sound was like a murmur and what was being said by the opposing demonstrators was indistinguishable. Both groups were praying to the same God or prophet to bless their opposing views.

The witnesses assembled at 6 a.m. and were led to a witness room, and they sat on benches or tan folding chairs. The area was under construction and the death chamber was being renovated. The intention was to allow death to be administered by lethal injection, and the electric chair had been moved to temporary quarters to allow work on the installation of the new, more humane instrument of death—the needle.

In about an hour, after the witnesses were seated, the curtain that divided the old oaken chair and the witnesses was pulled aside. Clem was strapped to the chair. It took a while for him to get his bearings and look about the room. There were a few people who coughed, but there was no other sound.

The prisoner was asked if he had any last words. Clem shook his head and smiled.

The warden nodded and a man in a white shirt placed a leather strap over Bondi's mouth and a hood over his head and then stood back. The Warden looked at the phone. It was a direct line to the Governor. The Governor did not interfere. The phone did not ring.

The warden nodded again and there was a jolt of electricity that caused Bondi to stretch at his leather restraints. Then Clem went slack and a second surge of electricity coursed through his body. Clem's fingers were clenched in a fist. The doctor removed the hood and checked Clem's vital signs. When the hood was removed, the witnesses could see there was blood that ran from Clem's nose and smoke rose from his bald head. The doctor pronounced the prisoner dead. The curtain was closed and the warden announced that the proceedings were over. Tom made notes of everything and the execution became part of his record and case file. Tom could not take photographs of the proceedings so he made a drawing of the event for his file. Tom's drawings were poor, but they sparked his memory of the events.

Tom overheard a guard taking questions from a reporter. "What had gone wrong?" the reporter asked. "I never saw blood or smoke before."

The guard said the machine did its job but performed imperfectly this time.

"Mr. Bondi died poorly." The guard explained, "It sometimes happens."

Tom's sketch of the execution of Clemenso Me Bondi.

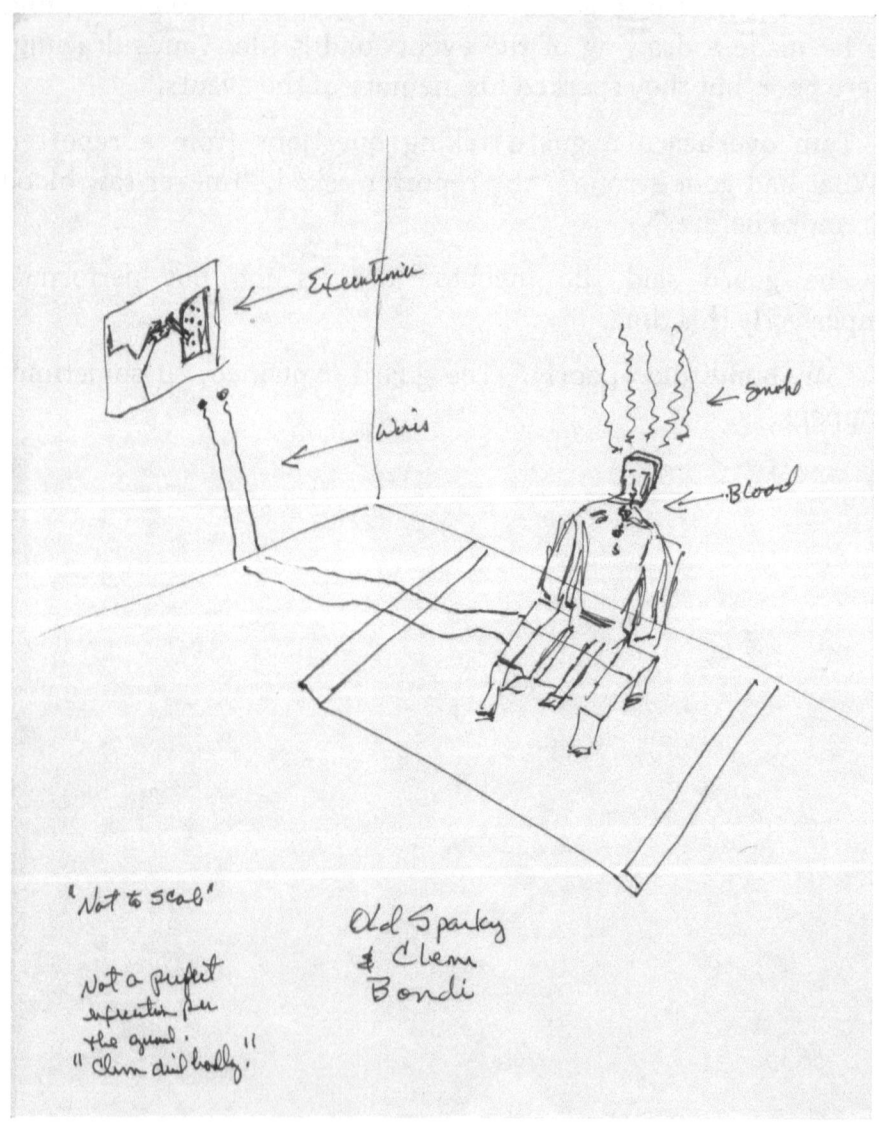

Part II
Strangulation by debt ...
cruel and unusual punishment

Chapter 16
Century Bank

Hiding facts from your wife is difficult when you are used to telling the brutal truth. But Tom had been unable to tell Darlene that the bank had called Tom for a meeting because the law firm had overdrawn its line of credit and the firm had done so in a spectacular fashion. He had to go in to the bank in Tampa and speak to the President and explain what had happened and how the deficit would be resolved.

In the past, if the account was overdrawn the resolution of the problem was simple. The bank simply increased the amount of the line of credit. Then Karen, the firm's bookkeeper, would draw down on the new, higher amount of the loan. The money was needed for payroll and costs of operations and it was properly spent, mostly anyway; except for a war here and there.

It seemed that at least once a year Tom would have to make a phone call to the bank to ask for an increase in the loan. In the beginning when asking for an extension of the line he had talked to a manager, and then he had to talk to a higher authority, a Vice President. Now, the President of Century Bank required him to appear in person to request an increase in the line. Tom had to drive over the bridge to Tampa and pay for parking and sit in an office with a view of Tampa's skyline from the 38th story of the Century Building, and grovel for a few more shekels so the firm could keep going.

This time was different. It wasn't going to be easy. The President said he was sorry to say that they would only extend the line of credit for another year and the total amount of new credit would be limited to $500,000. At the end of the year the firm would have to satisfy the arrearage owed (which at present totaled $2,857,253.07) and the portion of the new draw of $500,000 that the firm had used for the firm's operations. The firm would have to make arrangements with another lending institution for their future borrowing requirements. Century Bank would no longer make a loan to the firm.

The President was very specific that the loan was to be used for the law office only. "No more extra-curricular activities like fighting the guerrillas in Panama; the drug cartel in Belize, or whatever else you might be into these days." The president smiled.

The President also said that the bank required, "Sad to say," that Tom and Darlene would need to provide adequate collateral for the extension of the new line and for the amount that was past due. The collateral had to be provided before the firm would receive the new loan extension of $500,000.

"The value of the new collateral required before the bank will extend you the loan will be over three million dollars. Will you be able to provide additional collateral on short notice?"

"I suppose." Tom smiled his best debtor smile. "What collateral are you looking for to securitize the arrearage and the extension of the line?"

"You and Darlene have those two condos overlooking Tampa Bay." The banker was looking into Tom's eyes to gage his reaction to the words. "I understand the view is spectacular. We would like a mortgage on that property."

I bet you would, Tom thought. However he did not say that. What Tom said was: "When this bank first extended the line of credit to the firm, I gave the bank a mortgage on my office building. Is that property no longer sufficient collateral for the loan?"

"No. I'm afraid it's not sufficient," said the banker. "We are awash in small office buildings since the recession. I am afraid your office is not worth what it once was."

Tom felt the banker was wrong about the value of his office building. "I don't mean to argue, but have you appraised my office recently? It's free and clear of all debt except for Century Bank's mortgage."

"Sorry Tom, the appraisal on the building only came in at $350,000."

The banker put on his "I'm sorry" face and continued the spiel he made to customers daily. "I hated to ask you to come in to talk about this. We have had a banking relationship for many years."

"Yes," Tom interjected. "It's been decades that we have had this relationship. We have paid the bank a lot of interest over that time."

"Yes. Your firm has been a customer for decades," agreed the banker. "But you got way ahead of the bank's loan committee. It seemed like every time we would have to reign in your loan you would hit a big fee on a case and you would pay us back and you were current. But you have gone quite a while without a big fee and we have to do something. We are feeling insecure."

"Could you just let this ride for another year without asking for additional collateral?" Tom was embarrassed to say it but he did. "I will have to talk to Darlene about this." (A fate worse than death.)

"I do not think you are hearing me, Tom ... under our new proposal the bank will let it ride for another year. We will extend the line with an additional $500,000. But we cannot be left unprotected. We need collateral to cover the full amount of the loan or we cannot provide the additional credit."

"Understood," said Tom. "Sorry it's got to this point. It snuck up on me, too. I didn't think we owed so much."

The men stood up and shook hands and smiled.

"Nice seeing you again, Tom."

"Right," said Tom; firm handshake; no sweaty palms. Tom left.

* * *

The banker called his attorney and told him to prepare a mortgage and note indenturing Tom and Darlene's condo units. The banker was very clear with his attorney. He said: "You need to make sure the loan documents are iron clad. We can't afford to let this loan default if we do not have sufficient collateral."

"I'll do the best I can," replied the attorney. "Tom Night is a damn good lawyer. There will be a question if Tom and Darlene bankrupt as to whether the condos are their Homestead Property. Homestead property is exempt from the claims of creditors in bankruptcy."

"We need to get the legislature to change that loophole," said the banker. "I hope your best is good enough. Home office in North Carolina will have my hide if we cannot make collection on this debt."

* * *

As Tom drove back to St. Petersburg over the Howard Frankland Bridge, he looked at the number he had written on his legal pad:

$2,857, 253.07 plus $500,000 equals $3,357,253.07.

That is enough to bankrupt Darlene and me, thought Tom. I wish I had set aside the money I received when CCC Corporation was sold. But Tom had none of that fee left. The money seemed to flow through his fingers, to taxes and office expenses and a new Mercedes every few years.

It's hard to hold on to a chunk of cash. It's a good thing Alphonse, DeMarco and Jenny didn't sign the loan documents for the line of credit or they would be on the hook, too. I don't know what Darlene is going to say, thought Tom.

As usual, there was a traffic jam on the Howard Frankland Bridge heading back to St. Petersburg. As a result, Tom was stuck on the bridge.

As Tom sat in his brand spanking new 450SL Mercedes Benz convertible, which was now parked on the apex of the Howard

Frankland Bridge waiting for traffic to clear, he watched the recreational boaters in the bay below, who were enjoying the sun and the water and fishing.

Tom's mind wandered from the scene of pleasure to the problem.

It isn't like we aren't working, thought Tom. We just aren't making any money. Everyone is working 50-60 hours a week, but we aren't paying the bills.

The downfall, the killer (literally), had been the Mark Luke John Person fee dispute. The firm had been paid $400,000 by the child killer's aunt, and the money had been properly escrowed in the firm's trust account. The attorneys had worked hundreds of hours on the five murder cases and the money in escrow had been paid to the firm's operation account from escrow to pay fees and costs in the defense of the case as the money was earned. And then Person's aunt who had paid the fee from her retirement savings, sued the firm for the return of the money after her nephew was killed by the police in a shoot-out.

Person's aunt claimed her money was only to be used to pay for the trial in her nephew's case. Her nephew never went to trial. He was killed by the police prior to trial. So, she reasoned her nest egg should be returned to her. The fee agreement was unclear. DeMarco had handled the case at its inception and the fee agreement was in writing but it was only signed by Mark Luke John Person. The aunt had not signed a personal guarantee, and there was a question if the fee could be enforced against the aunt. It was her retirement money, after all. Her nephew, Mark Luke John Person was broke.

At first, Tom thought the suit for return of the fees was a joke. Then, after realizing it was a reality that had to be dealt with, Tom tried to settle the case before the firm had to file the answer to the lawsuit. But no luck ... then the case was in court and everyone had to hire a lawyer and it was like wild animals fighting in the bush in Africa on a moonless night. Everyone was wounded before it was over. Tom couldn't stand to watch the carnage. Six months into the litigation, without consulting or telling anyone, he went to the firm's line of credit with Century Bank and withdrew $400,000, and he returned the full amount of the fee to Person's aunt's attorney, Richard Sumter. It was better to settle the case and still have your ears. The aunt's attorney was a real bulldog.

And then there was the cost of the capture of Clem Bondi.

"Don't even ask me how much that cost," Tom had told Darlene as they argued about the expenditure after Tom was safely back in the country and Clem was in jail.

Now Tom had to talk to Darlene about the line of credit. It was a fate worse than death to have to be honest with your wife and admit there was a problem.

* * *

"Where is Tom?" asked Darlene.

"Tampa," said Karen.

"Why is he in Tampa?"

"He had an appointment."

"Who with?"

"The bank."

"Why?"

"To renew the line of credit."

"We never had to go to Tampa before to do that."

"It's something new."

Darlene looked Karen, the office manager, directly in the eye.

"Karen, tell me what is going on."

"The bank wants additional collateral to renew the line of credit."

"How much do we owe?"

"Best I can figure, it is about three million dollars."

"What does the bank want for collateral?"

"They probably want your condos."

"Well, Karen, don't tell anyone. "

"Okay."

"We will work this out."

* * *

"How was Tampa?" Darlene asked Tom.

"I got stuck on the bridge on the way back." said Tom as he walked to his room and began to look through his messages. He wondered which of the little pieces of paper on his desk would contain the name of the new client who would provide the work and the fee that would pay back the bank.

"Karen," Tom yelled out his door to his secretary.

"What?" Karen yelled back. Then she came to the door and stood there looking at Tom, waiting for him to compose himself.

"God, I hate the trip to Tampa. What in this mess of papers on my desk is important?"

"Tom, look at me," said Karen. "I told Darlene."

"Thank you," said Tom. "I can always rely on you to do the right thing."

* * *

A few days later, Century Bank's attorney delivered the new loan documents and the mortgages leveraging the condos and the office building. The bank also wanted Jim and Jenny DeMarco and Alphonse Alesse to sign personal guarantees for the debt. On Tom's advice, the three refused to sign. They refused to become obligated for the debt.

At first, the banker insisted all of the attorneys in the firm sign or there would be no $500,000 extension. But then Century Bank's attorney backed down. He knew the personal guarantees were not part of the oral repayment agreement that Tom made with the bank president at the meeting in Tampa.

"I can't fault you for trying to get more than was agreed, but my partners are not going to sign the guarantees," Tom told the lawyer testily. "I will pay back what we owe." Tom's pride had entered the equation and luckily, God intervened and Tom did not get in a fight, rolling around on the floor with the bank's attorney.

The bank's attorney backed down.

After the bank's attorney left with the loan documents that only Tom and Darlene had signed, Karen made copies and shared them with Jim, Jenny and Alphonse.

* * *

That night, Darlene and Tom were awake all night. They each sat in a chair with a cat on their lap and they listened to the cats' purr.

"And you were telling me I need to retire," said Tom. "I'll be lucky to retire when I'm 85 years old."

"Regardless. You will be 85 in any event."

"I hope I make it to 85. It reminds me of the client I once had who was sentenced to 60 years in jail. The man told the judge he couldn't do 60 years. The judge looked at the man and said for him to do as much of the sentence as he could."

Darlene smiled. She loved Tom's stories.

Part III
Salvation

Chapter 17
Introduction to Colin Frasier

Tom was at the door waiting for a response to his rapid and vigorous rapping. It was starting to rain ... autumn season ... sun showers.

A short, petite man answered his knock and said, "No soliciting," and began to close the heavy wooden door that fit into the main arched alcove of the 50,000 square foot Mediterranean style mansion on the bayou in Northeast St. Petersburg.

"I am not soliciting. It's Tom Night. I'm here to see Colin Frasier." Tom handed the little man a business card. "I have an appointment."

"Whatever." The man turned away from the open door and left Tom to make his way into the spacious alcove. The greeter threw Tom's card into a Venetian glass bowl sitting on a hand carved oak table in the center of the room. Though the rain continued, the entryway was lit with sunlight streaming through large stained glass windows. The very expensive, thick leaded glass bowl on the oak table was overflowing with other professional cards.

Tom closed the door. It latched and the lock clicked automatically and locked securely.

Tom, following the little man, wove his way into the sitting room through mounds of old magazines and newspapers and other ephemera stacked on the floor and the furniture. Tom had some difficulty using his cane around the obstacles in the way.

The tables were Mission Oak, probably original (Stickle), and expensive, Tom thought.

The butler (Maybe the rude little man was the butler, Tom thought) directed Tom to a chair.

"You will have coffee, cream and sugar," the butler guessed.

"Really, I prefer it black."

"Have it with cream and sugar or we'll be here all day arguing about the coffee." Tom heard a low, quiet man's voice. "The servants here do not know their place."

Tom turned to the man seated in the overstuffed wing back chair. The man seemed equal in size and height to the butler who had walked away to attend to the coffee. The man in the chair directed Tom to sit. Tom sat down and had a most uncomfortable feeling, like he had lowered himself onto a golf ball that was hidden under the thin velvet cushion in the seat. Tom stood and removed the cushion from the chair and, surprise, there was a ball. Tom inspected the dimpled orb. It was engraved with the term, "#3 Ben Hogan."

"Been looking for that." The man snatched the ball from Tom's left hand. When the man rose Tom could see his host was about four foot six inches in height.

"I am the man who asked you here to my home." The man stumbled over his words. "I am Colin Frazier." The little man was perfect in every way; sculptured and waxen and manicured.

Tom looked around the room. The man had a thing for collecting. The table lamps had glass shades that were created by Louis Comfort Tiffany. There were five shades covering lamps helping to illuminate the large room, and the walls were covered with paintings, all by artists who painted Florida subjects, and all very pricey. There were paintings by Martin Johnson Heade, Thomas Hart Benton, N. C. Wyeth, Harold Eter, Emmet John Fritz and Benson Bond Moore. As he stood after handing the little man the golf ball, Tom inspected the walls and absorbed the beauty of the oils. The paintings were of nature and women. Both subjects were pleasantly curving and titillating.

Tom sat back down carefully. He leaned back into his wing back chair and felt the smooth nap of the velvet upholstery. The feel of the material was distracting, almost sexual. Tom pinched the side panel of the chair and hooked the crook of his cane on the arm of the chair.

Another servant delivered a cup of coffee, black. Tom was pleased the coffee was black, but ignored the beverage, leaving the cup in the saucer on the walnut side table to his right, allowing the liquid to grow cold.

"I need your help, Mr. Night," the little man said. "I believe my family has been attacked. Perhaps an attack will be made on my life soon, too."

"Why would that be?" asked Tom. "Do you have enemies?"

"Oh, I have enemies, let me tell you." The little man was gesturing with his hands and arms.

"Really, you have more than one?"

Tom tried to look serious, trying to appreciate the man's concern, although Tom thought Colin could just be a nut. I'll humor him, Tom thought. But Darlene, his wife and partner, who he trusted, had told him he needed to see Mr. Frasier. She had told him he was known to be a bit strange but very, very wealthy and he would pay handsomely for advice. Tom may have grown too old to try criminal cases, but he would never be too old to give advice. Besides, the firm desperately needed fees to pay back the bank.

"Yes. Over the years, over the hundred and six years of my life, I have made enemies. My age has left me vulnerable."

"Have you considered a security service? I am just a lawyer. I don't carry a weapon and I could not protect you." Tom considered the question of the man's age. Really, thought Tom, Colin Frasier did not look a day over 70. His hair was black and only flecked with gray. He had few wrinkles.

"No one can protect me from a devil and that's who is after me—a devil."

"Maybe you need a priest." Tom knew he made a mistake referring to the clergy as soon as he mentioned the priest.

"Don't patronize me," lectured Frasier as his voice raised and crackled.

"I don't want to waste your time, sir. If I can't help you, I can't help you." Tom admitted then that he had physical problems. "I too am old and have neurological disorders affecting my balance and my speech. How do you expect me to protect you?"

"I am aware of your disabilities, but I know you are the one who can help me."

"Why are you so sure?" asked Tom as he fidgeted in the chair, anticipating he would have to use the bathroom soon.

"Do you know the British Honduras?"

"Yes. Belize. I am familiar with the country of Belize."

"You have a law firm in Belize, do you not?"

"Yes we do."

"You are acquainted with Andrew Prince Sr.? He was once the Solicitor General of the country?"

"Yes, his son, Andrew Prince, Jr., is a lawyer and my partner in Belize." Tom continued, "Mr. Prince Senior, works for us as the business manager for the firm in the office in Belize City. I was not familiar with the fact that you are a client or connected with the law firm. Have we provided you with service in Belize?"

"I am not a client at present, but I want to employ you and your firm in Belize to handle a matter that is important and grave. It involves my daughter, Coleen."

"Then you need help for your daughter, not for you?" asked Tom "Is your daughter in Belize?"

"I am not sure but I believe she is still in that country."

"Did you inform the police here in St. Petersburg that your daughter has gone missing?"

"She's free, white and nineteen, but ... I have proof that she is in trouble ... she invoked our private distress signal." Colin Frazier took a minute. "Besides, I think she is in Belize, not here in St. Petersburg."

"Belize has a police force, the Belize Defense Force (BDF). Their officers are well trained. You could just call the BDF."

"I am not going to rely on the BDF to recover my daughter."

"Why do you believe that your daughter is in danger in Belize?"

"I gave her a credit card to use in emergencies and she was to use it only if she was in danger."

Tom scooted forward in his chair to concentrate. "You mean if the credit card was used it was a signal to you that she was in trouble."

"Correct, Mr. Night."

"And the card was used?"

"Yes."

"When was the card used?"

"Two days ago."

"Where was the charge on the credit incurred?"

"At the Black Rock Rapids Resort in the Mountain Pine Ridge in western British Honduras."

"I have heard of the Black Rock Rapids Resort, but I have never been there. It's noted for the kayaking in the nearby Macal River, or so I've heard."

"Yes. It is so considered and has been rated 'top notch' for kayaking, they say. But I wouldn't know. I have never been there either," said Frasier.

"I understand," said Tom. He was aware that Frasier never left his house and he was a hermit known only to his staff.

Tom knew this personal information because he had asked Jim Faircloth, his investigator, for background on Frasier after the appointment had been scheduled. Tom had read the report as Faircloth drove Tom to the Frasier residence.

Per Faircloth, Frasier was a billionaire recluse leaving his home only after dark and then he was wrapped in the safety of a 1988 Silver Cloud Rolls Royce. He was the richest man in Florida. His vehicle was said to have been once owned by the Queen of England. The motor car was built like a tank and could withstand a heavy weapons assault. Frasier's chauffeur was trained, Special Forces, retired US Army.

According to Faircloth, the number of times Frasier left his residence during the daylight hours were few. Frazier's residence was like a small city. It was considered to be and was known as the most exclusive mansion on Razor Clam Boulevard, which was the most exclusive address and neighborhood in St. Petersburg, Florida. There was no reason to leave the mansion. It had everything.

Of his few trips from home, Frasier visited a doctor in Clearwater. The doctor refused to make house calls. Frasier had seen the doctor for over 40 years and Frasier believed his longevity was in part due to the care of this particular doctor and so he took the risk of a trip to the doctor's office during daylight. (According to Faircloth it was reported that Frasier also believed a teaspoon of turpentine was an elixir for what ailed him and he took a dose daily. However he took the turpentine against his doctor's advice.)

On a weekly basis, Frasier also visited a Jesuit priest who was in a nursing home. There in the health care facility, on the hard vinyl tile floor, Frasier would get on his knees and make his confession to the Almighty and beg for forgiveness for his sins. The priest was suffering dementia and Frasier had to assign his own penance. The priest was still able to present Frasier with the Host and Frasier took Communion.

Faircloth had failed to discover an official record that Frasier had any children, although Colin admitted on his tax returns to having one daughter. Faircloth could not find a record of any marriage.

* * *

Tom could tell Frasier was tired. The men had spoken for an hour and Tom was through with the interview. Tom had to know and be told by Frasier what it was Tom could do to help. Tom had to be hired to perform a duty for his new client. He had learned a hard lesson by not being hired by Mark Person's aunt. Tom needed Colin to say the magic words.

"Find my daughter, please," said Colin. "Please do that for me and I will pay you."

These were the magic words that made the employment contract legal and binding. Tom agreed to the engagement.

Tom asked for a photograph of Coleen, which Frasier provided from the mantle.

"Is there anyone else who would help us in the search? A single photo and the last known location is a little thin for us to successfully find your daughter."

Frasier had produced a vitae for Tom listing all the information Frasier had that Tom might need to locate her. "This is everything I know about my daughter." Frasier handed Tom a single sheet of paper with a few lines of data.

Tom looked through the notes Colin had written on the page: "Age- 19- female /Caucasian. Brown hair, brown eyes, 5'11" tall, slender- athletic- no scars or other distinguishing marks. She's rather plain looking."

"Where is her mother?" asked Tom.

"I know this sounds like my life is a soap opera, but a woman surrogate was implanted with my zygote. The female was hired for the purpose of carrying my heir, so that there would be a survivor of my line. The surrogate never saw the child, my daughter, after her birth."

Strange, thought Tom. Then Tom asked, "What about your daughter? What is important to her?"

"I don't know," said Colin.

"Is she artistic? A scholar? What motivates her?"

"I do not know who would know. I don't know. Why is this important? I would say she is athletic. She likes kayaking, I suppose." Frasier was becoming frustrated.

"You said she has a room here. Does she actually live here?" Tom thought he could find clues about the girl in the room.

"Sometimes she resides here."

"Can I see her room?"

"It's in the back." Frasier told the butler to show Tom the suite of rooms. Meanwhile Frazier fell into a daze-like sleep in the chair in the sitting room.

To get to Coleen's room Tom had to be taken down a long hall with large rooms to the left and the right. Each room was over-flowing with expensive items. Each of the rooms was identified with a plaque on the door: Relics, Artifacts, Books, Ceramics, et cetera. One room was filled with decorated Christmas trees.

The door to Coleen's room was locked. The butler went back and then returned with a key. As he opened the door he commented, "You are a lot of trouble."

And you are rude, thought Tom to himself as he ignored the man.

The bedroom was rather simple and contained no unique clues to identify the person who was Coleen Frazier. There was no picture of a boyfriend, or of any friends for that matter. There was nothing in the room which would tell a person who Coleen was; her heart and her soul. After inspecting the bedroom they returned to the sitting room where Tom again met Frasier.

Frasier handed Tom a check in the amount of $100,000.

"This is too much as a retainer for this work." Tom returned the check. "Deliver a check for $10,000 to my office at your convenience. If my fee is more than that we will settle up once I return from Central America."

"Why won't you take this check?"

"If I take $100,000 as a fee for a skip trace, it would appear I am guaranteeing the safe return of your daughter. I cannot ensure my efforts will produce a successful result."

Tom arose from the chair and, supported by his cane, he wove his way through the stacks of papers on the floor back to the front door. Tom thanked the butler for the coffee.

The butler smiled. "It's a special blend."

* * *

Tom was still not allowed to operate a motor vehicle by his doctor, so Faircloth was waiting for him in the car. "What did you think?" he asked.

"You know when that guy dies all they have to do is put a sign outside that says, 'ANTIQUES FOR SALE'. They will make a million dollars the first day." Tom looked at Faircloth. "Where did Colin Frasier make all his money?"

"Bob Barnes (the Secretary of the Department of the Interior) heard of him. He says he's in timber."

"Well we have to find his daughter. That will be our job for a while." Tom looked out the rear view mirror as Faircloth put the car in reverse and backed up, then turned the vehicle in the car circle and proceeded out the private drive of the 20-acre retreat and compound to the street.

"Boss, get the tag number of the car parked on the road."

"What's up?"

"The man in that car watched you go in the mansion and he got the tag number off our car."

"Okay. What's that all about?"

"As much money as Bob Barnes says that guy has, the man is probably a representative of the IRS and he is watching Colin Frasier's comings and goings," said Faircloth.

Chapter 18
Colin Frasier's Recent History

Tom Night rode directly from the mansion on Razor Clam Boulevard to his law office in downtown St. Petersburg. He wanted to speak to his wife Darlene and have his legal assistant, Karen, book the travel arrangements to Belize. Delta Airlines had a direct flight to Tegucigalpa, Honduras, from Miami in the evening. He thought he and Faircloth could take that flight out of Tampa. Then connecting through Miami, they could hire a pilot and a puddle jumper to take them from Tegucigalpa to the international airport in Belize City or better yet, they could call Rick Ibn and hop on one of his planes. Rick still flew an old DC-3 hauling cargo, mostly HVAC equipment. The plane was extremely reliable, and though un- pressurized, it could operate over the Mayan Mountains, which were only 3,500 feet above sea level.

Karen would handle the logistics. Tom just said he needed to go to Belize. She could read Tom's mind as to the particulars. She had been working with him that long.

* * *

When Faircloth checked the Internet he determined the man taking license tag numbers outside the Frasier mansion was driving a rental car, according to the DMV. The small car rental outfit that leased the vehicle was located at Albert Witted Airport on Tampa Bay. Faircloth called the rental agency and complained that the car was being operated unsafely and cut in front of him.

"Was there a collision?"

"No. Who was driving your car?" Faircloth insisted he be told.

The rental agent tried to avoid disclosure of the renter, but relented and gave Faircloth the information.

Faircloth knocked on the door to Darlene's office.

"Come in."

"Boss, Wackenhut Investigators Agency rented the car with the guy recording tag numbers at the Frasier's mansion."

"See if Wackenhut will tell us why they are doing that," said Tom. "I do not want to be in competition with another investigator working on the same case."

Darlene asked Faircloth: "Will your wife let you go to Belize on short notice?'

"I can go. Let me get caught up a bit in the office and I'll call home and ask her." Faircloth left the room.

"What do you know about Frasier?" Tom asked.

"He's a small man, physically," said Darlene.

"How would you know that? Faircloth says he never leaves the house. He's a hermit."

"I know because he has his clothes cleaned at Robert's Dry Cleaners and the owner commented to me that the clothes coming to the cleaner's from the mansion were the finest tailored clothing he had ever seen. Robert, the cleaner, said they were cut for a small person. The cleaner guessed he was less than five feet tall.

"He's old, probably over ninety," Darlene continued. "His butler shops at Colonial Pharmacy. The pharmacist mentioned his age. Colonial is a formulary, and it concocts drugs for the gentleman ... special dietary supplements. That fact being mentioned, he probably has Crohn's disease. Also, he is narcoleptic."

"He's wealthy?" suggested Tom.

"Fabulously so," replied Darlene.

"And he made his money, how?"

"Trees. He buys and sells timber. Deals are brought to him. Mostly they are risky ventures and involve brokers in the Third World. If you have timber to be clear cut in some far off, environmentally sensitive jungle, then he's your man. Recently, the organization Green Peace was angry with him. The NGO is trying to protect the lemurs in Madagascar and Frasier has cut the entire lemur habitat. He's like the fellow in the book about the Lorax.

"He's very intelligent," she continued. "It was his idea that after the loggers cut the jungle in the Amazon, that farmers from the Midwest US plant the land with soybeans. Frasier was paid handsomely for the timber and a second time for the farm land. The original land owners in Brazil thought they were cheated. They did not realize he intended to resell the land to the farmers for soybean production. The Brazilian landowners had left money on the table. They sold too cheaply."

"Then he does have enemies?" asked Tom.

"Yes, everywhere. His security agent, they call him 'Bosco', dates our Karen (it's a small world), and he tells her stories about close calls and the times he's had to save Frasier's life. But he may just be bragging. Bosco is the person who referred Frasier to us. Bosco told Karen that Frasier had a problem in Belize and Karen told Bosco about our office in Central America. They must have inquired and they called for us to talk about their problem."

"How did you know about Frasier and the timber industry?"

"His local accountant reviews his private accounts."

"Is that our accountant, Mr. Hardy?"

"Yes. Our CPA, Mr. Hardy, is a gossip."

"So I guess if Mr. Hardy shares Frasier's secrets we have no secrets either?"

"No. We have none that the CPA is keeping from the world. St. Petersburg, Florida is a small town."

"Does Frasier have family, married, et cetera?"

"Yes, a daughter. He is not married."

"I have his daughter's picture." Tom showed Darlene the photo.

"It doesn't do her justice," said Darlene. "Coleen Frasier is tall, athletic and beautiful. She would easily be hired as an international model if she was just a smidgen taller. She has sharp, Germanic features ... dramatic almost. You will never forget her face when you see her."

"Is she Intelligent?"

"She was well-schooled, but she has never been known to have any common sense. She's something of an airhead, but she went to the best schools. She is in her second year at Columbia Law School."

"How is it you have all this information?"

"Coleen Frasier is the dream daughter-in-law of every woman in St. Petersburg with an eligible son. The girl is wealthy, beautiful and connected to power. Coleen has been the subject of gossip in town since she was two years old."

* * *

Karen was motioning, trying to hand Tom the airline reservations.

"Karen says I have to go. I will miss my flight."

"Be careful. Listen to Faircloth," Darlene instructed Tom. He kissed her lips and she rubbed the kiss into her lips with her fingers.

As Tom went out the door he told Darlene to have their standard contract delivered to Colin Frasier for his signature. The contract also contained a clause stating Frasier guaranteed payment for the work the law firm performed on behalf of his daughter Coleen.

Chapter 19
Black Rock Rapids

The Black Rock Rapids Resort was small, with twelve cabins, but it had complete accommodations for visitors with varied epicurean tastes. Vegans' and meat eaters' appetites were satisfied in private rooms in the dining hall that was separated from the cabins. These vacation residences hung like Christmas ornaments in the Mayan Mountains above the Macal River. The cabins were located on the mountain so that each residence had a sightline to the mountains, the jungle, or the river without a view of the other cabins or their guests.

Privacy was the point; anonymity for the famous.

Tom's Belizean law partner, Andrew Prince, Jr., met Tom and Faircloth at the private airport in the city. One of Rick's pilots had ferried Tom and Faircloth from Tegucigalpa, Honduras over the mountains to Belize. When they landed it was 3 a.m., some 18 hours after Tom had received his assignment from Colin Frasier to find his daughter, Coleen. The private airport handled local traffic and small aircraft and it was located in town next to the Belize "Old River" which flowed through Belize City. (It was called the "Belize Old River" for some unknown reason lost to the ages.)

Andrew told Tom what he knew about Black Rock Rapids Resort, which was very little. It was constructed near a massive black rock in the waterfall on the Macal River, thus its name. The rapids in the river at that point were rated "top notch" in difficulty for rafters or kayakers. The resort tended to draw an athletic crowd that enjoyed healthy foods. Its guests flew into the

International Airport in private aircraft, or commercial if they were only noted in their field and not well known to the public. The Belizeans did not care for fame, but passengers on the Delta flight from Miami would recognize the movie stars and the politicians from television. For that reason they flew in private planes. These guests wanted privacy, yet hated the idea they would not be recognized in a crowd.

As requested, Andrew Prince had made an inquiry with the Belize Defense Forces (BDF) and the American Embassy, but no one was aware Coleen Frasier had entered the country, let alone that she was missing. Customs had no record of her arrival. There were no unclaimed bodies in the morgue or the hospital or rotting away in the insane asylum at Ladyville.

Andrew drove to the law firm's office in the center of the city. It was modern, built fifteen feet above the ground to protect against storm surge from a hurricane. The building was on concrete stilts. Tom was slow climbing the stairs. He did not want to fall and break a bone. Although he felt Ana Hernando's Medical Clinic was first rate, Tom did not want to be laid up in Belize.

The law office had a suite with a bedroom and bath with a shower. Tom and Faircloth cleaned up and changed.

Andrew had marked a map with directions to the river resort which was near the town of San Ignatius. He was loaning them his 1982 Range Rover. The roads were good to San Ignatius and this was the dry season. They would not encounter deep water in any streams they would cross near the Macal River. They should have no trouble once they were traveling on secondary roads and trails, or possible detours from the Western Highway to Belmopan and then past Spanish Lookout to San Ignatius.

Further, for their safety, Andrew loaned Faircloth the law firm's satellite phone. The pair could contact the office in Belize City, or for that matter they could call the office in St. Petersburg, Florida, using the phone. When Andrew knew the purpose of Tom's visit he had called ahead to the Black Rock Rapids Resort and arranged an interview for Tom with the manager of the resort. The manager told Andrew they did not have a guest named Coleen Frasier, but it was expected he would not identify his guests over the phone, even an unknown or non-famous guest such as Coleen Frasier. Tom would have to convince the manager in person that it was important that the resort reveal whether Coleen was there so he could assure her father she was safe.

* * *

It was 4:00 a.m. in St. Petersburg, 3:00 am in Belize. Faircloth was driving. There was no traffic on the roads in Belize City. Once he pulled onto the Western Highway it was a two hour trip to San Ignatius. Faircloth had slept on the plane from Miami but there were storms in the Mayan Mountains and he got no sleep on the trip as they flew in the six-seat Piper aircraft from the capital of Honduras to Belize City. Faircloth was tired, but Tom insisted they drive to the resort and be there first thing in the morning. Tom had no sleep.

Tom was upset that Andrew had called the resort and forewarned the staff of his intended arrival. As Faircloth drove, Tom folded his arms and tried to sleep with his head bouncing against the passenger window. Actually, the road was in good shape from the city to Belmopan and Tom dozed off for a few minutes here and there.

Tom insisted Faircloth fill the gas tank at the Esso Station in the capital. There were two gas tanks in the vehicle and Tom wanted both of them topped off. Gasoline was expensive ($2.00 per liter). Tom and Faircloth freshened up in the restroom and stopped at The Bull Frog Inn. Tom got black coffee and fresh bread and fruit and they were back on the road in an hour. He hoped they would make San Ignatius by 8:00 a.m. Tom hoped that he could speak to the desk clerk at the resort before the manager arrived for work, and try to talk to the staff and see what he could find out about Coleen before he had to argue with the manager. Tom anticipated the manager would tell him nothing.

"Careful on the road here, there are children," said Tom as they passed by the road to Spanish Lookout. The Mennonites had opened a school and the children from neighboring farms were welcome whether they were Mennonites or not. The parents in the area took advantage of the generous offer of a free, basic education.

There were a few boys walking along the side of the road. They wore white, long sleeve shirts and dark trousers and black shoes. There were no girls on the road hiking to school. Tom was pleased with the look of it. He smiled; Pennsylvania Dutch in Central America.

The road to San Ignatius ran along the Macal River. The river wound out of the Mayan Mountains from the Forest Reserve and tumbled down, curving left and right, slicing through the lime rock mountains.

Once in San Ignatius, Faircloth had to ask for the location of the resort. A young boy told them to look for the signs that said "Black Rock" and follow the arrows. The men felt stupid.

Up the side of a mountain, they found the main building and the guard at the gate.

Faircloth began. "We need to speak to the manager," he asked the guard.

"No one is in the office at this time."

"Then we will wait."

"Not here. Wait down the road." Their car was blocking the road.

Tom grabbed the steering wheel and told Faircloth to turn off the engine so that the Range Rover was blocking the gateway. Tom got out of the vehicle and walked around to the guard. Tom stood in the guard's face.

"We have come a long way to find the daughter of my friend, Colin Frasier. Have you seen this young woman?" Tom handed Coleen's photograph to the guard.

"Sorry, I can't speak with you about our guests or anyone who might be a guest."

Tom tried to read the guard's face for any sign he recognized the woman in the photo, but there was no indication.

"We know she was here. She charged for services here at the resort on her credit card." Tom showed the guard the copy of the receipt that Colin Frasier had obtained from the credit card company. Still the guard did not react.

"Where is the closest police station?"

The guard ignored Tom.

Tom tried a different tact. "The BDF ... where are they located?"

"Wait here." The guard walked to the office. When he returned he said, "I was told to tell you that Coleen Frasier left yesterday. She was alone. She rented our jeep and a driver and she visited the Mayan ruins at Caracal and then she was delivered to the International Airport. Again, she was alone. She spent all her time on the river. She is an expert kayaker. That is all we know. We respect the privacy of our clients."

"Thank you." Tom returned to the car and they left and drove into San Ignatius.

"Where to now?" asked Faircloth.

"Caracal, I guess." Tom had no reason to believe the information he was given by the guard was untrue.

To reach Caracal the map said Faircloth had to cross the river and head south. He came to a sign by the road with a vendor selling reproductions of Mayan artifacts. Tom said to stop. He bought a couple of items, Mayan faces carved in lime rock and a basket shaped like a bird. Tom talked to the vendor who was pointing to a road across the highway.

"Follow the road." Tom said to Faircloth as he re-entered the car.

Faircloth drove through a shallow stream and then came to the main branch of the Macal River. There was a man with a raft large enough for a couple of cars. Faircloth drove the Range Rover onto the ferry. The man would take them across the water for a few

Belizean dollars. Both Tom and Faircloth got out of the car for the trip. They paid the fare, crossed the river, and then drove on the road that continued on the other side and to a parking lot. There was an attendant standing in smoke from smoldering citronella oil lamps. There were many large mosquitos to greet visitors. The smoke repelled the insects. Tom and Faircloth got in the smoke, paid the attendant, and then walked to the ruins. They spent time taking photographs; looking like tourists.

Tom went back and spoke to the attendant and showed him Coleen's photo. The man rubbed his jaw and said he had seen her with a man from the resort in the mountain above the area known as Black Rock. There was nothing unusual about her that the attendant could remember except she said she wanted to go as soon as she was bitten by the mosquitos. The attendant thought it was funny.

Faircloth and Tom left the ruins; retraced their route, and headed back to Belize City.

Chapter 20
Backtracking for Coleen

As Faircloth drove over the Western Highway, Tom mulled over the situation. His conclusion was that unless Coleen Frasier felt being attacked by mosquitos was a sufficient provocation to alert her father that she was in danger, nothing had happened in Belize to cause her father any concern. Maybe she had run out of cash and had to use the credit card, or maybe she was looking for attention.

Tom enlisted the help of one more friend to track Coleen Frasier's movement. Rick Ibn was well regarded by the airlines that served the International Airport and he was friends with the customs authorities and the BDF. Tom asked Rick to track Coleen's departure from Belize.

Tom contacted Rick using the satellite phone. This was the first time he used the phone. The convenience of the phone was unrivaled. Tom did not believe any business person would travel internationally without the ability to communicate using such a phone. Rick and his wife had a satellite phone to communicate with the hospital in Big Creek and for Rick's air cargo hauling services. The communications base was at the hospital and at the surgical center in Belize City. Tom called and spoke to Rick's wife Anna Hernando, a medical doctor who had opened the hospital almost 20 years ago.

But first, before locating Rick, Tom and Anna talked about her three girls. They were all in a religious school in Panama City run by the Dominican Sisters, and they were well.

Rick was unavailable. Tom asked Anna to pass on the message that he needed help finding a young woman for a client in St. Petersburg. Anna said Rick was at the airport working for Delta Airlines repairing a new Boeing 757 that was having electrical problems resulting in the smell of smoke in the cockpit. Rick was a certified aircraft mechanic. He had attended school to attain the certification both at Embry Riddle College in Daytona Beach and also at the Boeing factory in Washington State.

"Rick will call you back when he has the information."

* * *

Tom drove back to the law firm's office in Belize City and spoke to Andrew Prince Jr. and was updated on the firms business and accounts. Tom and Darlene realized little profit from the Belize law firm after payment of salaries and expense of the office. The business was all risk and little reward, except when a client like Frasier came along. Colin's retainer would feed the office in St. Petersburg and Belize City for a few weeks. Tom was tired and he nodded off in the luxurious deep leather chair in the law library.

* * *

Tom was asked to come to the phone. Tom rubbed his face and his left hand began to shake. Time for a pill, he thought.

The extension phone rang. "Hello. Yes, Rick," Tom said. "Did you find out where this Coleen Frasier is? Did she leave Belize?"

"She left this morning on a TAN flight to Miami," said Rick.

"Were there any connecting flights?"

"Yes. She was scheduled to fly from Miami this morning. She should arrive there in Tampa early in the afternoon."

"Thank you, Rick. I owe you one."

Tom told Faircloth what he had learned.

"I wonder where she was for the last 24 hours?" asked Faircloth. "I would doubt she stayed at the airport all that time."

"It doesn't matter. She should be on her way home now and will land in Tampa in an hour or so, depending on how long it takes her to go through US Customs in Miami."

Tom took the satellite phone and called St. Petersburg to the residence of Colin Frasier.

The butler answered. "No soliciting," he said.

The man was a broken record, thought Tom. "I'm not soliciting. Mr. Frasier gave me this number to call him when I located his daughter."

There was a pause.

"Hello."

"This is Tom."

"Did you find her?" asked Colin.

"She should be arriving at Tampa International Airport today at around noon. She has a connecting flight out of Miami on Delta."

"Thank you. I will have Bosco retrieve her. What time is the flight again?"

"It should arrive at noon. Flight 207 from Miami. Bosco needs to leave soon."

"Alright. Mr. Night, come to the house when you return. I want to thank you in person."

"I may not be back until tomorrow. The next flight is not until tomorrow morning."

"Still, make sure I see you. It is important," said Frasier.

Tom hung up, then picked up the receiver and called the office and told Darlene what had transpired on a rather uneventful trip.

On the plus side, Tom was able to visit the San Ignatius area and he had never before been to the Mayan ruins at Caracal. Tom laid back and slept in the chair with his feet up on an ottoman.

Faircloth took a shower. They were stuck in the city for the night unless Rick had a cargo flight later to the States. Tom was pushing himself. He had done that successfully his whole life. But this trip was exhausting, His mind and body told him to sleep. Faircloth nodded off. He was tired too. They had not slept for two days.

Part IV

The story moves on . . .

Chapter 21
Shot Dead

"Boss, Boss, wake up."

"What is it?'

"Darlene is on the satellite phone," said Faircloth, holding the phone in Tom's face.

Tom rolled to the side of the bed and got his bearings. He was still in Belize. Someone had to have helped him into bed in the guest suite in the law office. Tom didn't remember going to bed, but remembered he had been exhausted by the trip to Belize and the search for Coleen Frasier. Tom put the phone to his ear and listened as his wife told him that Colin Frasier was dead.

"It's in the paper. It must have happened last night." Darlene began to read the newspaper to Tom.

"SHOT DEAD". That was the newspaper headline. The second line of the front page story said: "SHOCKING NEWS".

"The story is very short," said Darlene. The only facts stated are that Colin Frasier, Florida's wealthiest resident, was shot dead in his mansion on Razor Clam Boulevard last night. The police are searching for the killer."

"What else does the story say?"

"It's only background. It's obituary type material. The paper doesn't even report how old he was when he died."

"Why do we take that rag?" asked Tom. It seemed like he said that every time someone mentioned the Tampa Bay News Journal.

"Anyway, talk to Karen and see if she can talk to Bosco, Frasier's security guard. Bosco will know what is going on. He was supposed to pick up Coleen from the airport yesterday at noon."

"I'll call back soon," said Darlene.

Tom hung up and rubbed his head. He had a terrible headache. "What time is it?"

"Seven AM," said Faircloth.

"What day is it?"

"You slept 12 hours, Boss," said Faircloth. "I didn't want to wake you. Then your wife called with the bad news."

"Come get me when she calls back," said Tom.

* * *

Darlene had been in her office early working on an appeal with her paralegal. She had not seen Karen come in and they had not spoken, though Darlene had called her home phone on the hour since she talked to Tom. Darlene knew Karen would be a good source of news on the death. When Darlene went over to Karen's desk and asked, she was told she wasn't in but she was expected. She had not called in sick. It was only 8:30 a.m. so it was still early, but most of the staff assembled by 8 o'clock. Karen should be in.

"Try Karen and find out when she will be in, please," Darlene asked.

In a few minutes Karen was on the phone.

"Karen. Did you hear from Bosco about Colin Frasier's death?"

"No. I didn't learn of the death until I saw the paper this morning." Karen paused. "But I don't want to mislead you. Bosco did call last night when the police gave him his phone call. He said the police were interrogating him so he couldn't explain what had occurred. He was going to call me back in the morning, but I haven't heard anything yet."

"Did he say anything to you at all?"

"Well, I am afraid to say."

"Talk to me Karen."

"He called last night and asked me to go to the Bell Bar and pick up Coleen Frasier and bring her to my house. He told me to promise to tell no one." Karen paused and took a drag of her unfiltered Camel cigarette. "I went to the bar. I found Coleen there gossiping with the bartender, Paddy. I think Paddy was trying to pick her up. He was stroking her hand. I told Paddy I was there to take her home. Then, I did what Bosco said. I took her home with me and she's in my spare room, sleeping."

"Did she say anything about her father?"

"No, nothing. She was a little tipsy. I loaned her some night clothes and she went to bed."

"What do you know about Mr. Frasier's death?

"Nothing. Bosco said there was trouble at the house. He said there was an argument, but he didn't say there was any violence or a death."

"Did he say if Coleen was involved?"

"Apparently she had been drinking on the plane and was drunk when she arrived in Tampa, and there was a discussion about that. Her drinking was a source of friction between her and her father, I guess. This must have been early, before Mr. Frasier was shot. Bosco really didn't say there was an injury and Coleen didn't say much. She said she just wanted to go to bed to sleep."

"When did you hear Mr. Frasier was dead?"

"I saw the paper when I got up to go to work."

"Did you talk to Coleen this morning?"

"No. She isn't up yet."

"I will come over and we will go together to Karen and wake her up together. We will talk with her."

"I'm glad you called," said Karen. "I didn't know what to do."

Darlene grabbed her purse and scarf and was out the door. Then she realized she had not called Tom. She told her secretary to call the Belize City office and explain that Tom was to get back to Florida with all deliberate speed and she would update him when she could.

* * *

Back in Belize, Tom and Faircloth had both dressed and packed while they waited for the call from Darlene. There was a plane to Tampa in an hour. When Darlene's secretary called with Darlene's advice that they return to St. Petersburg ASAP, Andrew Prince Jr. volunteered to drive the pair to the airport. His secretary called and made reservations. The plane would leave at 9:00 am CST and arrive in Tampa in the early afternoon.

Chapter 22
Coleen Appears

Darlene and Karen sat in the living room in Karen's small bungalow located in the Old Northeast section of St. Petersburg, waiting for Coleen to awaken.

Darlene had received word that Tom and Faircloth were on the plane coming back from Belize. Darlene drove from the office to Karen's. Darlene had gone in to look in on Coleen. The length of her body was longer than the bed, her thin narrow feet and long toes were sticking out of the covers and her head was under a pillow. She was snoring. Best to let her sleep, she thought.

Meanwhile, Darlene called Jim DeMarco and asked him to gather whatever information he could about Colin Frasier's death, and if it was being investigated as a homicide and if it was thought to be a suspicious death; who was the suspected perpetrator. Finally, were there any wants or warrants issued for a suspect? Jim said he would ask Jenny to help. Jenny also knew people in the media and she might be able to get help from those sources.

Darlene and Karen continued to fill up the ashtray with foul, stale, half-smoked cigarette butts.

* * *

Jenny was the first to call with information. Her press sources at the Tampa Bay News Journal said they were going with a story in the a.m., a special edition, that Colin Frasier was murdered. Jenny was able to coax and cajole the reporter to read her his field notes. According to the notes, Frasier was shot in the head at close range, but he did not die immediately. He was sped to the hospital by Bosco in the Silver Cloud Rolls Royce. The reporter shared that the Rolls had been built for the Queen of England. Frasier was in surgery immediately upon his arrival at the Trauma Center. He died on the operating table from a heart attack. He was 106 years old. There were no named suspects, but the police were investigating. The reporter implied that the police were not getting any co-operation from the staff at the mansion.

* * *

James DeMarco said his sources in the State Attorney's office refused to comment but wanted to know what DeMarco knew about the murder. DeMarco said it was interesting that the assistant SA referred to the cause of death as a murder. It could also be a suicide or an accident or natural causes. DeMarco asked why the SA called it a murder and the SA said, "No comment." Demarco asked if there were any wants or warrants issued for a suspect. The SA said, "No", but refused to discuss the matter any further unless DeMarco revealed the identity of his client. DeMarco told the SA he did not have authority from his client to identify the person he represented. DeMarco said the SA was sensitive to questions about the care Frasier received in the Trauma Center. DeMarco asked if malpractice was involved as a cause of death. The SA refused to discuss it.

DeMarco said he called the police, but he could find no one who would speak to him about the investigation into Frasier's death, even off the record, except to say they were interviewing a person of interest. That led DeMarco to believe that the police had someone in custody.

* * *

Karen received a call from the office. Bosco had called and left a message. He asked Karen to bring him clothes for court. He was due in court in the morning. Karen and Darlene discussed the message. Darlene could see no reason for Karen not to do as she was requested and go get the clothes and deliver them to Bosco at the jail. Once she got to the station the police would tell her what Bosco would be allowed to have while he was in custody and how long he was expected to be in the custody of the police interrogators.

Karen left her house and did as she was instructed while Darlene waited for Coleen to wake up.

It was almost noon. Coleen still was not awake and Darlene became concerned and went in the bedroom and shook her, but to no avail. She was still dead asleep, but now she was breathing quietly. She would be out for a while was Darlene's guess.

* * *

Karen drove to the mansion. The mansion was only a few blocks from her house. There was nothing out of the ordinary. There were no police, only a man out front on the public sidewalk who was taking license tag numbers of the cars visiting the mansion. Karen knocked at the front door. The butler let her in. She explained Bosco needed clothes for court. The butler said he had also received the message and said they had prepared the clothes for Bosco from his room.

"We were waiting for you. If you see Bosco, tell him we are all doing okay under the circumstances." The butler handed her the box of clothes. When Karen started to ask the butler a question he told her: "Shush. You don't want to be a witness too, do you?"

Karen said she didn't think she wanted to be that involved and she left.

At the police station, the desk sergeant looked through the box and gave Karen a receipt for the clothes. Anticipating her question, the sergeant said visiting hours were on Saturday from 10 a.m. to 2 p.m. Karen left and returned home. She never got to talk to anyone other than the sergeant.

* * *

Tom and Faircloth's plane touched down at 3:00 p.m. in Tampa. They got in the car and drove to the office. Tom spoke on the phone to Darlene, who was still waiting for Coleen to wake up. Darleen told Tom what she had learned from Jenny and DeMarco and Karen. Tom asked if anyone had called to find out the charge that Bosco was being held on and the amount of the bail. When Darlene said "No," Tom put her on hold and called Lance White, the bondsman and asked him to check the amount of the bond; if bond had been set. Mr. White got on his other phone and discovered that Bosco was being held on a charge of interference with a police investigation and his bond was $5,000. The bondsman told Tom the charge sounded, "... like a bunch of BS. Sounds like your man isn't telling the police what they want to hear."

Tom got back on the line with Darlene. "It doesn't look like they think Bosco is the killer. They are trying to soften him up to get him to tell what he knows." Tom asked to speak to Karen.

"Karen, how well do you know that butler, Mike, at the mansion?"

"I know him just a little."

"Would you call him and tell him they can get Bosco out of jail if they post a $5,000 cash bond. Or it will cost $500 to a bondsman if they don't have the full amount of the bond."

"Oh. Well, I could do that," volunteered Karen. "I can pay the $5,000."

"No. Karen, see what the butler says. It would be better if the staff at the mansion bonded him out of jail."

Tom asked if Karen had a pen. "Give the butler this telephone number. It's for Lance White. He is a bondsman. It would be best if the bondsman got him out." Tom thought a minute. "I'm at the office. Call me if there are any problems." Tom paused to think. "Could you let me speak to Darlene, please?"

* * *

"So?" asked Darlene.

"Is the girl still asleep?" asked Tom.

"Yes."

"Do we represent her or who? I'm confused," said Tom.

"I've thought about this. I've had nothing else to do," said Darlene. "The way I see it, Mr. Frasier paid us to assist his daughter and after he paid us to do that we complied with the assignment in part—partial performance can establish our contract of employment. Then, as time has gone by, the type of assistance needed has changed. We are now providing legal assistance, whereas before we were acting more like an investigative agency. But we are still helping Coleen, which is why we were hired in the first place. We will have to confirm this with Coleen when she wakes up. I think our client is Coleen now that Colin Frasier is dead."

"Okay. That sounds fine." Tom asked these questions because he did not want to pay back any fees to a client ever again. He had been required to do that with Mark Person's aunt.

"I still do not know what Coleen knows about her father's death or if she had anything to do with it," said Darlene.

"So you will stay there and wait for her to wake up and you will talk to her first?"

"Yes."

"I'm going home for a shower." said Tom. "Make sure Coleen hires the firm to represent her."

"Yes, I will."

"Have her sign a contract."

"I will. I will."

Chapter 23
The Investigation

Tom heard the telephone ring from the shower. He turned off the water and went into the bedroom, tracking water on the strawberry colored wall-to-wall carpet. He picked up the receiver and said, "Hello."

"She's awake," said Darlene. "Do you want to come over here to Karen's?"

"No, you talk to Coleen. Let me talk to Karen."

Karen took the receiver and Tom asked, "Have you heard whether the butler was going to pay Lance White to bond Bosco out of jail?"

"I believe he will. He took the information about the bondsman that you gave me and he said he intended to call Mr. White."

"Good, good. Karen, you know that our firm cannot represent Coleen and Bosco together. There would be a conflict."

"I understand."

"I can talk to Bosco as a witness if he wants to talk to me voluntarily, but I would not be his lawyer. I could not give him advice, and anything he said to me would not, under most circumstances be privileged. I could maybe contend my interview with Bosco was work product and claim a privilege, but under certain circumstances the State Attorney or the police could subpoena me and compel me to testify about what Bosco told me."

"I understand. The police could force you to tell them what Bosco told you."

"That's right and that may not be good. Now on the issue of interviewing Coleen, it would be better if Darlene could talk to Coleen alone. I hate to ask you to leave your own home, but ... do you mind going to the office and waiting there until Darlene finishes the interview?"

"I had intended to go to the mansion and wait there for Bosco to bond out. I thought I would stay here and introduce Coleen to Darlene before I left. They never met. Coleen at least knows me. I picked her up at the Bell Bar at closing time. Then after I make sure they are comfortable with each other I will go to the mansion and see if I can help there."

"That would be a good idea," said Tom. "Sorry you are being treated like this."

"It's not your fault. I didn't have to pick up Coleen and bring her here from the bar. I got myself in this. I just don't want to be a witness against Bosco. I love him, you know. It's the first time for me ... being in love. I'm worried for Bosco."

"I don't think Bosco is involved in Frasier's death or the police would have charged him with something other than interfering with the investigation. They are just trying to force him to talk. They don't believe what he's telling them," said Tom.

"I don't think he would lie to the police," said Karen. "He might refuse to talk, but he wouldn't intentionally lie."

* * *

When Karen hung up the phone she heard voices in the kitchen. Coleen was sitting at the table smoothing the red and white checkered tablecloth stretched across the top of the old wooden table with her hands.

"How did he die?" asked Coleen. She was looking at her long thin fingers and twisting them into a ball. She avoided Darlene's gaze.

"Don't you know how your father died?" asked Darlene.

Karen interrupted. "Sorry," she said. "I have to leave for the mansion, I'm going to wait there for Bosco."

"Do you want me to stay here?" asked Coleen.

Darlene could tell Coleen was hoping she could stay at Karen's house. She didn't want to return to the mansion.

"Coleen, you stay here. That would be good," said Karen. "You can talk to Darlene. I will go to the mansion." Karen took her wallet from the counter and car keys and went out the back door.

Darlene looked out the window, trying to think of how to start the conversation. She had told Coleen her father was dead after she got her to sit at the table, but there was no reaction. Coleen just stared at her hands.

"Do you understand your father is dead?" Darlene repeated.

"Yes." Coleen showed no emotion.

"Can I say anything or do anything for you?" Darlene anticipated a need on Coleen's behalf for comfort. Darlene moved closer to Coleen. Coleen retreated and slinked into her chair.

"No. I just want to sit here and think for a minute." Coleen looked up with her soft brown eyes and asked, "You are a lawyer?"

"Yes."

"Can you represent me?"

"Yes, your father hired my firm to find you. He was worried you were in trouble because you used the credit card."

Coleen looked inquisitively at Darlene. "What are you talking about? What credit card?"

Darlene explained how Colin hired Tom and Faircloth to go to Belize and find her and that her father said there was a secret signal between Coleen and Colin involving the use of a credit card to signify that Coleen was in danger.

"This is bizarre," said Coleen. "I don't know anything about a secret credit card. I went to the Black Rock Rapids Resort to train on the kayaking course there. I want to try out for the Olympics. This is the first year the sport of kayaking will be an event in the games."

"I thought you were at Columbia University attending law school."

"I decided to take a break from school."

"Did your father know where you were going?"

"Not exactly. I told him I was going to Belize to practice but that was all I said. I did not say where in Belize. We had a fight. He wanted Bosco to go with me to Belize if I insisted I needed to go there to practice. I told him I was going to go alone. I'm a big girl now."

"And did you go alone?"

"Yes. Somehow he found out I was at the resort. Unfortunately, the hotel had a satellite phone and my father got the number. He kept calling the resort. It was embarrassing. Finally, after I was there for a few days, I left and went to Belize City and stayed at the Fort George Hotel for a day and a night to decide what I was going to do."

"What do you mean?"

"It was time for me to move out of the mansion and get on my own. I will be twenty next week. Most of my life I have been in a private school. I would only see my father in the summer and winter breaks. It was like I was an orphan. I don't know my mother. I wanted to start my own life. I thought that if I threw myself into this new sport I could make a name for myself."

"Do you know anything about the circumstances of your father's death?"

"No. How did he die?"

"The newspaper reports he was shot at the mansion."

"I don't know anything about that."

"No?" Darlene was surprised. "Were you at the house at all?"

"I flew in from Miami and I called Bosco and he took me home. My father was angry with me. We got into an argument and I walked out the door and went to the Bell Bar. I was there shooting pool with Eddie, the resident pool shark. I was wiping his clock." Coleen was bragging. "I took every dime he had. It took me to closing time to do it, though."

"Had you been drinking?"

"Yes, but I was tipsy, not drunk. Paddy, the bartender said he would drive me home. But I knew how that would go. I didn't want to get in a wrestling match with him groping me for the price of a ride. So I called Mike. He said he would get me a ride."

"Did he say anything was wrong at the mansion?"

"No ... nothing. He just said Dad was still upset and I should give him a chance to cool down. So that's what I did. Karen picked me up. She said Bosco called her. It's all confusing. I came over here. Karen is very nice."

"Your dad was shot." Darlene paused and then she asked a second time: "You don't know anything about that?"

"No."

Darlene showed Coleen the newspaper and told her what the law firm had learned from the police and the media. Coleen said there was nothing she could add to what had been said.

Darlene called Tom with Coleen in the room and she explained to him what Coleen had told her.

"I have a question. Ask her if there were any guns in the mansion." Darlene did not ask the question. She handed the phone to Coleen. (From the horse's mouth, thought Darlene.) Tom repeated the question.

"Guns? Yes," said Coleen, "my dad was an antique gun collector. I think Bosco had modern weapons but I never saw them. I heard them talking about a Glock, pistol. It's German manufactured, I think."

"Have you ever shot a gun?"

"No."

"Okay. Thank you."

Tom asked for Darlene.

Coleen transferred the phone to Darleen.

"What now?" asked Darlene.

"We wait for the police to act and we wait to see if Bosco will volunteer to talk to us after he is out of police custody." Tom wondered about having Coleen submit to a paraffin test to see if she had recently fired a firearm but he thought better of it. If the test showed powder residue, and if Coleen was arrested, Tom might have to give that information to the State Attorney as part of the rules of discovery if Coleen were charged with a crime. Best to let the police prove their case, thought Tom. The police have the burden of proof.

***

To Tom, nothing Coleen said sounded right.

Chapter 24
More Statements

It was the afternoon after. John Bosco and Tom were sitting in Tom's office drinking coffee. Bosco had bonded out of jail. He agreed to speak to Tom. He understood the conversation was not privileged or confidential. Bosco acknowledged Tom was not his attorney. Bosco said he wanted the record to be clear. That is why he gave the statement. This is what he said:

"I was in the kitchen at the refrigerator getting a glass of milk when I heard the gunshot. I ran down the hall to the sitting room and Mr. Frasier was holding the side of his face with both of his hands. There was quite a bit of blood seeping through his fingers. I went in the bathroom and grabbed a towel and went to him and looked at the wound. It was through his right cheek. It was not a tear but a puncture of the wall of his cheek. I used the towel to apply pressure to the wound and the bleeding stopped. I had seen an injury like that on one other occasion. In that case, the victim was yelling when a gun discharged and a slug entered the man's mouth at an angle and penetrated the mouth and exited through the cheek. Odd things happen, is all I can say."

"Who fired the shot that hit Colin?" asked Tom.

"I wasn't in the room when the shot was fired so I do not know who shot Mr. Frasier."

"Who was in the room with him when you entered the sitting room?"

"I did not see anyone at first, but when I came back in the room from the bath with the towel I saw that Mike, the butler, the cook, Bess, and Mr. Frasier and his daughter Coleen were in the room."

"Do you know who fired the shot?"

"I did not see who did it but I guess it was Coleen. She was crying and she had the gun in her hand."

"Which hand?"

"The left hand."

"Can you identify the gun?"

"Yes, it was a Glock 9mm."

"Who owned the gun?"

"I would expect Mr. Frasier purchased it. It was kept in the drawer of the table near where Mr. Frasier normally sat."

"Did he purchase the weapon for his protection?"

"Yes. That was its purpose. Mr. Frasier feared he would be murdered. That was the reason I was hired, I believe. Colin wanted me to protect him."

"Were there any attempts on his life that you were aware of?"

"Yes, there were."

"Were the police ever involved or called when those attempts occurred?"

"No."

"In the past, had Coleen ever attempted to kill her father?"

"No."

"Did Coleen admit she shot her father?"

"No."

"Did she say who shot her father?"

"She said he must have shot himself, but that didn't seem likely."

"Why is that?

"If he intended to shoot to kill himself he would have aimed into his mouth, in and up to destroy the brain. The wound was to the cheek. This wound should not have been fatal. It was just a flesh wound. If he shot himself he shot a hole in his cheek. I don't think the injury he suffered would kill him. I think the doctors must have screwed up and killed him when they were stitching him up."

"You mean malpractice?"

"Yes."

"Do you know who the doctor was who treated him?"

"It was a plastic surgeon, but I don't know the doctor. I never saw him." Bosco asked Tom if he should continue with his narrative.

"Please continue." said Tom.

I got the bleeding stopped at the mansion and drove Mr. Frasier to the hospital. It was only five minutes from the house."

"Did Mr. Frasier say anything?"

"No. He couldn't talk. At least, I don't think he could talk."

"How did the hospital obtain the history of the injury?"

"I told the nurse he was shot and they took him to the back of the ER for treatment. They showed me to the waiting room. I was waiting out front. Then the police came and they took me to the police station. I didn't say anything to the police. They asked me questions for four hours. I never answered any of their questions. I didn't know what to say so I kept my mouth shut. You know, I gave them name, rank and serial number. Finally they said I was under arrest for interfering with their investigation and they set bond and the cranky old butler paid to bond me out."

"Did the police talk to the staff?"

"No. The police didn't know the injury occurred at the mansion. I didn't say anything to anyone, except to the nurse. The nurse asked me what happened. I told her, quote: 'I think he was shot,' end quote."

"So the only name the police know is your name?"

"I also told the nurse Mr. Frasier's full name and then the cops took me to the station to question me."

"Karen picked up Coleen at the Bell Bar. Are you aware of that?" asked Tom.

"Yes. I asked Karen to do that."

"How did you know Coleen was at the Bell Bar?"

"I didn't know for sure, but I figured she would be there. If Coleen gets upset she goes there and shoots pool with Eddie. She thrives on competition. When the cops got through with me I got to use the phone and I called Karen at her house and asked her to check and see if Coleen was at the bar and if she was, to take her to Karen's home, her home, until I got out."

"Did you tell Karen about the shooting?"

"No. I just said there was an argument."

"How did you find out Mr. Frasier was dead?"

The police told me. After I talked to Karen, the police came back in to continue the interrogation and said that now this was really serious ... that the man I took to the hospital was dead. I still didn't say anything. Finally, they gave up and the bondsman came and got me out of jail."

"Have you talked to Coleen since your release from jail?"

"Yes. I asked her again if she shot her father."

"What did she say?"

"She said she did not shoot him."

"Do you have any basis in fact to disbelieve her statement?"

"No, except Coleen has a tendency to prevaricate."

"Are you saying that she lies?"

"Yes. She will try to paint an unflattering picture in the best light for her, particularly if the misstatement will be to her benefit."

"Would the situation involving the death of her father be one of those situations?"

"Well, yes, unfortunately. If she shot her father she would deny it."

* * *

Following his conversation with Bosco, Tom made the following list of things he had to do immediately:

1. Re-interview Coleen

2. Speak to the homicide detectives who interviewed Bosco. What did he tell them?

3. Obtain the history from the ER. What did Colin tell the nurses and doctors?

4. Open an estate for Colin Frasier

5. Glock firearms. Defects?

The most important "to do" item was the re-interview of Coleen, thought Tom.

* * *

Tom went to the law office to verify what Coleen had told Darlene and to tell Darlene that Bosco contradicted Coleen's story in substantial ways. First, Bosco had the impression that Coleen shot her father because she was seen with the smoking gun. Second, she was in the room after her father was shot. She had to know he was shot before she left for the Bell Bar. At least that was how Bosco spun his statement.

Darlene was in Alphonso Alesse's office. They were discussing opening an estate for Colin Frasier. The Florida Statutes required that Colin's last will and testament be filed with the Clerk of Court. The firm also had to petition the probate court for the appointment of Coleen, the only heir of Colin Frasier, to be appointed as the personal representative of the estate. Further, Coleen would need to file a petition to allow her to hire the firm of Night, Adams, Street, Alesse, DeMarco and Barnes as the attorney for the personal representative. They prepared a separate contract for representation by the law firm to act as her personal criminal attorney if she was charged with killing her father. This separate contract in the criminal case was not filed with the court.

Tom asked Alphonse to stay while he spoke to Darlene about Bosco's version of events. Bosco's statement opened the door to a prosecution of Coleen for the unlawful killing of her father, whether by accident (negligence) or with intent (murder).

Darlene confirmed that she spoke to Coleen and verified that Coleen specifically denied knowing her father was deceased until she was told by Darlene that he was dead. Further, Coleen denied she shot her father.

Alphonse raised his hand to get the group's attention. "You know, the law will not allow Coleen to benefit from the death of her father if his death was the result of a homicide and she is the perpetrator of the crime."

Both Tom and Darlene became quiet. Alphonse was known to floor a fellow attorney with his immediate, unconventional application of the law to a particular set of facts. Darlene and Tom had never considered that the Probate Law stated if Coleen were convicted of her father's murder that she could not inherit from his estate.

"Alphonse, tell us, in your opinion, what is the best way to handle the matter?" asked Darlene.

Alphonse thought for a minute and then said: "Two things. First, Coleen has to control the estate. If she is the only heir and she is named as the beneficiary under the will, then she has priority for appointment as long as she is competent. She is 19 years old, so she is an adult, but this is a billion dollar estate. It's my opinion the court will want another entity, a lawyer or a bank or a trust company, to act as co-personal representative to help her administer the estate. It would probably be better if we get ahead of that issue and find an institution that would agree to act as co-personal representative and have the institution file a petition for the institution to be appointed personal represent-ative together with Coleen."

"We can do that, we could hire the Trust Company of St. Petersburg," suggested Darlene.

Then Alphonso said, "The other thing to worry about is estreature by the State."

"How could estreature become an issue?" asked Tom. "There is an heir by intestacy (Coleen is Frasier's next of kin) and a will with a beneficiary (all parties assumed there was a will). How could the state of Florida make a claim for the assets of the estate or estreature of the assets?"

"Follow this," said Alphonse. "If Coleen is disqualified as Colin Frasier's heir, under the law of intestacy and as a beneficiary under his will because she murdered her father, then there is no heir or beneficiary and the assets of the estate go to the state of Florida."

"How can we anticipate that happening?" asked Darlene.

"The state will have to file a motion to disqualify Coleen as a personal representative and as an heir and as a beneficiary."

"When would that happen?"

"As soon as Coleen motions for appointment as personal representative the state would file its motion to disqualify if the state believes she murdered her father."

"Then what would happen procedurally?"

"There would be a trial in the Probate Court to determine if she killed Colin intentionally. If the court finds she killed her father intentionally she receives nothing and the state of Florida gets it all."

"Doesn't the state of Florida have anything better to do with its time than to sue orphans?"

"Actually, the state is just doing its job," said Alesse, "it's the state's duty to collect every asset that is legally due to the state.

Besides, a billion dollars would make a large contribution to the state's rainy day fund."

"Well, how do we get hired to represent Coleen?" asked Tom.

"We have to file a petition in Probate Court."

"Well, you two work on that and Faircloth and I will try to establish and understand what the true facts are involving the death."

* * *

Tom always figured the best way to answer a question was to hit the issue straight on. Tom sent Faircloth over to the mansion to interview Bess, the cook, and Mike, the butler, and get their story. He would go to the Bell Bar and talk to Paddy, the bartender, and Eddie, the pool shark and see what they remembered.

Meanwhile, Darlene came in holding a letter addressed to Tom. The return address on the envelope was for Colin Frasier at the mansion on Razor Clam Boulevard.

"You will want to open this envelope before you leave," said Darlene.

Tom opened the envelope after looking at the post mark. It was postmarked at 3:00 p.m. on the day he called Frasier and told him his daughter was on the plane returning from Belize City to Tampa.

The letter stated:

Dear Tom,

Thank you for your help locating my daughter. Bosco just brought her in the door. She's upset with me for sending you to find her, but I am at my wit's end with the girl. Unfortunately, she is not an intelligent child and having an independent, stupid child with her own mind is a difficult proposition.

It's not all her fault. Coleen has had a lonely life. I spent no time with her. I was in my early eighties when she was born. I did not know her mother and I had no relation with any woman in my life. Love is a foreign concept to me and I never learned to establish a relationship or to share love with my daughter.

As I explained when you visited, the purpose Coleen was conceived was to create an entity to receive the assets of my estate and to save estate taxes. I have enclosed instructions as to the location of my original will. I trust you to file the will with the Probate Court when I die.

I want you to represent my estate when I die. Please do that for me.

I gave Coleen a story for her life, that she's athletic and intelligent. Actually she is lazy and has not been able to complete any of her schooling. She has difficulty concentrating. She has no common sense and she has been taken advantage of by men since she reached puberty. She had her first abortion when she was 15 and another at 17. I hope she understands her need for contraceptive measures in the future.

She is also a liar and she is good at lying.

I have enclosed the original check I presented to you when we met in the amount of $100,000. I have decided that is the appropriate value of your service to the date of this letter. You will earn every penny you receive representing my family.

Thank you for your help. Come see me. We need to talk.

Sincerely,

Colin Frasier

***

Tom handed the letter to Darlene.

Darlene read it through and then turned to Tom and said, "I guess since he's dead we should retrieve the will from the safe deposit box and file it with the court."

"Yes, but first let's deposit this check against our debt on the line of credit with Century Bank."

Chapter 25
Florida Politics

During the two days Tom Night had been out of the office in Belize, Karen had taken several messages from Bob Barnes and his mother, Bea Barnes. All of the messages said it was important that Tom call them.

When Tom returned from Belize he saw the messages among numerous other notes, letters and court pleadings, but he did not understand the messages to be a priority. Members of the Barnes Family were known to wait until the last minute to ask for assistance and by that time it was too late to get in front of the problem, because they had already been sued or threatened with a lawsuit.

Tom did try to call Bob but he was told he was on the road.

Robert "Bob" Barnes saw more of Florida after his appointment to the Cabinet as Secretary of the Department of the Interior than he had while running operations for CCC Corporation or Barnes Lime Rock Inc., and during that time his family lived in the state of Florida.

The federal government had large landholdings in the state of Florida, including the Everglades, the Ocala National Forest, Elgin Air Force Preserve and the Cape Canaveral Space Coast. There was a large, successful, Native American contingent in South Florida and Tampa that was active in pursuing gambling operations and farming. These government interests brought Bob to the state often. He was well liked, open and honest. If he could help you and it didn't hurt the department or the citizens of the US he would throw his weight into the battle, and he usually was successful.

Bob would have liked to settle down in Florida with his wife and adopted son and his recently born daughter. Since he was appointed Interior Secretary, he and Smiley had purchased a home in Alexandria, Virginia, so he was close to the office in Washington, DC, but it would be easy to re-sell the home and move back in the Homestead. There was plenty of room for Bob's family, and Bob felt there was a need since Frank had died and Bea was alone in the large two story house on the 800 acre tree farm and dairy operation. Bea did not complain when she was alone, but it was evident she would enjoy the company of Bob and Smiley and the kids. If he ran for governor, it would mean Bob would move back home and he would be the head of the Barnes Family.

Politically, the main impediment to his election in the state of Florida was his political affiliation. Bob Barnes was a Republican, as was his father and grandfather and great grandfather. Florida was still in the control of the Democrats. The Republicans con-trolled the White House and the US Senate. The Democrats controlled the US House of Representatives.

The Republicans targeted the "sunshine states" and the Deep South to expand their political base. At the same time the Republican Party was campaigning to win over Florida, Bob Barnes was working and speaking throughout the state, and he was well known statewide. It was serendipitous that the opportunity for elected office fell into Bob's lap. The thought in the Republican Party was that he should run for the office of Governor of Florida. He had 30 years of experience in executive positions, first in private industry, then in a public corporation, and now in government service. That experience gave Bob an edge over Democrats, who normally had no experience running a large organization.

The other matter that tripped up candidates was the lack of proper and in-depth vetting. Bob Barnes' background had been investigated and he had been scrutinized when he sat for the position in the Interior Department. He had withstood the investigations and public questioning and private inquiry without any evidence of scandal. The political activists in Florida were happy with Barnes' story as a man, a husband and a father. Even the fact that he was adopted was compelling. He had faced many obstacles and prevailed.

The question was whether elected office was what Bob and his family wanted. According to the experts, the governorship of Florida was attainable if Bob wanted it.

Chapter 26

The Estate of Colin Frasier

Tom asked Faircloth to drive Coleen back to the office from the mansion after the investigator spoke to Mike, the butler, and to the cook named Bess.

Typically, a witness had a different take on the facts of a shooting because of the tendency of the witness to become excited by the event. In this case, both witnesses were interviewed separately and privately and the statements were recorded. Their statements were essentially similar. While the statements were being taken of Bess and Mike, Coleen was not present. She was in her room.

Both witnesses were in agreement with Bosco that at the time Colin was shot, Coleen was the only person present in the sitting room with her father. They saw her after they heard the gunshot and raced into the room. Both witnesses assumed Coleen was in the parlor when the shot was fired. Neither of the witnesses actually saw Coleen shoot Colin, and they did not see her in the room when they came in. They both noticed her when they heard her crying. When they looked in her direction she was holding the Glock pistol in her left hand. They agreed she was right handed. Coleen did not say she shot her father, but they both remembered her saying Mr. Frasier shot himself. They agreed that they both panicked and that Bosco took action, staunched the bleeding with a towel, and they worked together to put Colin in the Rolls Royce and Bosco drove him to the hospital.

When Bess and the butler got back in the sitting room after Bosco and Colin left the Mansion, the pistol was on Mr. Frasier's favorite chair. They put the gun back in the drawer of the table where it belonged, and began cleaning Colin's blood from his chair and the carpet.

It was then that they noticed that Coleen was gone. It was about midnight. The large "Regulator" wall clock beat out the midnight hour and they looked around and Coleen was missing. Their best guess was that the shooting occurred at 11:45 pm.

Mike, the butler, added that in the early morning he took a call from Karen regarding Mr. White and he dealt with the bondsman so Bosco could be released from jail.

Both witnesses were unaware that Mr. Frasier was dead until Bosco returned to the Mansion and told them the detectives who interviewed him said he had died. All of them thought Colin would live. The wound did not appear to be fatal and Colin did not appear to be at death's door. Colin Frasier walked out to the car for the trip to the hospital needing little assistance. Bess said all she did was guide him, while Mike opened the front door to the vehicle, and Mr. Frasier got in the car for the trip to the emergency room. Colin was sitting up and holding the towel to his face when he was last seen by the witnesses.

Mike and Bess had no other information. They had not talked to Coleen about the incident again since she returned to her suite in the residence. They learned from Bosco that she had left the house and walked to the Bell Bar. They agreed that she often went to the Bell Bar when she was in town and she was depressed. She enjoyed shooting pool. They admitted that earlier in the day Coleen had been drinking and she had an argument with her father about her intoxication.

Faircloth thanked the witnesses for their cooperation, and he retrieved Coleen from her room and drove her to the office, as Tom had instructed.

Then, Coleen spent more than two hours working with Alphonse and Darlene on the papers to be filed in probate court so the estate could be opened. They then drove to Century Bank and retrieved important papers from the safe deposit box and drove to the Trust Company so that a vice president could execute the petitions and other documents to begin the court proceedings. After the documents were finalized, Alphonse and Coleen drove to the clerk's office in the courthouse and filed the legal paperwork and Frasier's Last Will and Testament in the public records.

* * *

When Coleen and Alphonse returned to the office, Tom wanted to speak to Coleen alone in his office.

Tom gave her copies of the transcripts of the tape recordings of the statements taken from Bosco, Mike and Bess. Tom had underlined the portions of the three statements that contradicted her statement to Darlene. First, the witnesses said that she was present in the mansion when the shooting occurred. Second, that she was seen with the gun in her left hand after the shooting. Third, that she said her father had shot himself.

After reading the statements Coleen turned her head and blushed a deep red. "Well, if that's what they said, I guess what they said is true."

"Did you shoot your father?" Tom asked in a matter of fact way.

"No. The gun was on the floor when I came in the room. I picked it up and I assumed my dad shot himself accidentally and then dropped the gun. That's what I told Mike, Bess and Bosco."

"How did you get to the bar?"

"I walked. It's only ten blocks."

"Did you stay there at the bar until Karen took you to her home?"

"Yes."

"It's important that you tell me the truth to this question." Tom looked Coleen in the eye. "Did you talk to anyone in the bar about what happened to your father?"

"No. I positively did not say anything to anyone at the bar about my father."

"Did you talk to Paddy, the bartender?"

"Well. Yes. I didn't think you meant Paddy."

"What did you tell him?"

"I guess I did say that my father was shot accidently."

"Who did you say shot him?"

"I told him I didn't know for sure."

"Did you talk to Eddie about the shooting?"

"Why would I tell the pool shark?"

"Did you tell Eddie anything about the incident at your house?"

"I said there was a lot of excitement at my house."

"What did he say?"

"He ignored me. He was concentrating on the game and that's when I went and talked to Paddy." Coleen looked at her hands. "Paddy won't say anything. We go way back."

Tom did not feel assured. "Okay. Thank you, Coleen. Please do not talk to anyone about the shooting unless I am there." Tom looked at Coleen to make sure she understood. "Faircloth will take you home."

God, thought Tom, there is no telling what Coleen said about the shooting, or to whom. Tom smiled at Coleen as she went out the door with Faircloth. "She's dumb as a rock," Tom whispered.

* * *

Alphonse was at the door to Tom's office.

"Is it true?" asked Alphonse. "When we were at the courthouse Coleen said Mr. Frasier may have shot himself?"

"That's what she says," Tom replied. "At least that's what she says now."

"He was shot with a 9mm Glock. Is that correct?" asked Alphonse.

"Yes, everyone seems to agree with that fact."

"Are you aware the Glock has been criticized for having a trigger that is very light?"

"What do you mean when you say 'the trigger is light'?"

"The Glock has a hair trigger."

"Who says that?" asked Tom, with great interest.

"I think it was the FBI," said Alphonse. "They said at one time that the sensitive trigger and the engineering of the safety would allow the gun to fire at a time when the user did not intend to shoot."

"Give me an example."

"I remember in the FBI report, that anecdotally, a police officer said his Glock 9mm fired when he bent over to tie his shoelaces. Further, the statistics show an increase in accidental shootings and lawsuits when police departments change from having their officers armed with a .38 Caliber revolver to being armed with a semi-automatic Glock."

"Will you see what you can find out about the possibility that Colin's Glock fired accidently?" asked Tom. "That's what Coleen told the witnesses."

"I will," said Alphonse. "I had a chance to talk to Coleen when we were having the documents signed for the Estate. Did you think about requesting Colin's medical records from the hospital?"

"Yes, I thought about it."

"Well. of course you did. I shouldn't presume ..."

"Presume all you want." Tom became agitated. "What is your thought, Alphonse? Spit it out."

"I think the staff at the hospital will have some information about how the shooting occurred."

"Maybe not," Tom contradicted. "They say Colin couldn't talk because he was shot in the face."

"Well. Maybe he wrote an explanation of what happened."

Tom perked up. "You're right. He probably filled out a written questionnaire for the ER and the questionnaire would have asked Colin how he was injured. Colin would have given his version of the events leading to his injury. Do you have any idea how we could obtain the medical records quickly and confidentially?"

"We could make a request for the medical records under the guise we are investigating the case as a possible malpractice action," said Alphonse.

"Yes, it's sounding like that would be appropriate in any event," said Tom. "Bosco said he was surprised Frasier died of the wound to the face. Bosco thought it was a superficial injury. He thought malpractice must have been involved."

"We need to have another doctor look at the records to see if the doctors made a mistake and failed to comply with the standard for care of a patient with a gunshot wound. That is our duty. And while we are getting the records to give them to an expert for an opinion, we will find out what Mr. Frasier told the nurses and the doctors about how he was injured.

"We also need to hire a firearms expert and have him look at the Glock pistol. We need to have the expert obtain custody of the gun from the estate. And most important, we can see if Colin wrote a history of the shooting from his perspective."

Tom continued, "Alphonse, will you help me? I can't keep up with this case. This one is like a train going by me so fast that it will rip my arms off if I grab hold."

"You know I will help, Tom. I owe you." Alphonse turned to leave and then remembered another fact. "You know I read all the notes to the file."

"Yes? What else did you see?"

"Did you see the note from Jenny? The newspaper was going to write another story claiming Frasier's death was a murder. You may want to send a letter to the publisher stating that you object to that conclusion being drawn based on the facts that exist at this time?"

"Yes, I should do that."

"I could help," said Alphonse. "The letter would need to be delivered this afternoon to make sure it arrives at the newspaper in time for them to change the story before the paper is printed."

"Please do that. I have to go to the Bell Bar to talk to the bartender."

"I think you will see Faircloth at the bar. He was going to meet the homicide detectives there to talk to them about the case."

I need to stop that interview, thought Tom. Paddy will get right in that conversation and tell the detectives what Coleen told him. Tom dialed Faircloth's office, but he had missed him. Tom put his head in his hands. Tom felt very tired ... exhausted. How in the hell do I stop Faircloth's interview of the detectives at the Bell Bar? thought Tom.

* * *

Darlene came into Tom's office and interrupted his thoughts. "Tom, I'm trying to fill out the forms for the Inventory that we need to file in the estate. How are we supposed to know what assets are in the estate?"

"Call Mike, the butler. He may know." Tom snapped his fingers. "I know. Call the CPA. Isn't Frasier's CPA our CPA?"

"Yes."

"Darlene, call and make an appointment for both of us to meet with the CPA. The CPA should know Colin's assets and his liabilities. Meanwhile, I need to go to the Bell Bar and talk to Paddy."

Chapter 27
Bell Bar Redux

The Bell Bar was an example of an economic use of business leasehold space. It was 25 feet wide and 80 feet long (2,000 square feet). You entered in the front door on 4th Street and the back door opened to the alley. There were restrooms in the back together with storage for bar stock inside a locked room. Coming forward from the restrooms, on the north side of the bar there was a room with a pool table. In front of the billiards room and storage room there was a long bar. There was a work area behind the bar and there were stools on the opposite side of the bar. There were booths along the north wall and the bar and work area on the south side and an aisle down the center between the bar and the booths.

The Bell Bar was actually built on a right of way for a road. The land which was intended to be a roadway was vacated by the City and sold and the bar was constructed where the roadway would have been.

It was 2:00 p.m. in the afternoon. The Bell Bar was full. The chairs and bar stools were filled with US Postmen and retirees nursing beers and discussing the news of the day. Eddie was chalking his pool cue and he nodded as Tom came in the back door from the alley.

Tom noticed Faircloth was sitting in a booth facing two homicide detectives. They were drinking scotch and water. As Tom walked to the booth the police excused themselves. They said they had to return to work. The detectives were not going to talk to Tom about Colin Frasier.

Tom sat down and Paddy, the bartender, slid into the booth next to Faircloth.

"Watch the bar," said Paddy to Eddie, the hustler. "Don't let these rats steal us blind."

"Happy to oblige," said Eddie as he poured himself a free beer.

"Turn up the noise," Paddy ordered. There was a control for the juke box behind the bar and Eddie turned up the sound of the record on the machine. Patsy Kline was singing "Crazy."

Paddy had grabbed a bottle and two glasses. He slid into a seat at the booth and poured a Johnny Walker Red for each of the men. Tom deferred. "All the more for me," chortled Paddy, and he pulled Tom's glass in front of him and drank it down and wiped his fingers with his lips.

Paddy looked at Tom and Faircloth and offered his view: "Those cops don't know shit." Paddy was commenting on the detectives who had now left the bar.

"And what do you know, Paddy?" asked Tom.

"Everything," Paddy assured Tom.

Faircloth tried to turn the conversation to another topic. Paddy was intoxicated. It was good he had the early shift and clocked out today at 4:00 pm. If he worked until 2:00 am, they would have to roll him out the back door at closing time.

"Is Paddy right?" Tom asked Faircloth. "Were the detectives able to tell you anything?"

"Paddy may be right. The police did not tell me much. Actually, they were looking for information. They wanted to know who we represented."

"What did you tell them?"

"That we represented the Estate of Colin Frasier."

"What did they say?"

"They laughed. The cops almost fell out of the booth thinking you were doing work in probate court. They said that now you were stealing money from widows and orphans."

Tom smiled. It was funny that he was doing estate work. Tom got the conversation back on point. "Were you able to find out what they know about the shooting?"

"They don't know much. They haven't got enough information to charge anyone. At least, that is what they said."

"Did they seem to be interested in Bosco as a suspect?"

"No. They have nothing on him, but they are pissed. They couldn't get any information out of him except his name and social security number and date of birth."

"Do the police think Frasier was murdered?"

"The jury is out on that question."

"Why don't you go back to the office," Tom said. "I'll be along in a bit. I want to speak to my friend, Paddy."

"How did you get over here to the bar?" Faircloth asked Tom as he squeezed out of the booth.

"I walked." Tom tapped his cane on the table. "I'll call you if I need a ride."

Faircloth stood up to leave. Tom took a hundred dollar bill from his pocket and laid it on the table. Paddy's eyes lit up.

"Well, Paddy, you will have to earn this Ben Franklin."

Faircloth left out the front door into the bright sunshine. It was agony to walk out in the bright Florida sun after a few drinks. It felt like your eyeballs would crack.

Tom motioned for Paddy to lean close to him, and he asked, "What did Coleen tell you happened to her father?"

Paddy stared back at Tom. "I don't know nothing about nothing on that score."

Tom opened the conversation with what he knew. "Coleen told me she told you her dad shot himself by accident."

"If you are telling me what your client told you, you are violating a confidence. You can't tell me what she said. It's a lawyer/client communication."

"That's true," said Tom. "Are you going to say anything about what she told you?"

"She was drunk. Anything she told me falls under the bartender/drunkard privilege. I don't reveal anything that is told to me by a brother drunk ... or from a sister drunk for that matter."

"We will see if you are a man of your word." Tom slid the $100 bill to Paddy. Tom hoped the bill would seal Paddy's lips, at least if Paddy was asked a question during idle conversation. It would be different if Paddy was subpoenaed by the Grand Jury.

* * *

Tom arose, grabbed his cane, and tipped his head to Eddie as he passed the pool table. It had been more than one time over the years that Eddie had driven him home from the Bell Bar because Tom was so intoxicated that he couldn't operate a motor vehicle. But that had been in the distant past.

Tom went to the restroom in the back. He used the facilities. The loo was small with a toilet and sink. Then Tom became dizzy. He put the cover down on the toilet seat and wet a paper towel and sat down and wiped his face with the wet brown paper. No good. He wet the back of his neck. He had never felt fatigue like this. He had some trouble breathing ... shortness of breath.

Normally Tom could arrest fatigue by walking. It was only four blocks to the office if he cut through the alleys. Tom decided not to use the pay phone at the rear of the bar to call Faircloth for a ride. Maybe a little exercise would make him feel better. He walked out the back door and headed south to Central Avenue and then east to Beach Drive. In a short time he was to the side door of the office.

But honestly, the exercise did not make him feel better. He felt shaky, nauseous and he had a clammy sweat on his brow. After Tom got in the office he was able to smile at the staff and he made it to his room. He laid down on the couch and he slept.

* * *

At 5:00 p.m. there was a rush of noise and activity as the clerks and legal assistants and secretaries closed up shop. The attorneys would continue their work, but the hourly workers left the building. Tom awoke and he could hear his wife asking for him and he tried to call to her, but he could make no sound.

Darlene opened the door to his office and looked in at his desk. Tom wasn't sitting there and she could not see him lying on the couch. She turned off the light at the switch by the door and closed the door.

Tom closed his eyes and fell back to sleep. Whatever, he thought.

Darlene went looking for Faircloth. She had booked an appointment with A. Hardy, Colin Frasier's CPA. She went to locate Faircloth because he was supposed to be with Tom, and Darlene did not want to talk to A. Hardy alone. Hardy was the kind of man who got in your face like he was a drill sergeant – he made you very uncomfortable.

Faircloth was finishing dictating his memory of the interview he had with the homicide detectives. The detectives would not let him tape record the interview. It really pissed Faircloth off that the police refused to give a taped interview. What did they have to hide? He thought.

Darlene came to his door. "So where is the boss?"

Faircloth looked up from the Dictaphone receiver. "I left him at the bar. He was talking to Paddy about Coleen."

"Well, let's swing by the bar. If Tom is out wandering and we cannot find him, I want you to come with me when I talk to the CPA."

Faircloth grabbed his coat. As chief investigator, Faircloth held a position at the same level and pay grade as an associate attorney. He wore a coat and tie and he worked a lot of hours, but he was paid more than the Chief of Police at SPPD. He was satisfied.

* * *

The pair went out the door and drove to the alley behind the Bell Bar. Faircloth went in the rear door. He saw Eddie. Tom had left, Eddie said. Faircloth came out quickly and hopped back in the car. "Eddie says Tom was there and spoke to him for a minute but Tom left an hour ago."

"He didn't know about the appointment with the CPA so he may have gone home," surmised Darlene.

"Do you want to go to the condo and get him?"

"Let him sleep. He's sitting in the recliner watching the ships going to Tampa. We'll catch him after we talk to the CPA. I need to get the Frasier business records so we can file the Inventory of the assets and liabilities of the estate."

Besides, thought Darlene, Tom would not get much sleep at home. The Barnes clan was invited over to the condo for dinner. Bob Barnes intended to make a pitch for a campaign contribution for his campaign for governor.

* * *

Jenny Barnes thought she was the last attorney in the office, but Alphonse met her at the front door. He was looking for Tom to sign the letter to the publisher of the local newspaper objecting to any story that alleged Colin Frasier was the victim of a murder, unless the newspaper had a good faith basis for such an allegation. The letter argued that Colin's estate would be slandered if the newspaper reported Colin was murdered.

"Just sign his name," said Jenny. "You both agreed to what he was going to say in the letter didn't you?"

"Yes. I need to hand deliver the letter to the newspaper now anyway."

"Then it's good," said Jenny and they left the building. As they left the downstairs entrance the cleaning service was on the way into the building. They were cleaning the rugs and would be there all night.

Chapter 28
A. Hardy, CPA

A. ("A" is for Allright) Hardy's office was in a house tucked in among a neighborhood of two story bungalows in the Old Northeast section of town. The architecture mimicked neighborhoods in the state of Illinois and the Midwest, and what would generically be called "up North."

A. Hardy's neighborhood was not zoned for business but everyone ignored the zoning regulations as long as the violation was not too egregious. There were many offices in the neighborhood for lawyers, doctors and professionals.

As soon as Darlene and Faircloth entered A. Hardy's living room with the fireplace, they were met with a fierce greeting by this bear of a man. Hardy had in fact been a drill sergeant in the war. Afterward he went to college on the GI Bill and sat for the CPA exam. He passed the first time he tried. An accomplishment, as it took numerous attempts to pass the test by many applicants.

Hardy's greeting could be described as "glad handing" or a pumping of the arm of the recipient. This went on for several minutes until Hardy got it out of his system. During the greeting he would also get his face as close as he could to the other person and "eyeball him."

As soon as Darlene got in the room and Hardy began his assault, she got out of the way and let Faircloth receive the full force of the CPA's attention. Finally, he would calm down and the red blood would drain from his face and he would ask, "What can I do for you?"

Darlene had a folder. She opened it and withdrew a typed document on 8½ by 14 inch linen paper. The paper was signed by the local probate court judge and was entitled "ORDER" and went on to say that Darlene Street and the firm were appointed as the attorney for the Personal Representative of the Estate of Colin Frasier. The order was directed to all interested parties to cooperate with Darlene to allow her to complete her duties as attorney for the Personal Representative. One of her duties was to marshal the assets and records that belonged to Mr. Frasier so the property owned by Colin Frasier could be collected and the assets could be used to pay his debts, taxes and expenses and finally, the balance of the estate would go to his heirs as Colin's will or the Florida Statutes directed.

Darlene gave a true copy of the order to Mr. Hardy.

"Darlene," said A. Hardy, "I didn't know you and Tom handled estate work. I would have sent you referrals if I knew."

Darlene knew that CPA Hardy did not refer cases to the firm, but she did not know why.

"Alphonse Alesse regularly handles estate work in our office," said Darlene. "However, everyone in the office will be handling this case as big and complicated as it will be. You can see from the order that Coleen and The Trust Company are co-representatives of the estate. The Trust Company has its own attorney."

Hardy began to speak and waved his arms. "This will be by far, the biggest probate matter in these parts, maybe in the whole state of Florida. Are you aware the attorney fee could be as much as three percent of the value of the estate? Why, if the estate is valued at one billion dollars, the attorney fee could be as much as thirty million dollars."

"Don't count your chickens," said Darlene.

"A billion dollars is an amount of money," said A. Hardy, "that will bring the cockroaches out of the wood work."

"I think they are already scratching around," said Faircloth under his breath, but so loud that Darlene heard his comment, and smiled.

"Well," said Hardy," you will need the records I have. But, I will want to make copies so I know what I gave you."

A. Hardy rose from his seat and gestured for the pair to follow him and they went to a room upstairs. In fact, the room was the entire upstairs. It was a room 20 feet by 40 feet and it was crammed with file cabinets. Hardy pointed to the cabinets. "Of course, we also copied the records on discs and we use a computer. It's amazing but everything in this room is held on less than 200 floppy discs."

"Do you have any suggestions regarding portability?" asked Darlene.

"I do not want the liability for these original records now that Colin is deceased. The Trust Company has a huge vault and they could handle the paperwork. I have no objection to allowing the Trust Company to hold the original papers. You and I could work off the discs ... you could take one set and I will have another."

"That sounds logical and simple. We can let the bank hold the original files."

Hardy agreed. "Much of the information is proprietary and confidential and the lists of assets and debts need to be sealed by the Probate judge. The discs have been encrypted to prevent the wrong eyes from seeing the information."

"This meeting was a good first start. Let me talk to the Trust Bank and I will get back to you in the morning."

"Darlene, could I ask a question?" A. Hardy looked very serious and his eyes twirled.

Darlene nodded. "Yes."

"Did Colin commit suicide?" Hardy patted Darlene's hand.

"Why do you ask?" She pulled her hand away.

"Well, you didn't know him like I did. I talked to him just about every day of his life. He was the most driven man I have ever known. He had only one thought and that was to win at business. He was so angered by the thought that someone would steal from him that he would almost have a physical attack if he perceived that was even a possibility."

"I don't understand what his proclivity to apoplexy has to do with Colin's death being a suicide," said Darlene.

"Well, he was 106 years old." A. Hardy was almost in Darlene's face as he spoke and he wiped spittle from his chin. "Every day was his last."

"Yes."

"Well, he was upset that the government would assess a tax on his estate after he died."

"Yes?"

"Well, we are almost at the end of the year."

"Yes, we are at the end of the year. I do not understand. What is your point?"

"This year the tax rate on an estate is ten percent of the value of the non-exempt property."

"And next year the rate is higher?" asked Darlene, anticipating his point. "So the taxes would be less if he died this year."

"Yes, next year the tax rate increases to sixty percent. "

"So you think he took his life to obtain a more favorable tax rate?"

"Well, yes, he would save his estate fifty percent in taxes. I figured he might have killed himself to save $500 million."

"I don't think his death was a suicide, but we will look into all possibilities."

"Well, call me in the morning regarding the files." Hardy gave a little bow.

* * *

When the cleaning crew came to Tom's office they immediately noticed Tom. The lady went over to him.

"Are you okay, mister?"

Tom was having difficulty talking, but was able to ask for an aspirin. They brought him one white Bayer pill and he put it under his tongue with a shaky hand and then he laid back and hoped it would do some good as the medicine dissolved under his tongue. Tom's doctor had advised him to take an aspirin if he felt weakness in his arms and drooping of his face. Tom asked the lady if she would drive him to the hospital.

The crew got him down the stairs and to the cleaning van and to the ER.

* * *

The admitting nurse recognized Tom. He had been at the hospital over the years taking depositions of the medical personnel who took care of the victims of Tom's clients' evil deeds. Tom hoped the nurse did not hold it against him ... the fact that he represented mostly bad people who committed criminal acts.

"Let's get him in the wheel chair and into the back for treatment." The nurse could see the signs of a stroke and wanted a doctor to see Tom immediately. The cleaning crew told the admission personnel where they had found Tom and what they had done.

"You probably saved his life giving him that aspirin," commented the nurse.

* * *

Darlene's condo had filled up with guests. Bob and his wife and their two children, and Jim DeMarco and Jenny and their three girls and Bea were there when Darlene opened the door.

"Where is Tom?" asked Darlene.

"The housekeeper let us in," said Bea. "Tom wasn't here."

Darlene hoped Tom hadn't decided to take this night to go on a bender. They had been married for over 25 years now and he had stayed on the wagon that whole time. Darlene thought, he will be along soon.

There was a spread of simple food laid out for the group and they dug in when they were directed. "Tom will be along. We have had a couple of hectic days." Darlene went over to Jim and Jenny and asked if they had seen Tom.

"No," they said.

Darlene excused herself and called the office. The answering service picked up. There were no messages. She tried Faircloth. He had not heard from Tom. He said he would make a call or two and get back.

Jenny asked her brother to try out his pitch for campaign contributions. Bob Barnes stumbled through the speech and the guests clapped and then ponied up their checks for the campaign.

The phone rang. Darlene answered it. "I'll be right there," she said into the phone.

Tom was at the hospital, she announced to the guests. Jenny told Jim to drive Darlene there.

"Call us when you know anything." No one thought the situation could be that bad.

Part V
The run for governor

Chapter 29
Tom's Illness

"The carotid artery supplies blood to the brain," explained the neurologist. "There is a fork in the artery, and plaque can build up at that location. The plaque can break off and lodge in a blood vessel in the brain. If the blockage is temporary, the patient can have a transient ischemic attack, known as a TIA. If the blockage is not temporary, the result could be a thromboembolic stroke. Many times a TIA is a precursor to a stroke, which can cause permanent damage and/or death. Normally the stroke occurs within a couple of days of a TIA. "

"What is the treatment for the TIA?"

"Rest ... no smoking. We will control his blood pressure and see how things progress. He will be in the hospital for three days."

"Is there medication available?"

"He will be taking one aspirin daily to thin his blood and Hydrochlorothiazide for his high blood pressure. No more smoking," said the doctor. "Tom has to quit smoking."

"He doesn't smoke cigarettes," said Darlene.

"He admits he does."

"He said he quit," Darlene insisted.

"Well, I don't know. You need to talk to him. It would probably be best if you did not smoke in his presence."

"Is there a procedure to prevent a blockage from causing a stroke or is there an operation that will reverse the blockage?"

"They are using a stent that is inserted into the carotid artery to correct the blockage, or there is a procedure to remove the blockage. If we can correct the problem with medication and avoid surgery that is the best course."

"How will we know what to do?"

"We will just have to wait and see how he does."

"What about work?"

"You need to buy him some books to read. Escape novels, history. I do not want him to think about the practice of law.

"Thank you, doctor." Darlene watched the doctor leave the waiting room and then she lit a cigarette. I don't guess I will be smoking many more of these, she thought.

* * *

Within a day after the probate court entered its order appointing Coleen Frasier and The Trust Company as co-personal representatives of the Estate of Colin Frasier, there was file activity in the court file. Alphonse had anticipated the state would file an objection to the appointment of Coleen as personal representative alleging Coleen killed her father.

Instead, an attorney in Miami had filed a petition with the clerk of court alleging Coleen was not the only legal heir of Colin Frasier. The attorney alleged he represented another heir, a woman named Jesse Jones Smith. The allegations of the petition rambled about but the kernel of the argument was contained in the following paragraphs of the petition:

"83. Petitioner further states that she co-habituated with the deceased and that they established a relationship as husband and wife under the Common Law existing in the state of Florida at that time.

"84. Petitioner further alleges that she and the deceased consummated the said Common Law relationship and they had a child named Coleen Frasier.

"85. Petitioner and the decedent's common law marriage was never legally dissolved."

The Petition then prayed (requested) that the probate court recognize the common law marriage between Colin and his widow, Jesse Jones Smith, and that the probate court determine that said Jesse Jones Smith has rights as the wife of Colin Frasier to a life estate in the homestead property of the deceased consisting of a mansion located on Razor Clam Boulevard in St. Petersburg, Florida, and that she has a right to a child's share of the net assets of the estate. As there was only one child, a child's share was equal to one half of the estate. One half of the value of the estate would be at least half a billion dollars.

Darlene, DeMarco and Alphonse spoke immediately after the law firm was served with a copy of the petition filed by Mrs. Smith's attorney, Arthur Maxwell Battle, Esq.

The trio decided to divide Tom's workload in the Frasier case as follows: Alphonse would handle the probate matters, DeMarco would act as Coleen's criminal lawyer, Jenny would handle the malpractice action against the hospital, and Darlene would handle research, pleadings and briefs.

The first issue they would face was the request from Mrs. Smith's attorney to depose Coleen.

DeMarco said they should file an objection to the request because a deposition would subject Coleen to questions under oath regarding the circumstances of Colin's death. Darlene thought it best to avoid any hint that Coleen feared prosecution for the death of her father. She suggested they file a motion for a protective order. The basis for the objection was that Coleen knew nothing about her mother and she could offer no testimony regarding the claim of Mrs. Smith that she was Coleen's mother. The deposition would be harassment and not lead to relevant discovery. DeMarco would further allege in his pleading that the cause of Colin Frasier's death was irrelevant to Mrs. Smith's claims.

Further, Alphonse suggested they needed to get Faircloth involved. They needed to send him to Miami and conduct an investigation of Mrs. Smith. Alphonse also would follow up with the medical records from the ER at the hospital to see what Colin reported to the nurse as the circumstances of injury when he was admitted with the gunshot wound.

DeMarco would keep a low profile representing Coleen on possible criminal charges. He would have completed his job successfully if no charges were filed. He would have to stay connected with the State Attorney and the police without appearing to be concerned that the authorities would press charges. DeMarco and Alphonse would also develop the plan for a preemptive attack against the Department of Revenue of the state of Florida. Alphonse still believed the department would file a petition to cause an estreature of the assets of the estate to the state.

The positive aspect or good news that flowed from the petition filed by Mrs. Smith was that the department's claim for estreature would be defeated if Mrs. Smith had a valid claim as the common law wife of Colon Frasier. If Mrs. Smith had a valid claim as a beneficiary there were two heirs to the Estate of Colin Frasier—Coleen and Mrs. Smith. The additional heir would defeat the state of Florida's claim for estreature. At least, that's what Alphonse thought. (But would it? Would the state still have a claim for Coleen's share?) That would be the first issue for Darlene and her clerks to research.

Darlene would also file a motion to dismiss the petition filed by Mrs. Smith. The basis of the motion was the failure to attach as an exhibit to Mrs. Smith's petition a certified birth certificate naming Jesse Jones Smith as the birth mother of Coleen Frasier, or any official record that stated the petitioner and Colin Frasier were the parents of Coleen Frasier or a "Jane Doe" child.

Darlene set the motion to dismiss on the earliest docket the probate court had available. That date was several months away. "That should set them back on their heels if they are looking for an early disposition of the case," said Darlene to her scheduling secretary.

* * *

Faircloth had entered the tomb.

As he exited the elevator into the basement of the hospital his fellow traveler, a doctor in a white coat, said, "God, I hate it in here."

"Yeah," said Faircloth. "It smells moldy."

"It's the smell of old medical records, maybe."

"I don't think so. I think this is where the contractor broke into the burial chamber of the large Indian mound the hospital was built on." Faircloth shivered. "We are in the middle of a grave down here."

They entered a small cubicle. Faircloth deferred to the doctor. The doctor obtained his patient's file quickly. *I could be so lucky,* Faircloth thought.

It was Faircloth's turn. "I'm Jim Faircloth with the law firm of Night, Adams, Street, Alesse, DeMarco and Barnes. I have an appointment to receive copies of the medical records of Colin Frasier."

"Do you have a release?" asked the clerk.

"Here is the Release and an Order from the Probate Court authorizing the release of the records, and I have a certified copy of the Letters of Administration appointing our client Coleen Frasier as the Personal Representative of the Estate of the patient Colin Frasier."

The records clerk asked Faircloth to have a seat.

Twenty minutes later the clerk was back and asked Faircloth for his identification. Faircloth produced his driver's license, his license from the state of Florida as a private investigator, and a letter of introduction from the law firm stating he was authorized to obtain Mr. Frasier's records for the firm.

The records clerk asked Faircloth to have a seat.

Twenty minutes later the department head came out and apologized for the delay. "The hospital's attorney had to review the records. There is a letter for Mr. Alesse in with the records that we have provided."

"Do you mean you have not provided all the records?"

"That is correct. We did provide some of the records, but not all of them. The letter from our attorney explains our position."

* * *

Faircloth drove directly back to the office and went in to see Alphonse. Alphonse opened the large, thick, waterproof envelope and removed the contents, which included about an inch of records and x-rays and other test results.

Darlene and DeMarco heard Faircloth was back and they entered Alphonse's office. Darlene picked out the cover letter from the hospital attorney, which tried to explain why the hospital was withholding certain of Colin Frasier's records. The hospital based their decision on new legislation known as "The HIPPA Law". Darlene yelled the content of the letter to the group to a resounding groan. No one understood the HIPPA law.

"Well, is the ER record included?" asked Alphonse. "Or did they object to us receiving those records too?"

Alphonse fanned the one inch stack of records and found the nurses notes. In between the pages was a plain sheet of paper with hand printing. The printing stated the following:

"I was brought to the hospital for treatment of a gunshot wound to my right cheek. The wound was caused by a bullet from my Glock pistol. I had taken the pistol from the desk drawer intending to clean it. When I sat down in my chair the gun fell from my hand and hit the floor and the gun discharged and I was shot accidentally in the cheek."

/S/ Colin Frasier.

Alphonse read the note signed by Mr. Frasier to everyone in the room, which was now filled with secretaries, clerks and attorneys.

There was a huge cheer that rose from the people in the room. Colin's statement exonerated Coleen. Colin said the shooting was accidental.

While the group still erupted, Darlene continued to read the letter from the hospital's attorney.

"Listen to this. Listen to this!" she yelled to the group. "The letter says that the hospital is deeply disturbed by the death of Mr. Frasier and apologizes for any hurt, anguish and pain the family has suffered. They want to mediate the estate's malpractice claim. They are conceding liability for Colin Frasier's death."

There was another huge cheer.

Tom's firm had been appointed by the court as the attorney to represent the estate against the hospital. The firm was due a separate fee in the malpractice case equal to one-third of the amount collected from the hospital or the hospital's insurance company to compensate Coleen and the estate for Colin's wrongful death. The malpractice fee would be a bonus to the firm, on top of the probate fee. The fee in the malpractice alone would pay off a substantial portion of the line of credit owed to Century Bank.

* * *

Darlene was not an emotional person, generally. She was very worried about Tom, and in particular, she was worried because she did not have Tom to rely on to get the firm through the intricacies of the representation of Coleen Frasier for the death of Colin Frasier. She was worried they would be embroiled with the state of Florida in an estreature battle and Tom would be unable to argue the case.

After they received the correspondence and the medical records from the hospital, Darlene felt a great flood of relief. She would not be confronted with the issue of estreature or the defense of a homicide. She had not had a cigarette in days, but she could not stand it. She just had to have a smoke. She snuck into her office and closed the door. She found a pack of Newport's in her desk and opened the window and lit a cigarette and inhaled the smoke deeply into her lungs.

She began to cough.

Chapter 30
Jim Faircloth

James Faircloth drove his 1992 Ford Station wagon down Interstate 95 south on the west coast of Florida to Alligator Alley, then headed east across the Everglades to Miami. He intended to set up his base of operations in a motel on US 1 and search for Jesse Jones Frasier/Smith.

He had tried to locate her using the obvious sources ... the phone book and the City Directory, but no luck. At the time the Internet was a limited source of information. There was no reference to Frasier/Smith or her attorney in any search engine. He thought he would have better luck staking out the attorney who had filed the petition on Frasier/Smith's behalf. Faircloth would find Smith through Attorney Battle.

Before Faircloth left St. Petersburg for Miami, DeMarco called a friend in Ft. Lauderdale who was a member of the Bar Association of South Florida. He had been a member of the Board of Directors of the Bar Association, and he would know all there was to know about Frasier/Smith's attorney, Arthur M. Battle, Esq.

It turned out that attorney Battle had a checkered career as a lawyer. He had been suspended from the practice of law for a period of time for failure to provide services as promised. Mostly, he failed to attend hearings resulting in the dismissal of his clients' cases. His excuse was that the client failed to make fee payments as promised and Mr. Battle had withdrawn as counsel. The problem was that Mr. Battle did not set a hearing on the motion to withdraw and no judge had relieved him of responsibility in the cases he walked away from. Other infractions involved allegations that when Battle showed up for court he was intoxicated. Battle had completed serving a 90 day suspension just before he filed the petition on behalf of Frasier/Smith. Battle was not known as a probate lawyer. Mostly, he handled criminal cases and some personal injury clients.

Mr. Battle had an office in a run-down strip center in the Little Havana section of Miami on Flagler Street, near the river, across from Jackson Memorial Hospital.

Faircloth's idea was that a search of the records of the Clerk of the Criminal Court of Dade County would bring up records connecting Frasier/Smith to Attorney Battle, and he could get an address for Ms. Frasier/Smith and begin his surveillance of the woman.

Faircloth would have to go to the clerk's office and search the dockets for a reference to Frasier/Smith, hoping that there would be an entry for a criminal case. If she had been prosecuted she would have a SPN number, and once he found her "spin number" Faircloth would be led by the official records available on computer in the clerk of court's office to all cases in which Frasier/Smith was a defendant, no matter what name she used. From the SPN number Faircloth could obtain information from the city police and the sheriff and the DMV (Department of Motor Vehicles), and then he would obtain her fingerprints, criminal history, driving history and a photograph and even a list of probable acquaintances and last known addresses. He could even get business records, corporate filings and such.

It would be a slog, but when Faircloth found the SPN number he would know all there was to know about Ms. Smith. She would be legally hacked.

* * *

Unfortunately, no person with the name Jesse Jones Smith or Jesse Jones Frasier or Jesse Jones Frasier/Smith had a criminal record in Miami. There was no SPN number for her. Faircloth thought he struck out. He tried Civil Records. The names were not listed in the Plaintiff/Defendant Index.

Then he tried marriage records and hit the mother lode. There were five marriages that had been dissolved in Miami/Dade County involving Jesse Jones Smith. She was also known as (aka) Jesse Jones Koslowski, Jesse Jones Marz, Jesse Jones Battle, and Jesse Jones Diamond. Her maiden name was Jesse Jones Olsen, and she was 43 years old. If she was Coleen's birth mother she was 24 when she delivered Coleen. Colin Frasier, was 83 years old at that time.

Interesting, thought Faircloth. In the past she had been married to a person named Arthur M. Battle and his occupation was listed as an attorney at law. Therefore, it appeared she had been married to her attorney 21 years before and they were divorced 17 years before his search was completed. If the dates were correct, Attorney Battle and Frasier/Smith were legally married to one another at the time Coleen was conceived and born. Further, this meant that Frasier/Smith was married to Attorney Battle while she was married by the Common Law to Colin Frasier.

Upon understanding, and after confirming these facts, Faircloth immediately called the office and spoke to Alphonse. Alphonse told Faircloth to give him time to speak to Darlene and DeMarco and he would call him at his motel. He was told not to do any more investigation until they called him.

Faircloth drove back to the motel, put on his swim trunks and waited by the pool.

* * *

Alphonse spoke to Darlene and DeMarco about Faircloth's discoveries. DeMarco felt they needed more facts. They needed to talk to Mike at the Frasier mansion. The butler seemed to have been with Colin the longest and he might be able to identify Jesse and Attorney Battle and their relationship to Colin and Coleen.

Mike was a little odd. He was full of himself and his importance to the Frasier household. The lawyers felt the best person to speak to Mike was Tom, but he was out to pasture at this point and so the duty was left to Darlene.

Darlene drove the 20 or so blocks to the mansion and parked in the car circle in front. She was allowed in by Mike. "Hello," he said. "Come in and have a seat." The sitting room had been cleared of the stacks of magazines and newspapers. It appeared Mike was now in charge since Colin's death.

"We are trying to figure out who Maxwell Battle and Jesse Jones Frasier/Smith are in relation to Colin and Coleen," said Darlene.

Mike explained what he knew: "Mr. Battle was Colin's lawyer about 20 years ago. Jesse was Maxwell's wife. I believe Jesse was the surrogate, the person who carried Coleen to term, and she delivered her successfully. "

"How was Jesse impregnated?"

"Oh, I do not think Colin Frasier had sexual relations with the woman. There was a doctor at a clinic in Naples, Florida, who provided the medical services that allowed Mr. Frasier and Jesse to have a child. "

"Is the doctor still in practice?"

"Unknown."

"There needs to be an egg and sperm? I guess that is elementary. Was Jones/Smith's egg impregnated with Colin's sperm?" Darlene asked.

"I believe the egg came from another source but the sperm belonged to Mr. Frasier." Mike then shrugged. "But what do I know. These are things I picked up from Mr. Frasier and from letters and notes and phone calls I overheard."

Darlene scratched her head.

Mike touched Darlene's shoulder and made sure he had her attention. "I know this all sounds absurd, but rich folks don't think a thing about acting in an absurd manner. They are like crazy folk."

"Okay, I get it. But what is the level of confidence that you have that you are correct ... that Jesse Jones Battle was impregnated with a zygote produced from the egg of another woman and Mr. Frasier's sperm?"

"Fifty, maybe 60%."

"That's all?"

"Yes."

* * *

Darlene went home. Tom was in the chair with the view of Tampa Bay. He was asleep. He spent a lot of his time resting and reading novels by Edgar Rice Burroughs and Zane Grey.

"You're home early." He heard her enter.

"Yes." Darlene hesitated. She was concerned she would upset Tom if she asked him a legal question.

Tom anticipated her worry and said: "So, you need to talk to me about the Frasier case but you are afraid it will kill me if you tell me what you know and ask the question."

"Yes," admitted Darlene.

"Just tell me the facts and ask me the question," said Tom. "I'm not that fragile."

Darlene went through the facts they had compiled.

Tom sat quietly and mulled over the facts and then he smiled. "So the facts establish an ironclad defense to Jesse Jones Smith's petition. We win."

"Explain, please."

Tom rested the "Tarzan" book on his lap. "The allegation that she was married to Colin Frasier is defeated because she is a bigamist."

"What do you mean?" asked Darlene. She was perplexed. "I thought we would only win the case if we could show Jesse Jones Frasier/Smith was not Coleen's mother if she did not produce the egg that was impregnated with Colin's sperm."

"No, that is not the ultimate issue. As I see it, the relationship that matters is whether Jesse Jones Frasier/ Smith was ever the wife of Colin Frasier. The issue is not whether she was Coleen's mother."

"I am still unsure I understand."

"Smith claims she was Colin's Common Law wife. But according to the records, at the same time she alleges that she was Frasier's Common Law wife, she was legally married to Maxwell Battle. She cannot establish a legal relationship to Colin as his wife if she was already married to Mr. Battle. Jesse Jones Frasier/Smith's claim for rights under the Estate has to be predicated on a valid marriage between Colin and Jesse. If there is no marriage, there is no right to homestead in the mansion or to a child's share of the estate."

"How would you use this argument?"

"You do what you do best, Darlene. You draft a Motion to Dismiss Jesse Jones Frasier/Smith's petition. Make the argument in the motion very simple so that Jesse and her lawyer can understand the logic of our position.

"The argument is that Colin Frasier and Jesse Smith could not be legally married or establish a common law marriage because she was still married to Mr. Battle when she gave birth to Coleen. Therefore she has no rights to Colin's estate. You also need to allege in the motion that Smith and her attorney are attempting to defraud the estate. You want to say that Jones/Smith is a bigamist and her attorney is aware of that fact and yet they are attempting to assert this false claim in order to extract money from the estate."

"Do we file the motion with the clerk?"

"No. You send Mr. Battle a copy of the motion and you set an appointment for me to go to Miami to meet with Mr. Battle for the purpose of settling his client's claim."

"I do not understand. We send Mr. Battle a copy of the motion to dismiss but tell Mr. Battle we want to settle even if we can defeat him in court?"

"Yes. It's better to settle this now than let it drag out and then be appealed for ten or so years," said Tom. "Battle is to be instructed to have his client at the meeting and I need three cashier's checks that I will take with me to Miami. The checks should be in the amounts of $50,000, $75,000, and $100,000 and the checks need to be made payable to Mrs. Smith and her attorney, Maxwell Battle. Last, I will need an ironclad release and satisfaction of claim to be drafted by Alphonse to be signed by Mrs. Smith and Mr. Battle."

"Why does Attorney Battle need to sign a release of claim?"

"Because if Battle was married to Jones/Smith at the time she was impregnated with the zygote, Battle would be presumed by law to be Coleen's father," said Tom. "We need to cut off any possible rights Battle has to the estate through Coleen. The court is hot on equal rights. If Jesse has a right under the law as a mother and a wife, Battle could possibly successfully argue he has a similar right under the law as a father and a husband. A person's sex cannot bar a person from a right or privilege."

"We had not thought of that," said Darlene.

"Neither did Mr. Battle. By law he could argue that he is Coleen's father. We need to have him sign a release so he does not make a claim in the future, should Coleen die before Mr. Battle."

"Do you think it is wise that you travel to Miami? Do you feel well enough physically?" Darlene hoped Tom said yes, because he seemed to have the best grasp of the law and the facts in the case.

"I will be fine," said Tom. "By the way, when was Colin's funeral?"

"I haven't been told anything about a funeral or a burial."

"It may be the body hasn't been released by the Medical Examiner. You remember he was allegedly the victim of a murder. Call the Medical Examiner." Tom thought a minute and then asked, "Did we get the medical records from the hospital?"

Darlene was embarrassed, "I forgot to tell you. We were given some of the records. There was a note written and signed by Colin in the ER records. Colin said the shooting resulted from the accidental discharge of his pistol when he dropped the gun."

"Then Coleen is not the suspect. Who are the police invest-igating?"

"I have no idea about criminal charges. The hospital wants to mediate any claim the Estate has for malpractice that contributed to Colin's death."

"Are you saying a nurse or a doctor committed a criminal act that constituted manslaughter and the State Attorney is invest-igating the hospital and its staff?" Tom rubbed his chest. "I don't think so."

"I do not know what I am saying." Darlene was confused again.

"Well, it is very important that we find out how Colin died. We need to know who or what caused his death."

"The medical records the hospital's attorney provided do not include an explanation of how Colin died," Darlene conceded.

"Tell Alphonse that he needs to send a letter to the hospital which states that if they do not release all of Colin's records, the estate will not negotiate a settlement of the wrongful death claim." Tom thought a minute. "You know something must have happened to Colin that was so bad that the hospital is trying to hide the facts from the public. They want to pay the estate and require us to enter into a confidentiality agreement to hush this all up."

"That would be all right, don't you think?" Darlene wanted a simple solution. "What do we care if the public knows what the hospital did that caused Colin's death?"

Tom ignored his wife. "You know, we might be able to find out what happened from the autopsy report." Tom was not going to give up on establishing what caused Colin's death.

Darlene relented. "You go to Miami and speak to Mr. Battle. Alphonse and I will find out the cause of Colin's death." Darlene tried to satisfy and assure Tom that they would obtain the medical records.

Chapter 31
Colin's Stay in the ER

Most humans are out of their element when they are in a hospital emergency room. Being in the ER conjures up dark passages of pain and anxiety and even thoughts of the possibility of death. A billionaire is no different than most other humans in this circumstance, except they have more to lose.

Colin Frasier, being a physically small man and over 100 years old, was treated with more gravitas and gentleness by the hospital staff than ordinary patients. Colin was provided with a fleece cover and an extra pillow. The rails were secured at the side of his hospital bed and he was asked, "Comfortable?"

Colin did not respond to the question in depth. He had a gunshot wound to the cheek and the doctor discovered he lost two teeth. Colin nodded his answer and he mumbled, "Yes."

The ER doctor examined the wound and asked if the history Colin wrote was correct. "This gun shot was an accident. Is that correct? We have to be very careful when a gunshot is reported. We wouldn't want to misstate the cause of the wound. You are sure you were not the victim of a criminal assault?"

Colin shook his head to emphasize that, no, he was not assaulted.

"I will need to bring in a plastic surgeon and a dentist. I don't want to leave you with a bad scar. And I am worried that your jaw may have been fractured when you lost the two teeth. "

Colin began to tear up at the thought of a round scar on his cheek.

"You are not in danger of dying," assured the doctor. "I see many gunshot victims here in the ER and you will weather this injury. I would bet my life on it."

To assure him he would survive, the doctor gave Colin a magazine, a new one that had just been delivered, and told him to relax. He gave him a shot of topical painkiller to ease the throb and anxiety.

* * *

Light purple drapery divided the ER Room into cubicles and offered visual privacy; however, you could hear everything that was said in the large room. After Colin began to read his never-used magazine, the orderly rolled a patient who was truly the victim of a criminal assault into the space beside Colin. The man was breathing heavily, sucking in oxygen, and he complained he was in acute pain. As the orderly settled the new patient into his space the drape was accidentally pulled aside and Colin was introduced to his roommate and his molested face. He had suffered bite wounds to the nose and ears and eyebrows and lips.

A police officer was with the man and he was trying to obtain his statement.

"So, you were home?" asked the cop. "What happened?"

"Yes, my dog was outside and he was barking at a man on the street. I called the dog and the man ran at my house and dove through the window where I was standing and he began to attack me."

"Did you resist?"

"Of course I resisted. But he was as strong as an ape. He threw me around and then he began to tear at my face and he began to bite me."

"Were you able to push him off and get away?"

"No, not by myself. I was saved by my neighbors and my roommate. They pulled him off and held him down until the police got there. He kept yelling and screaming that I was the devil and he was going to kill me."

The ER physician came to the side of the bed and began to staunch the man's face, locating the wounds and cataloguing the work that would have to be done to repair the damage. They had not found the tip of the man's nose, but parts of his ears and lips were on ice in the operating room waiting to be reattached. The ER doctor's job was to stabilize the man and assess him before sending him upstairs to the plastic surgeon.

The doctor apologized. He could not give him any painkiller. The doctor promised the man he would be first in the surgery queue.

The victim asked the policeman, "Where is the man who attacked me?"

"They are bringing him here for treatment," said the doctor.

"What is wrong with him?"

"Angel dust," said the cop.

"Phencyclidine," said the doctor." Enough of it and it will make you crazy and think you are invincible ... and the drug will make you strong as an ox."

Colin interrupted the conversation by tapping the doctor on the back. Colin managed to convey his alarm that the crazy man was going to be treated in the ER.

"No problem. We can control him. We have done it before."

The victim also objected and said, "I don't want him anywhere near me."

"You will be upstairs before he arrives for treatment," said the doctor.

"You spoke too soon," said the officer.

You could hear the man as he came out of the elevator. His scream brought the hair up on the back of your neck and your hair would quiver. The scream caused a fear like doom was upon you.

The doctor chuckled nervously. "There he is. There he is."

The cop went over to help control the man. The crazed individual was able to get his feet under him and he had three cops trying to hold on as he swayed, shifting his weight from side to side. His hands were cuffed in the front. He was nude. His muscles rippled. The man saw his victim and he hooted, "Devil, devil, DEVIL," and attacked.

The four cops were thrown aside and the animal jumped on the victim who was lying on an ER cart and began to ravage the victim again.

Colin tried to move away but the animal was pushing the victim's cart and Colin's cart together through the room, toppling IV bottles and medicine carts and wires and equipment and diode screens to the floor. The more noise the better. The animal seemed to desire the sound of destruction. Tin and glass and wood and metal were crushed and destroyed as the animal bit into the breast of the victim, who was howling in pain.

The animal continued to push the carts until he finally hit a solid wall and the cops who were trailing behind were able to catch his feet and legs and pull him to the hard terrazzo floor. One cop took his night stick and began to beat the animal's head to no avail. The men then used every set of hand cuffs they could find for restraint. Finally, the animal collapsed. The doctor felt the suspect's neck for a pulse. It was shallow but it was present.

Unfortunately, the cops thought, the animal will survive.

The victim of the assault by the animal was deceased. The animal had bitten a hole in his neck and the man bled out, spurting his life onto the purple drapes.

Colin was still on his cart. He too was dead. The preliminary determination of the cause of Colin's death was a heart attack. Colin was scared to death.

* * *

Alphonse was not able to convince the hospital's defense attorney that the hospital should voluntarily give up Colin Frasier's records and so the next day the attorneys were before the judge in probate court arguing about production of the medical records.

Judges do not want to have to decide disputes involving production of discovery. The attorneys should be able to work it out themselves. But here, where the hospital's lawyer refused to give well over half of the records without any good, substantive reason, offering merely technical arguments, the court was left with little choice and heard the motion to compel production. Without the records, the Estate would have difficulty prosecuting the case since their main witness, Colin Frasier, was dead and unable to testify. The records were necessary. Further, these were Colin Frasier's records. Colin owned the records. The hospital merely had Colin Frasier's records in its custody.

The judge ordered the hospital to deliver the records forthwith and for emphasis the judge ordered the hospital to pay the Frasier Estate $5,000 for the legal fees necessary to bring the motion to court.

The hospital had 30 days to file an appeal of the court's order compelling production, but they relented and delivered the remaining records the following day. They also sent along a copy of the hospital's malpractice insurance policy and a letter stating the insurance company was tendering (making an offer to pay) the policy limits of $5,000,000 to settle the case. The hospital would require the Estate and Coleen Frasier to enter into a confidentiality agreement as a prerequisite to collection of the money.

Once Tom and Darlene were able to see the records it was obvious the State Attorney and the police were investigating and building a case against the drug addict who had attacked Colin and his roommate. They were not looking to prosecute Coleen.

The police were waiting for the decision of the Medical Examiner as to whether Colin's death by heart attack was caused by the assault by the animal who was under the influence of PCP. The police had charged the addict with the death of the man he had chewed to death. The authorities had charged him with murder in the second degree for that death. They were unsure they could prove premeditation because he was out of his mind on the drug when he killed the victim.

Colin Frasier's death seemed to be incidental to the attack by the addict on the "devil". Perhaps it was a felony/murder.

Chapter 32
Settlements

Faircloth had been told to return to his motel room in Miami to wait after he discovered that Coleen's birth mother was married to Attorney Battle at the time of Coleen's impregnation and birth.

It was raining ... a low pressure front was passing through. Faircloth sat in the room in an uncomfortable Swedish styled chair, watching TV and waiting for the phone to ring. He was there, bored, for a week. While he sat and watched re-runs of "I Love Lucy," the problems for the law firm and the Frasier estate were being eliminated. Coleen was no longer a suspect in her father's death. Tom was feeling better and back to work to the same extent as before he suffered the TIA.

Alphonse and DeMarco had settled the malpractice claim against the hospital for failure to protect Colin Frasier from injury and death by the hands of the known phencyclidine addict, and Century Bank had been paid a substantial part of the debt the firm owed on its line of credit.

The State Attorney was waiting for the opinion of the Medical Examiner before charging the addict with Colin's death. The question was whether Colin's heart attack could be attributed to the fear and anxiety caused by the assault. Colin had not been injured in the attack except that he fell off the cart at the end of the ordeal.

To assess blame in a civil wrongful death case there must be impact or an injury to the victim before there is liability for damages.

This was a criminal case and the burden of proof on the issue of causation would be more strict. There was no physical effect that could be shown that Colin incurred from the attack by the drug addict except Colin's heart was seized by fear and arrested. The argument from the defense would be that Colin would have just as likely had the heart attack as a result of the gunshot to the cheek as from the fall off the cart. The State's Attorney had a solid murder case against the addict for the death of the poor man who had had a hole eaten in his neck. The victim bled to death. Why muck that case up with the issue of whether Colin's heart attack was induced by fear of an impending attack from the addict? thought Faircloth.

One new, odd and suspicious piece of news. A. (Allright) Hardy, Colin Frasier's CPA, was found dead in his bathtub. He had slit his wrists. Naturally, upon his suicide, everyone suspected he had embezzled from Mr. Frasier. But Frasier had so much wealth they could not find the property that the CPA had stolen, if he had.

Allright's body was found by his secretary at the office when she went in to use the restroom. Apparently he had cut himself the night before and expected his loyal worker would find him. The Trust Company had advised Hardy the day before his body was discovered that they would be conducting a routine audit of the assets and accounts of the estate. The audit did not involve Tom's law firm.

The last major issue to be resolved for the estate involved the alleged common law marriage of Colin Frasier to Jesse Jones Smith. The partners were preparing for the settlement conference with Mr. Battle. They had decided that Tom would be accompanied to Miami by Alphonse. Faircloth would drive, but first he had to drive his station wagon back to St. Petersburg to act as chauffeur for Tom and Alphonse. Faircloth did not mind. He was happy to get out of the motel room in Miami.

Darlene had spoken to the attorney who represented their co-counsel at The Trust Bank. They agreed that if Tom could settle the probate case for anywhere under a million dollars Tom would save money for the Estate. There were so many attorneys involved in the litigation that every time any legal work was performed the cost was exorbitant. Ultimately the fees would all be paid by the estate. The estate was the only source of funds. Tom figured that every phone call cost the estate $500. Of course, from the attorneys' viewpoint, you can never have enough attorneys or reasons for the attorneys to charge legal fees.

* * *

The Fontainebleau Hotel on Miami Beach provided a three room suite and conference room for the law firm while the team was in Miami for settlement discussions with Mr. Battle. They would also provide secretarial services, if needed. The meeting with Mr. Battle was set in his office in the strip mall off Flagler Street in Little Havana. Darlene had scheduled the conference for 9:00 a.m. on Monday.

Tom's group arrived at the hotel in the late afternoon on Sunday and had a relaxing meal on the terrace overlooking the Atlantic Ocean. They did not discuss the case during dinner. The lawsuit had been the topic of conversation on the six hour drive from St. Petersburg. At this point it was up to Smith and her attorney to convince Tom and Alphonse that they were owed money and the amount they should be paid. Tom had limited settlement authority.

* * *

After they arrived at Battle's office, Faircloth was shown a seat. It was a vinyl-covered chair set next to a stack of magazines in the reception room. Faircloth's job was to wait patiently. Tom and Alphonse were taken to a small conference room. The room was lit with harsh fluorescent bulbs and contained a table with five chairs. There was another small table with a telephone. The floor was covered with a snarled shag rug. Everything in the room was a shade of green, but the colors still did not match. There was an incense stick lit and smoldering in an ashtray next to the telephone to mask the smell of stale tobacco smoke.

Shortly after the receptionist had returned with their drink orders (Cuban coffee, black), an attractive man and woman in their forties entered the room and made introductions. Maxwell wanted to be called "Max" and the woman said, "Mrs. Smith, I'm Mrs. Smith," and she sat in a chair and tried to hide by melting into the wall.

Because this was a settlement conference, Tom wanted to establish rules in the event no settlement was reached. First, Tom insisted the parties enter into a written agreement that stated that whatever was said by the parties during the negotiations was confidential and could not be used as evidence in court. Tom insisted Max and Mrs. Smith sign the agreement before they started to discuss anything, even the weather.

"I don't know why we need to sign this agreement." Max made a show by standing and gesturing while he spoke.

Tom was not going to argue. "Sorry, that's just the way it is. We have no authority to offer money to your client if she doesn't agree and sign the settlement conference agreement. We also need a copy of your client's drivers' license or other photo identification."

Max cracked a smile. "What? Don't you trust us?"

Tom and Alphonse broke up laughing. Max and Mrs. Smith joined in. The mood had changed. Everyone signed the paperwork and provided copies of their identification. Max also agreed that he wouldn't stand when he addressed the parties in the room.

Since Max's client was asking for money he had to present Mrs. Smith's case first. Max's argument was circular. The nub of his thought was that Mrs. Smith had carried and delivered Coleen and she had not been fully, completely and properly reimbursed for the act. He offered no case law or authorities that formed the legal basis for the argument. It was simply that it was inequitable that the Frasier Estate not compensate her in some way. It just wasn't fair that the law did not allow Mrs. Smith to share in the assets of the multi-billion dollar estate. Put another way, the enormity of the estate should allow for Mrs. Smith to share in its largess. It was simply not fair.

Without being obnoxious, being as matter of fact as he could be, Tom replied to Attorney Battle's argument. Tom explained that according to the law, Mrs. Smith had no legal standing or basis to obtain compensation. Tom showed the documents that proved Mrs. Smith was married to Max at the time Coleen was born. His point was that unless Mrs. Smith could prove she had a viable, legal, marital union with Colin Frasier she had no right to compensation under the Probate Code. Mrs. Smith could not be married to two men at the same time. Tom agreed that if Mrs. Smith had provided care and support for Coleen at any time until she reached adulthood, she could be reimbursed, but she had never cared for Coleen after she was born. Coleen was with Colin and supported solely by him after she was born.

Faircloth had also obtained a copy of an agreement signed by Mrs. Smith nineteen years earlier at the time of Coleen's birth. That document stated Mrs. Smith had agreed to act as the " birth surrogate for a zygote" implanted in her womb that ultimately resulted in the birth of the human infant named Coleen Frasier. The document stated that Mrs. Smith was paid $25,000 for the service she provided, acting as the birth mother, and that the $25,000 was full and final compensation for that service. The document was titled: Release and Satisfaction of Any and All Claims.

Tom then went on to say that though Mrs. Smith had no right to additional compensation the Estate was willing to discuss her claim and they had authority to make a small monetary settlement.

Mrs. Smith, an attractive woman, began to sob and said, "You don't understand. This is my only chance."

Max tried to quiet her.

"It's my only chance," she repeated.

Tom understood and felt for her. This was her one chance at the brass ring, at the kewpie doll, at the pot of gold, and she didn't want the chance to pass her by.

Tom looked at Max and asked, "Can I speak to your client directly?"

"Sure." Max had no objection because he had no control over his client and he knew he did not have a winning position. They were at Tom's mercy.

"What do you think would be a fair settlement, Ma'am?"

"I have to pay Max."

"Assume we pay Max," said Tom, trying to coax the amount it would take to obtain a release for the Frasier Estate from Mrs. Smith.

"I would settle for $100,000."

"That is fair." Tom turned to Max. "What do you want for your fee?"

"I think $100,000 would be fair."

"I don't think so." Tom smiled. "You did not give birth to a baby, Max." Tom looked at him intently. "Remember, this is probate court. You are going to have to prove to the court that your fee is reasonable."

Max took a minute and then said he would agree to a fee of $50.000.

Sold, Tom thought to himself. He told Max, "That's more than we had budgeted. I will have to make a call for permission."

"Fine," said Max. "Make the call."

* * *

Tom called the Vice President at The Trust Bank of St. Petersburg, who was in charge of the Frasier Estate account, and discussed the status of the settlement discussions. Tom recommended the Estate settle for the amounts demanded by Mrs. Smith and Attorney Battle and that he use the checks he had been given to pay the parties and secure their signatures on the releases that Alphonse had prepared. The VP had no objection.

The parties signed the documents and Tom left two cashier's checks totaling $150,000 to satisfy the debt. Tom took possession of the Release and the Settlement Agreement and the Stipulation to Dismiss the claim against the Estate that was signed by Petitioner Smith and a General Release signed by Smith and her attorney. Tom pointed out to Attorney Battle that he was releasing any and all rights he had to fees or for compensation he might personally have in the case. Battle acknowledged that fact by initialing a special clause in the release. The group shook hands and left the room. Tom nodded to Faircloth as he exited the room.

Faircloth noticed that Tom was a little slower leaving the building than he was when he entered.

"You okay, Boss?"

"Let's get in the car. I need an aspirin."

Tom took water and then put a single pill under his tongue and let it dissolve. The gritty residue coated the inside of his mouth. Tom had read that the active ingredient in aspirin was the bark of the willow tree. Whatever it was, the pill provided relief almost immediately. Tom took another sip of water and laid down in the back seat of the Lincoln Town Car and he closed his eyes.

"Should we go to the hospital?" Alphonse was worried, but deferred to Faircloth. Faircloth had become Tom's medical companion and he could read him almost as well as Darlene. Faircloth had had experience with Tom's TIAs and knew he would need a couple of hours rest before the effects of the attack fully subsided.

"Lucky you got out of there when you did," Faircloth said to Alphonse.

"The opposing party did not have much to say," said Alphonse. "Tom doesn't waste time."

"I'll take US 1 North," said Faircloth. "It will be slower but we will be closer to a hospital or clinic than if we drive through the center of the state on the turnpike and we are out in the middle of the woods. He needs a few hours of sleep and he should bounce back. We'll just have to wait and see how he does."

* * *

While Tom stretched out in the back of the Lincoln Town Car he was listening to Alphonse and Faircloth. Rather, Tom listened as Alphonse was talking nonstop and Faircloth was exhibiting the best attribute of an investigator. Faircloth was listening and nodding his head and watching the road.

Alphonse was explaining his relationship with Coleen. He was in love but he didn't know what her feelings were for him.

"What about your ages. Isn't that a problem?" asked Faircloth. Alphonse was 50 years old and Coleen was 19.

"It, the age difference, never comes between us. I think she is beautiful. I am far from handsome. My looks and the difference in our ages do not seem to matter to her."

"Why is she interested in you, do you think?" asked Faircloth.

"I listen to her. I think Colin was very critical and picked on her. He may have thought it was for the best, but he drove her away from him. Colin was a strange man. He didn't think the way we do. If she is different from him then it's probably for the good."

"But then, she misses him," wondered Alphonse out loud. "Coleen is afraid to do anything now that Colin is gone. He thought for her. She says she didn't have a life unless she rebelled and took a path opposite to what he wanted for her."

"Are the two of you serious?"

"I am, but I don't know if she is. It's killing me, really. It hurts. I probably should not be her lawyer."

"You represent the Estate, not her."

"That's a technicality. After today's settlement with Max and Mrs. Smith, she's definitely the only heir to the estate. "

"You need to talk to Tom and Darlene."

"I guess." Alphonse was quiet, then he said, "You're right. Thanks for listening to me, Faircloth."

Tom began to stir. He sat up.

"You okay, Boss?"

"Fine, fine," said Tom. "How close are we to home?"

"We are coming to Arcadia. We are heading west from there to Bradenton."

"It will be good to get home. I need to get some rest."

"Why don't you lay back down," offered Alphonse.

"Good idea." Tom laid back and he fell into sleep again.

* * *

Following Faircloth's advice, Alphonse sat down and conferred with Tom and Darlene about the fact that he was in love with Coleen.

"Have you had sexual intercourse with the client?" they asked simultaneously.

"Of course not," said Alphonse.

"You realize she is our client in that she is the sole heir of the Estate. You cannot fall in love with her or we will lose this fee. If we lose this fee we will be bankrupt," said Darlene in a matter of fact way.

"I understand."

"Then we do not need to fire you?" Tom pointedly stated. He was smiling but he was serious.

"No. you do not need to fire me. I understand. Love will have to wait until the estate is closed."

"Correct."

Tom interjected. "You might also consider that if she asks what to do with all her money you might suggest she establish a foundation. I would hate to see Coleen blow all that money. If she blew all the money, some attorney would probably sue our law firm because Coleen did not establish a foundation to protect the money in the Estate."

"We'll think about that," said Alphonse. "It will be her decision."

Chapter 33
The Blood Sucking Banker

For the last six months, since the law firm had been retained first by Colin Frasier and then by the Frasier Estate and finally, by Coleen, the firm was flush. The president of Century Bank had called Tom and asked if the firm wanted to increase and extend the $500,000 line of credit. The banker had suggested the bank would allow a $2,000,000 credit line. When Tom hesitated about accepting a loan, the banker insisted that he come to St. Petersburg and take Tom and Darlene to the Yacht Club for dinner so they could discuss a new loan or credit arrangement.

"I'm not a member of the Yacht Club," said Tom." They wouldn't have me."

"I'm a member," said the banker.

"That's alright," Tom said. "Instead of increasing the loan, we want to satisfy the loan, pay it off and open a savings account that will pour over to the office checking account."

"Why do that? The line of credit is convenient."

"The younger lawyers in the firm don't like the credit arrangement," said Tom. "We would rather collect interest on our office account."

The banker had no answer to that statement.

***

When the Estate of Colin Frasier settled, Tom's law firm agreed to a fee of fifteen million dollars. The firm was on a cash only basis from that time on. But the banker was persistent.

"I insist," said the banker, "that you let us help you with your banking needs."

"But now that we were paid the fee by the estate we do not need a loan."

"What about the needs of your new client, The Frasier Foundation?"

"If you want to talk about the foundation you will need to speak to Alphonse Alesse. He is handling that account."

"I tried to phone him but he doesn't take my call."

"Did you leave a message?"

"Yes."

"I'll tell him you called."

The banker couldn't stand it. He had to ask. "Is it true The Frasier Foundation was funded by the Estate of Colin Frasier with three billion dollars?"

"That was the figure that was reported in the court records. Yes it was. Three billion dollars was the correct amount," said Tom.

"We could do good things for the foundation, helping it with its money and investments," bubbled the banker.

"I am sure you could," said Tom.

"You know I am an environmentalist?" offered the banker. "I am very interested in trees."

"You must have heard that Coleen Frasier's purpose for the foundation and as the director of the Frasier Foundation is to re-plant all the trees that were cut by Colin Frasier's companies during his lifetime, and repair all the damage he caused to the environment."

"Yes. We are all for that goal. Century Bank would even make a contribution in the amount of one million dollars to the foundation. But I would need to have an appointment with Mr. Alesse to discuss the matter."

"I will be sure to tell Alphonse."

* * *

Tom picked up the receiver and dialed Karen. No answer. He walked to the front of the office. Darlene was at Karen's desk writing out checks ... paying bills.

"Where is Karen?"

"She is on her honeymoon with Bosco."

"That's right. I forgot."

"How could you forget? We paid for the wedding."

Tom smiled. Without Karen's help referring Colin Frasier to the firm through her friend Bosco, the firm would probably still be trying to figure out how to pay off the bank and save Darlene's condos and Tom's office building. Paying for the wedding was the least the firm could do for the couple.

* * *

Tom had not been concerned with money matters since the firm had been paid for the work on the Frasier account. The firm had earned $1,666,666.67 for representing the Estate in the malpractice case against the hospital for their negligence in care resulting in Colin Frasier's death. The firm had also been paid $15,000,000 for its representation of the Estate in the probate court and in the probate litigation filed by Coleen's surrogate mother. Last, they earned $100,000 for the skip trace, locating Coleen for Colin Frasier when she left the United States to practice kayaking in the Macal River in western Belize.

The total sum of the attorney fees Frasier paid was $16,766,666.67. The firm was rich, and Tom and Darlene were at ease and slept well at night.

In addition to the large fee, the firm had future security because the attorneys represented The Frasier Foundation, which had been endowed by Coleen Frasier with most of the residue of the estate assets once the estate was closed. It seemed to take forever to close the estate.

In addition to the work with the foundation, there was litigation of all sorts. Everyone in town felt Colin owed them for some debt or tort or slight or oversight. The probate court set aside $15,000,000 for the alleged creditors to fight over. Tom handled the litigation and dealt with the court on resolution of the claims.

* * *

On Tom's advice, Alphonse had suggested that Coleen consider a foundation as a way to preserve a large portion of the Frasier Estate's assets, protected from taxes and controlled by professional managers and by Coleen and her heirs. Coleen was aware of the damage her father and his companies had done to the forests in third world countries, in the Amazon and in Indonesia, particularly Sumatra, and also in Madagascar.

Coleen had argued with her father when she discovered as a teenager what his business was, and the harm he was causing as a result of the way he harvested natural resources. She also learned of the collateral damage that he caused to the animals and living creatures when the forests were clear cut and replanted in a monoculture such as eucalyptuses or pine or soy beans. There was a question if any human knew the best way to regenerate the rain forests. The foundation could preserve lands and attempt to re-grow what had been destroyed and establish the best regime for the regeneration of flora on the planet.

But, the process would take a lifetime.

Chapter 34
Alphonse Alesse and Coleen Frasier

Alphonse Alesse was a quiet man. He had practiced law for over twenty years. That whole time, he was employed at the firm of Night, Adams, Street, Alesse, Demarco and Barnes.

He didn't seem to date any one woman steadily and had not remarried after his wife divorced him. The reason for the divorce was a lack of trust. Alphonse was charged but not convicted of a crime, to wit: aggravated battery. Alphonse had never pled guilty to the felony, but he pled no contest to the misdemeanor charge of simple assault. The plea had been sealed by order of the court and he had no conviction for any crime, but his wife thought he might somehow have been involved in the crime of cutting an exotic dancer with a razor.

His wife harbored an irrational fear of Alphonse and she lost all desire for intimacy with her husband. She also felt he did not understand how the criminal charges had impacted her life and the scrutiny she felt from her friends and neighbors. Last, and most im-portant, she was angry that he entered the plea without discussing it with her. She felt that if he were to admit to a crime, even if it was a minor misdemeanor, she should be part of the decision.

Alphonse knew their marriage was at risk as a result of the criminal charge. He did not want a divorce, but he would not contest a dissolution and he left the divorce decision to his wife. He put up no fight and offered no defense to her allegation that their marriage was irretrievably broken.

After the divorce the consensus among the staff at work, who had nothing better to do than to gossip, was that Alphonse was homosexual, but there was no factual basis for the assumption. In fact, the one openly gay associate told his friends in the secretarial pool that he had made a very overt pass to see if he could entice Alphonse to exhibit any sexual interest in him and he was politely rebuffed in a way that told the associate that Alphonse had no interest in the associate and that he was not interested in an affair with a person of his own sex.

Alphonse spent his money on music, old music, opera, classical, the longer hair the music was the better. The atmos-phere in his office had an undertone of Mozart, Brahms and on Friday it was Tchaikovsky.

In his practice of the law, Alphonse was reserved. At hearings, he always waited to be asked by the judge to respond to the argument. If he was in a group of lawyers, he would not butt in; rather, he would raise his hand to his face and wait to be recognized and then offer his opinion. He would not offer an argument that had been covered earlier in the legal discussion. He wrote his legal briefs in the same thoughtful, careful, concise manner as his oral argument, which was appreciated by the judge, and his argument was most often successful.

Alphonse did not drink alcohol, but he did smoke marijuana. Sometimes he took a little toke during a break at work in the men's room, but he mostly avoided weed at work. After work, however, he always had a joint while he sat in his car in the covered parking lot before he drove home at the end of the day. He was the last to leave the office and there was no one to observe him as he sat in the car and sucked away at a joint with the windows up. He smoked to take the edge off. It made him mellow and it improved the sound of the classical music that he enjoyed so much.

* * *

The day Alphonse first met Coleen he had worked all day and into the night preparing the paperwork to file with the Clerk of

Court in order to open the Colin Frasier Estate. Coleen needed to stay with Alphonse because he needed her signature on the pleadings. Afterward, he discovered that she had no car, and regardless, her driver's license was suspended. She needed a ride home to the Frasier Mansion and Alphonse obliged. It was late and dark and when they entered the car, Alphonse opened the ash tray and there in plain view was an assortment of rolled dope. Alphonse didn't even think about it. He motioned for Coleen to choose their poison and once she made a selection, the two shared the joint. Neither said a word.

Afterward, Alphonse fired up his four cylinder Toyota and pushed in a CD – Rachmaninoff – and started to back out of his parking spot.

"Don't take me home yet. I have the munchies," said Coleen.

"Hamburger?" suggested Alphonse.

"Yes, big and greasy with cheese."

Alphonse drove up 4th Street to a sports bar and the pair shared burgers and onion rings, vanilla milk shakes and a serious case of the giggles.

"I won't be allowed to eat for a week." Alphonse rubbed his gut. "I blew my diet."

"I seem to burn calories off without a problem," Coleen explained. "I get plenty of exercise with the kayak."

"I'm interested. I would like to try that. Where can I buy a kayak?"

"Jason's (a local sport's equipment store) has everything you need. They even have a pool with a continuous wave machine so you can practice at the surf shop."

"Really?"

"Do you want to try it? They are open 'til midnight."

"Great."

That was their first date.

* * *

Alphonse was 50 and Coleen had just turned 20 years old. Because of the work they were doing on the Frasier Estate they saw each other several times a week. Coleen always came late in the day and she and Alphonse would ride home in his car after work. They would share a meal and they always shared a joint.

Coleen would invite Alphonse into the mansion and Bess would make them a meal. Usually it was something simple like a sandwich with a large glass of milk.

The staff at the house enjoyed Alphonse's company. To a great extent he was like Colin Frasier. He was quiet and contemplative. He thought things through until he had a solution to a problem, and then he went forward methodically to attain his goal. He was tenacious. Mike, the butler and Bess, the cook, agreed he was like Colin. They enjoyed having Alphonse around and encouraged his relationship with their boss. Coleen was open to suggestion and she broached the subject of a trip with Alphonse.

"What would you like to do together if we went on a real, serious date ... a vacation?"

"I would like you to take me kayaking out in the Gulf of Mexico." Alphonse had bought a kayak, a simple plastic craft to paddle around and he had been going out in a bayou in the bay near his house early each day before work.

"You have been practicing?" asked Coleen.

"Yes. I bought a rack for the car and I thought we could go up north to the Suwannee River or to Old Town and follow the trail of Islands in Deadman's Bay near Steinhatchee. The assistant at the surf shop at Jason's gave me the idea."

"I have an ocean kayak," said Coleen. "We could use my kayak."

* * *

To the pair this was real; a serious date. They went to Deadman's Bay. There were islands covered with virgin pine trees and saw palmetto and wiregrass and trails in the wetlands to the

Gulf of Mexico through the sawgrass and salt marsh sedges. The water, though salty, was pure and clear and there were millions of fish; also otter and manatee. There were also Florida birds: ibis, wood stork, rosette spoonbill and osprey, bald eagles, falcons and hawks. It was Florida in its pristine and untouched state.

Most of the land was owned by a company called St. Thomas, Inc. There was more than 250,000 acres of land on the east coast of Florida, south of St. Augustine and almost another 250,000 acres in the Big Bend area on the west coast of the state. After paddling around and then renting a plane and flying the property over the next several weekends, Coleen asked Alphonse if he could see what it would cost to buy the land?

Alphonse explained it would take a good deal of research, but that he thought he knew who could help. He told Coleen about the relationship the law firm had with the Barnes family and with Marla and James Reynolds and that they would probably volunteer to help Coleen determine if the land would make a good investment for The Frasier Foundation. Alphonse offered to set a meeting for her with them.

Things seemed to gel. Coleen wanted Alphonse to be with her and be a part of the decision process regarding the purchase of the five hundred thousand acres of forest and natural wetlands from the St. Thomas Company. She thought he was brilliant, but also very nice. Coleen felt she could trust Alphonse, and she could. Alphonse was smitten.

The purchase seemed to be a great idea. Marla and James Reynolds offered inside information on St. Thomas, Inc. The company's assets consisted of land, land and more land. St. Thomas was a timber company. The company was land rich and cash poor. Most of the land had been purchased in the early 1900s. The land was raw and untamed with few roads offering access to the timber. Included in the 500,000 acres, St. Thomas had some 10,000 or so acres of prime development property that was located on the Gulf Coast, but that land was isolated and had few inhabitants and no infrastructure, no entertainment, or any venue other than the natural beauty of the property itself. St. Thomas' idea, going into the future, was to develop the 10,000 acres into towns and get out of the timber business. Frasier Foundation was a perfect fit since the foundation wanted to own raw land, which the foundation intended to keep in its natural state.

Once the CPAs got involved they were able to take advantage of tax loopholes so that St. Thomas could make a gift (that's right a gift) of most of the wildest, most untamed land to The Frasier Foundation. As a for profit company, St. Thomas would have a tax deduction for the contribution (gift) of the wild land to The Frasier Foundation, which was a charitable foundation. The charitable deduction would be set off against the cash paid by the Frasier Foundation for the balance of the land that was to be developed by St. Thomas into a residential property, St. Thomas generated much needed revenue from the transaction to develop the 10,000 acres into a city in north Florida. The cash from the sale was pretty much tax free. Because of the tax advantage of donating some of the land to The Frasier Foundation, St. Thomas could sell the land cheap.

The foundation was able to purchase the half million acres for an average cost of $200 an acre, or $100,000,000.

It was a steal.

Part VI
With his boots on

Chapter 35
Hello Sister

Bob Barnes was in town on the campaign trail for governor of Florida and he was at the law office of Night, Adams, Street, Alesse and DeMarco for a meeting with Tom Night. But first he walked into the office of Jenny Barnes DeMarco to say hello to his sister.

"It seems like every time I drop by you are getting ready to have another baby."

Jenny and James DeMarco had three children and were expecting a fourth soon. Due date for the birth was just shy of a month. Jenny hugged her big brother. She reached up and rubbed the top of his head. He had a receding hairline that had moved to the back of his head. Bob's only concession to the baldness was to cut his hair very short and accept the inevitable. He would probably be totally bald at some point soon.

"How you doing brother?" said Jenny smiling. She was proud of her brother. Since being appointed and confirmed by the US Senate as Secretary of the Interior three years ago, Bob had been nominated as the Republican candidate for governor of the State of Florida. Since their adoptive father, Frank Barnes, had died, Bob and his family were living with Bea in the Homestead in Holly Hill.

"I came to see the boss. Last time I was in town he was in the hospital with a TIA," said Bob. "I wanted to see Tom for a minute if he's available."

"He is in. I'll take you." Jenny talked to Karen and then motioned for Bob to follow her to Tom's office. Tom looked up from his desk and pushed himself up on unsteady legs. He grabbed his cane and walked to the door and invited Bob into his room. Bob and Tom and Jenny sat on comfortable leather chairs after Bob and Tom shared a bear hug.

"How's the race? Interesting?" asked Tom.

"I think we are making some progress but we are the minority party and the polls show we are behind. For us to win, we have to get some of the Democrats to vote for our side."

"The Democrats have been in power now in the state of Florida for a long time," Tom said, recognizing the fact that Bob's grandfather, Senator Francis A. Barnes, had been voted out of office thirty years earlier by the Democrats and his state senate seat had remained in the hands of the Democratic party ever since.

"You're right Tom. The Republican Party seems passe. The best thing I have going for myself is that the public may want a change in the government. Florida keeps getting hit with these recessions. The downtowns are worse than in the rest of the country. I'm trying to make the public understand we can make a difference."

"Pocket book issues are important to the voters," agreed Tom. "Plus, your party has had many new converts and many Republican retirees have moved to the state. The fact this election has a short two-year term could also help."

Tom nodded his agreement. "I came by to thank you and Darlene for your contribution. You were very generous."

"You are welcome. The recent times have been good for us."

"Could I speak to you a minute in private?" asked Bob.

Tom nodded his head toward Jenny. She excused herself and closed the door.

Tom waited for Bob to speak.

"So," Bob began, "I don't know if you are aware that a number of years ago, before I was married to Smiley, when Marla was running CCC Corporation we were an item. We dated and then we broke up when she married Reynolds." Bob cleared his throat. "Then Marla and Reynold's had some difficulty in their marriage and Marla moved back to the old Plantation house in Ormond with her mother. Reynolds stayed in New York. They never divorced but they lived separate lives. During that time Marla and I lived together at the Plantation."

"Did you have separate domiciles?" asked Tom. "Separate legal residences?"

"Yes, I got my mail at the Homestead in Holly Hill, but Marla and I shared a bedroom at the old house on the river."

"So, what of it? Marla and Reynolds are together now, living at the old house at the plantation. They bought the business and are living as husband and wife. What happened between you and Marla is a private affair. The person who is going to say anything will probably have a history of their own. 'People who live in glass houses shouldn't throw bricks' is what they say."

"That's true. My problem is with Marla. She is always appearing at events and she comes over to me and grabs my arm and introduces me to everyone."

"She's always tried to run the show," said Tom.

"It's more than that. It's like she thinks she's my wife, the way she acts. My wife, Smiley, has noticed it, and I can tell my wife is hurt by Marla's attention to me."

"And what do you want?" Tom shrugged his shoulders," Do you want my advice as to what you should do?"

"Really, what I am here to ask is if you would talk to Marla."

"I was afraid of that. When do you have an event where you expect Marla to be present?"

"In Orlando next week ... it's the Lincoln dinner. It's a big event."

"Darlene and I will come to the dinner and I will try to talk to Marla. Will Reynold's be there?"

"He should be. He always follows her around like a little puppy dog."

"Well, whatever. I don't think that is a fair assessment of Reynolds. Marla has a strong personality." Tom wondered how he had come around to now supporting Reynolds. Tom had been jealous of him for years. Tom was also jealous of Bob.

Tom pulled out his day calendar and marked the date. "We'll be there."

"Also," said Bob, "the Democrats may sue me claiming I am not a resident of the state of Florida."

"Well, where do you live now?"

"We live at the Homestead in Holly Hill, Florida. I have had my legal residence there for almost 50 years. My wife and I have a house in Washington, DC, that we purchased when I was the Secretary of the Interior. The house is listed for sale, but we still own it."

"Where are you registered to vote?"

"At the Homestead, in Holly Hill, Florida."

"Where does personal mail come to you?"

"The Homestead."

"This sounds like a harassment suit."

"I will still need a lawyer."

"Send me the Complaint if suit has been filed," said Tom. "And do not delay. I will need time to defend you."

* * *

Bob climbed in the rear seat of the Ford Crown Victoria that had been loaned to the "Bob Barnes for Governor Campaign." In the front were his campaign manager, Herman Moines, and his security man, Gene "Smitty" Smith.

"Where to next?" asked Bob.

"Home Shopping Corp. invited us over to do a 'Meet and Greet' any time we want," said Moines.

"Sounds good. Maybe we can get on the TV and get some exposure with the viewers on the shopping network. We need the publicity. "

Home Shopping had 6,000 employees and a huge canteen. Back in the day, Bob went to school with the owners and he had permission to hook up with their PR department and meet the employees at lunch, say a few words, and hand out brochures. Bob had spoken to the morning shift on a past trip to the area and they had time to get to the facility at the Gateway area of the city to meet the workers who worked the second shift through the dinner hours. The operation at Home Shopping was on air 24 hours a day.

"Where do you want to go after that?" asked Bob.

"We could go to the Yacht Club and shake some hands," said Herman. "That will be enough for the day. I don't want to wear you out."

"I intend to win. I can't win if I don't meet the voters. I also want to see the new TV spot advertisements. I don't want to go negative on our opponent."

"Greg Teague will pound you to death with negative ads. You have to be prepared to fight fire with fire. They already started the rumor mill going in North Florida with the 'half breed' jokes, making fun of Smiley and her son, Robert."

"My wife and I have talked about that. She has had success visiting schools and churches in the Panhandle and up in Tallahassee and Panama City and Apalachicola. She's been welcomed into the peoples' homes and has had good press coverage. I think those jokes will backfire. Members of the Seminole Tribe are even voluntarily showing up at events and campaigning for us. The tribe was voting Democrat before Smiley got on the campaign trail for me. The polls say they are voting for me now."

He's fooling himself, thought Herman, but he did not contradict Bob. Herman just smiled.

"I want to work," said Bob. "Let's go see some folks."

"Fine," said Herman. There was always a crowd of people at the Pier, Herman thought. "We'll head to the Pier after the Yacht Club."

* * *

While Bob worked the banquet hall and dining rooms of the Yacht Club on Tampa Bay in downtown St. Petersburg, Herman Moines was on the pay phone in the lobby.

"No," said Herman into the receiver of the phone. "He's still working and he wants to hit another event tonight. There's a concert at Janus Landing and then he wants to shake hands at the Pier."

In response to the next question Moines said he had nothing concrete yet that they could use against Bob Barnes, but he had his suspicions after the first stop of the day when they visited attorney Tom Night.

"Why?" said Herman into the receiver. "Well, because Tom Night is the Barnes' Family fixer. My guess is Bob spoke to Thomas Night about something that could damage his chances to be elected.

"Why? Well, because he told us to stay in the car and when I asked the purpose of the visit for the campaign log, Bob told me to make no mention of the visit. He said it wasn't related to the campaign. It was personal."

Moines continued, "Yeah, it sounds like I may be on to something. I told you this guy has something we can use against him. I just hope I can find out what it is before the election is over."

"Yeah," Herman said, "I realize I don't get paid by you if he's elected. I'm trying to slow him down, but he has an ambitious streak."

Unfortunately, Greg Teague is not as ambitious as Bob Barnes, thought Herman.

"When I know more about Tom Night's secrets, you will be the first to know."

Herman hung up the receiver on the phone and exited the phone booth and headed into the main dining salon to pick up Bob and Smitty, the security man.

Smitty was a retired baseball great and he helped Bob gather a crowd. Besides acting as security in case there was a problem, he was a greeter and he seemed to know everyone on the West Coast of the state, mainly because he played baseball in the majors and the teams all had camps and leagues that practiced for the summer season in Florida on the west coast: Tampa, St. Pete, Clearwater, Naples, Bradenton, Sarasota, Ft. Myer and Haines City.

Smitty knew everyone.

"Time to go," said Herman and he waved his hand. He interrupted Bob, who was answering a voter's question.

Bob cut in to say: "You go. Smitty and I will head over to Tampa after Janus Landing and the Pier."

"You're nuts," said Herman. "You are going to burn out."

"He'll be okay, Herman. I'll get him home by midnight." Smitty thought Herman was wrong to boss Bob around in public.

"I'll meet you at the hotel." Herman apologized to Bob. "I just want you to survive the campaign."

* * *

Smitty took the comment from Herman about Bob surviving the campaign personally. Smitty had been hired to keep Bob safe and secure during the run-up to the election, and he took the job seriously. Lone men had been deciding elections, even gubernatorial contests, with a gun. Killers were not relying on the ballot box to effect change. The Kennedy brothers, Martin Luther King and the attempts on Gerald Ford, Ronald Reagan and George

Wallace were fair warning to any campaign of the importance security was to the campaign to add security to the budget.

Bob Barnes was not a controversial candidate. He really came across as a nice guy who offered a voice of reason, fairness and above all, change for the voters. But he was expected to lose, so it would seem there was little need for the opposition to kill him. Though there were doubts about the need for security, no one in the Republican Party wanted to be the one who rejected protection for their candidate for the highest office in the state if Bob was assassinated.

When Smitty had the chance to take Herman aside he expressed his displeasure at the remark regarding a lack of security. Smitty poked his finger in Herman's chest and asked him if he had any reason to think Bob was in danger and would not survive.

"Was there any reason to believe Bob was in danger?"

"No. Of course not. Bob Barnes is safe. I do not know anyone who wishes him any evil."

In fact, Herman thought, the Republicans could not have picked anyone better than Bob to assure the Democrats would be re-elected to the Governor's office. To Herman, Bob was not electable because he was too likable. He wasn't taken seriously by the voters, according to the polls. He had no name recognition in the parts of the state where he should have had strength. The voters had not become familiar with his life story. Jacksonville and the I-4 corridor from Daytona Beach to St. Petersburg was the area of Republican strength, but for some reason Bob did not click with the voters in that part of the state.

Herman thought Teague's men were crazy to worry so much about Bob as to hire him as an insider to bring them dirt on Bob and his campaign. But Herman was happy to be collecting a paycheck from both sides in the race.

Chapter 36
Greg Teague

Greg Teague always had a pleasant smile on his face. And why should he not smile? His life was perfect. He had a perfect marriage. There was no baggage. His wife was from Gainesville. Her family toiled as professors in the political science department at the University of Florida. They had taught Teague in college and thought him to be the most intelligent and gifted political science student who ever attended the university.

While in college, Teague was a member of The Blue and Orange Key Society, an incubator for students who would later be involved in politics in Florida. He was active in political campaigns in school, helping his fellow Blue and Orange Key members, and in his senior year he was elected Student Body President with the help of the members of the club.

Greg Teague was almost six foot tall, strong jaw, blue eyes, a full head of sandy hair and a strong speaking voice.

When Teague left Gainesville upon graduation, he married and he took his bride to his hometown of Ft. Lauderdale, and ran for a seat in the House of Representatives of the state of Florida. He was elected the first time he ran. He was only 23 years old. His opponent even admitted later that he had voted for him. "Teague," said the opponent, "was the better man for the job."

Teague and his wife had twins, a boy and a girl. Teague was loyal to his wife. The kids went to public school and thrived in South Florida. They were in the scouts and played sports and every step of the way Teague was by their side when he was at home. His wife cared for the twins with great devotion when he was away.

Teague was known as "GT" in the legislature. He was a leader. First, he was appointed as committeeman to the appropriations committee, and then he moved up to lead the House as Speaker in six short years. He attained his position fair and square. There was no baggage collected along the political trail. People owed GT because he helped them. When he ran for Speaker of the House they voted for him. He did not owe the speakership to others except the house members who loved him.

After his election as Speaker, he was known to have his finger in every political pie, and to share the pie with his cronies. Nothing got through the House without his approval. No legislation was scheduled for a committee hearing or for a vote without his approval. The control he exercised over the agenda could prevent any bill from moving through the legislature and the text of all bills had to be approved by GT before they could become law.

GT wielded power by giving his members what they needed back home to be re-elected in return for their vote. And if they did not vote his way and smile when he told them how to vote, then he assigned them an office in the basement of the old capital building and cut off funding for their campaign and removed them from chairmanship of a committee; or he assigned the recalcitrant member to a committee with no power or panache. The wayward member would be at the bottom of the totem pole and out of office come the next electoral cycle.

Since Teague had the power and fortitude to say no, he could control the entire agenda in Tallahassee. Even the Senate and the Governor had to kowtow to his wishes. Most important, during this last session, the Governor's buddies wanted to pipe water from the Suwanee River south, to sate the thirst of the housing developments in Orlando and Miami. To accomplish this theft of water from the voters and citizens in North Florida, the Governor had to obtain the permission of the legislature and that meant GT had to approve the bill. To get GT's approval, the Governor's buddies had to make political donations to GT and his cronies for their campaign funds or PACs.

* * *

The legislature had only one thing it was required to do, which was to pass the budget. GT played chicken with the Senate and forced the Senate to approve the budget he proposed by withholding support for the Senate's budget proposal in the House, which he controlled. After the disruption happened one time and the senators felt the public's wrath because the Senate failed to pass the budget, the Senate agreed to the budget proposed by the Speaker of the House year after year. It became the norm. GT controlled the content of the budget.

GT even figured out a way to exercise power over the press, though he was only partially successful. He would hold court at a local steak house and only invite the reporters to the press corps dinner who followed his company line. In return for slanting the story his way, Teague gave the reporters he invited to dinner a heads up on the agenda for the year, and he announced who would be carrying the ball for the party. He would also dish out dirt on his enemies and he used the media to undermine anyone who crossed him. GT was amazed that everyone had some dirty laundry he could throw in the public view to sabotage his opponents. Most of the media toed the Teague party line, except for the Tampa Bay News Journal. The newspaper bucked Greg Teague, but didn't have much success reporting his activities to its readers because he cut off their information and leads.

However, Greg Teague realized that he too was vulnerable. He could be attacked because he was the person who manipulated the politicians and the press. He fingered the strings that caused the elected officials to enact policy. GT was the king-coon, the paternal politician. He was in charge, but he was vulnerable if the public knew how he exercised unfair control over the state from the back room. He dreaded hearing the nickname, Boss Teague.

The image Teague presented was that he was not a threat. He played at being a "bubba". GT knew voters were fickle. The public could vote him out of office. In order to retain his position as a supposed lowly legislator, GT gave his constituents in Ft.

Lauderdale every piece of pork they could possibly want. He bought the voters with parks and schools and ball fields and industry and jobs. He lavished his district and consequently, he was elected every two years to the House without fail, and then once elected to the lowly House of Representatives, he was elected Speaker and he had the power and the political platform he needed to control the state of Florida.

* * *

GT had everything he wanted, until he lost his health. Greg Teague noticed a lump on his neck. It was cancer. Though not particularly aggressive, the cancer was deadly and would kill him in six or seven years.

He considered his options and decided he wanted fame as his final tribute. He wanted everyone to know he was the king coon. He wanted the title "Governor" on his gravestone.

He would run for Governor of the great state of Florida.

* * *

The old Governor's mansion was the scene of a bloodless assassination one week after Teague received the bad news from his physician that he had a finite time to live due to his medical condition.

 GT called the sitting governor on his private line and invited himself over for a private conference. The private conference was a violation of the requirement that any meeting of two or more public officers where policy was to be discussed was to be open to the public. Further, the public had to be given notice of the meeting.

This law did not concern the Speaker or the Governor because they regularly violated this law. They weren't stupid; if the public attended the private conferences they would know the Speaker and the Governor were violating other laws, such as the laws against criminal conspiracy.

When they met at the mansion and Teague shook hands and smiled, Governor Adams was a little reticent. "How can I help you, GT?"

"I was thinking I would run for governor next term."

"I have another term. It would be four years from now before you could run." Adams was confused. It must be four years from now, he thought.

"No, I intend to run for the next term. That's in a year," insisted GT.

"Well, I say again, we had agreed I get two terms. The next term is my term."

"There are no guarantees in life," said Teague. "You can run again if you want, but I will oppose you for the nomination and we both know you will lose."

"I was nominated and elected in a landslide last time." Adams pushed out his chest in pride.

"You won with my support and my votes on the Democratic Election Commission got you the nomination. You will not have my support in the future," said Teague. "You can bet on it."

"I don't think you will run against me," threatened Adams. "I know everything you have ever done, particularly in selling the water from the Suwanee River to the developers."

"Don't wag your finger in my face. You were divvying up the pie right along with me. If you want to bring that up we will both be sharing a jail cell."

"I don't intend to give up this job. It's due to me. It was promised," said Adams.

When the talk came to threats and blows GT always had a back-up plan. "You know the governor appoints the US Senator under certain circumstances?" Teague laid the bait.

"What of it?" Adams was sniffling. "Senator Nelms is in office in the US Senate for four more years. Nothing will pry him out of his US Senate seat."

"If you were to retire as governor and I were elected Governor, I would cause Senator Nelms to resign and I would appoint you to his seat in the US Senate."

"I could go for that, if you could deliver," brightened Adams. "How do you know Senator Nelms is going to resign?"

"Trust me, it's true. If I want him to resign, he will resign."

Insider knowledge is the currency of political power.

What GT had was dirt. Senator Nelms' home town was in St. Petersburg. Nelms was known to frequent Little St. Mary's restroom near the pier. GT knew Nelms would resign if he was threatened with the revelation of his homosexual acclivities. GT had saved this gem of dirt for use at the right time and this was the right time.

GT and Governor Adams agreed to their trade of the senate seat for the governor's chair.

After their discussion, the Speaker and the Governor adjourned to the front porch of the Governor's Mansion and stood and shook hands and smiled for the entire world to see. If asked, the men always said that at these meetings they discussed college sports. There was no policy discussed. GT backed UF and Adams rooted for his alma mater, FSU. The excuse for the meeting was lame but plausible to the rabid sports fans in the state. Teague and the Governor would never be convicted of a violation of the open meeting law for making a little wager on a game between the two top college franchises in the state.

Chapter 37
Lincoln Dinner

The Lincoln Dinner was held in the Marriott Hotel Auditorium in Orlando on International Drive. Three Thousand of the faithful attended the event and listened to speeches from the candidates for statewide office.

The keynote speech was given by Bob Barnes. He knew most of the people in the room from his time as Secretary of the Interior. He was known to be honest and he was well liked. His wife, Smiley, and her older child, Robert, circulated in the room, shaking hands and greeting the diners before the event. The Barnes Family's roots in business and agriculture stretched back to the 1830s and the political genealogy was highlighted by "The Senator," the late Frances A. Barnes, who had represented Volusia County in the legislature for almost twenty years.

Bob Barnes had purchased tickets at the dinner for the clan. Included at the table were seats for Tom and Darlene and Marla and James Reynolds. Bob controlled the seating arrangements and he placed Tom and Marla together surrounded by Jenny and Jim DeMarco and their three children. The seating arrangements would allow Tom and Marla to talk without being overheard.

Bea Barnes did not attend the dinner. Frank, Jr. had passed more than a year back from a heart attack when he was fishing with Robert, Jr. Bea still did not feel right going out in public.

Tom re-jiggered the seating arrangements and put James Reynolds in a place of honor next to the party's candidate for Governor. Reynolds was well respected in the business community and was known internationally as the former President and CEO of JRD Corporation, which was still a huge conglomerate.

Reynolds was aware Bob and Marla had had an affair while he was still working for JRD. During that period he spent most of his time at company headquarters in New York City and he quietly dated other women. Marla was expected to remain in their residence in Upstate New York and keep quiet. She would have none of that.

While pressured by duties at work, Reynolds was too busy to pay any attention to his wife. He was only aware his wife was having an affair because she told him when she explained she was moving back to her house at the Plantation in Ormond Beach, Florida. As their separate lives played out, Reynolds was relieved that Marla and Bob were discreet and they caused him no embarrassment and did not embroil the company in a scandal. Reynolds was able to complete his term in office at JRD uneventfully. The stockholders and the directors of the corporation were pleased with his performance, and he and Marla came to an arrangement about their lives after he retired. They were happy together now. Marla and Reynolds enjoyed running Plantation #7 and living in Marla's old house near the beach.

Bob Barnes was not much of an orator, but he had learned to keep his political speeches short and on point. He had a stump speech that he would massage to the event and the audience. The themes were fewer taxes, less government restriction on business and more individual freedom.

This dinner was the main gathering of the Republicans after the Republicans had nominated Bob as their candidate. Further, this was the first time that the Republicans were aware Governor Adams would step aside and not run for re-election. Speaker Greg Teague would be the Democrat's candidate for governor. Therefore, this was Bob's first chance to comment on Greg Teague as his opponent.

The following was the punch line of Bob's speech:

"If I had known that Greg Teague was going to be my opponent I may have thought twice before running." There was laughter.

Then Bob looked out over the crowd from the podium and continued. "But having Boss Teague as my opponent allows us to confront head on the deadwood in Tallahassee. GT, as he's affectionately known in the capital, has been in office too long. And so have the Democrats. Power corrupts, they say. The Democrats have been in power long enough. The state of Florida needs change!"

Bob concluded with a vow to protect the environment and bring clean jobs to the state, and to not forget Florida's heritage in agriculture and ranching and timber, which were all renewable industries and compatible with the Republican pledge to protect the lands of the state.

There were cheers and even enthusiasm from the crowd.

* * *

After the speech, Tom and Marla sat at the table and talked about how proud they were of Bob's political accomplishments, and all in such a short time.

"The fact that Bob could be the Governor takes my breath away," said Marla.

"You have not been known to be so easily impressed in the past," said Tom as he took aim with an arrow at her heart. "You know the Democrats will look for any way they can to embarrass Bob. They would not be beyond attacking him as a fornicator and an adulterer."

Marla sat back in her chair and placed her fork on her plate. She looked in Tom's eyes and said, as she blushed, "Is it so obvious that I still love him?"

"Yes, it is apparent that you love him when you are near him and when you listen to him speaking."

"I do not want to cause him any problems." Marla lowered her eyes. "I didn't realize it was obvious. What do you suggest?"

"I didn't mean to suggest it was intentional on your part, Marla. Probably it would be best if you did not see him until the election was over. It would also be good if you kept attuned to the fact that the opposition may try to talk to you about your feelings for Bob. You could reply to a question in an innocent way, but they may get you to say something that would compromise you and Bob."

"What should I do if that happens?"

"Avoid the subject of your feelings for Bob. Just say you intend to vote for him and leave it at that. Later, call me."

"I will. This is pretty rotten, don't you think?"

"Yes it is," said Tom as he cut the chicken on his plate.

* * *

Herman and Smitty were seated in the very back of the room at the Lincoln Dinner with the other operatives—campaign managers and such. By the time the chicken and peas reached their table the food was ice cold.

Herman pushed the food away and pulled out a cigar manufactured up the road at the Have-A-Tampa factory. He blew smoke across the table and aggravated the guests. Herman had been sipping Old Granddad bourbon, and he didn't care if he was obnoxious.

Smitty asked him to put out the cigar and Herman poked it out in the mashed potatoes. Herman leaned back and sipped his drink and watched his boss's table. In particular, he was interested in the woman Tom was speaking to so intently. "Who is that woman?"

"Marla Reynolds."

"Is she one of the Barnes'?"

"No. she's married to James Reynolds. She was Tom's secretary for a number of years and then she worked for Frank Barnes and she was the trustee of the Barnes' Trust, which controlled CCC Corporation and Plantation #7."

"Did she ever work with Bob?"

"Yes, for a number of years."

"Did they date?"

"I don't really know for sure. Why do you ask?"

"Just wondering," said Herman as he set his glass on the table. "I need to make a call."

"The pay phone is in the hall," said Smitty. "Don't get lost, we will be going soon."

Chapter 38
Herman Moines

Herman Moines was a quick study in the ways of men and women. He surmised that if Marla Reynolds and Bob Barnes had worked closely together early on in their careers then they could have been attracted to each other and fallen in love.

For Herman's purposes, if he could prove the existence of a relationship between Bob and Marla and if the relationship existed at a time when either or both of them were married, then Greg Teague would have an issue they could exploit to undermine the Republican candidate's credibility with the voter, particularly in the religious communities along the I-4 corridor. Proving Bob Barnes to be an adulterer would make a big splash in the press.

The question for the Democrats was whether they should use Herman Moines to obtain more information and confirm the relationship and risk him being caught as an inside operator for GT's party, or have him quit the Republican's as Bob Barnes' campaign secretary and go on vacation in Bimini at the expense of the Democrats until the election was over.

Of course, nothing Herman Moines was doing, acting as a spy for GT, was ethical, but it was expected GT would have a spy. This was Florida politics, and even what was unfair was anticipated. But GT was smart enough to distance himself from Herman now that he had the information he needed. Greg Teague thanked Herman for his services and paid him with cash and told him to visit the islands and work on his tan.

What GT needed at this point was someone who would verify a relationship between Bob and Marla, and establish the dates of the affair. It would be best to trap or trick Bob or Marla into an admission. His hope was that he could use a newspaper reporter to ask Bob the embarrassing question. It was expected that Bob would lie to the reporter and deny the relationship. Then once GT's camp provided proof of the affair to the press, Bob Barnes would be branded a liar. His credibility would be destroyed.

GT authorized his campaign committee to fund the cost of a private investigator. Cash only.

Because Bob did not anticipate there was any reason to conceal the love he felt for Marla before he ran for public office, he never tried to hide it. He did not anticipate ten years past that he would run for public office, and he had never been asked questions about his early love life when he was being considered for the cabinet post in the Federal Government. To the Federal Investigators the affair was too remote.

In short, it took very little work for the investigator to confirm the information about the relationship between Bob and Marla and that they lived together in the old house at Plantation #7 while Marla and Reynolds were married, but separated.

* * *

Tom Night knew exactly how GT would play the game, and he knew he had to gain the cooperation of Marla and James Reynolds to undermine the political attack. Tom had to obtain their agreement that if they were asked a question about the affair they would simply say they had no comment regarding the allegation. They would neither admit nor deny the allegation. They would not address the allegation and lie about the affair and thus they would render it irrelevant as a campaign issue.

Marla would not bring up the issue and if Marla did not raise the issue a reporter would seem to be crass to ask a question about her love life out of the blue. If a reporter did ask if she had had an affair with Bob Barnes, Tom advised that Marla should ignore the question. Marla would stand mute and the reporter would be left with no follow up question and would be left to stare at Marla. The reporter would have to go to a relevant question.

* * *

Lucy Hale had a daughter. The Pulitzer Prize winner had named her daughter Lucy Hale, Jr. (She thought she made a statement calling her daughter "Junior".) When the prize winning reporter was gunned down by Clemenso Me Bondi in the park in front of the newspaper's office, young Lucy was eleven years old. The newspaper became her mother and father, and she was hired as a reporter as soon as she graduated from college.

Young Lucy first worked as an obituary writer, and then she handled crime and local tragedy, and then the court system and now she was 30 years old and she was reporting about Florida politics. Lucy's editor assigned her to run down the rumor that Bob Barnes had had an affair with a prominent citizen who was married to the retired CEO of JRD Corporation.

"Sounds like good gossip." Lucy looked at her editor. "But where's the story? This doesn't seem relevant to me. Is it something the people of Florida have a need to know?"

Lucy's editor seemed annoyed. He didn't like playing in the mud, either. "Look, the Editorial Board wants to run down the rumor and see what comes of it. You need to ask the questions and earn your pay."

"Right, Chief." Lucy saluted sarcastically.

Lucy had no intention of asking Bob Barnes or James Reynolds or his wife Marla about their private lives. Lucy knew someone on the Editorial Board was trying to stir the pot and grab an exclusive story and headline. Lucy wasn't going to oblige if she could avoid it.

Lucy knew the Barnes Family was close to Tom and Darlene and she decided to call and see if they would set up an interview. Darlene said she would be happy to ask. "Who do you want to talk to?"

"Marla Reynolds," said Lucy.

"You want to talk to Marla Reynolds about Bob Barnes?" asked Darlene.

"Yes." Lucy hoped they would take the hint and refuse the interview.

Darlene told Tom about the request and Tom explained what he anticipated the questions would involve. "Let's give young Lucy an exclusive interview with the candidate and let her ask her question to the candidate."

Darlene set up the meeting. Bob came to Lucy's office and he answered all her questions, the relevant and the ridiculous, but when she asked about the rumored affair, Bob did not admit or deny a relationship existed, he simply said, "No comment."

When Lucy brought the rough draft of her story to her editor for review he read the copy and there was nothing about Bob and Marla's affair. When asked, Lucy repeated that Bob said he had no comment on that subject.

"If he did not make a comment that should be part of the story," said the editor.

"How is it relevant? He did not comment on the matter. He did not raise the matter and he did not deny the matter. Therefore, it is not relevant."

"We decide what is relevant," said the editor.

"I'm not going to include it in the story," insisted Lucy. "I agree that if Bob said he did not have an affair when he did, and if he was caught in a lie, then the lie would be relevant to the issue of his character. But if we can't prove he's a liar then I refuse to put that content in my story."

Although there was a row at the paper, young Lucy stuck to her guns and the issue died and went no further in the press. The question about Bob Barnes' philandering did continue to swirl about as a rumor among the politicos, the political operatives and those in the know, but there was no proof that the rumors were true, and the voters did not become aware of the non-issue. Bob and his wife ignored the issue and both reaffirmed their love for each other and their children and their family when asked.

* * *

Meanwhile, GT was having problems with Senator Nelms. The senator was having second thoughts about agreeing to resign his seat so that it was available for GT to use to fulfill his promise of a US Senate seat to Governor Adams. This reluctance on the part of Senator Nelms became known when GT demanded the senator give him a written acknowledgement of his promise to resign and the senator refused.

Then there was a rumor of the oral agreement between GT and the senator and Governor Adams to trade seats, and then the rumor became a fact when the senator denied he would resign, "under any circumstances ... particularly, I will not resign under pressure from the Speaker."

Although, the senator, GT and Governor Adams never admitted the agreement between the three men was a fact, the senator's denials were so weak that the voters became convinced the rumors were true. What Senator Nelms realized was that the way to preserve his senate seat was to deny GT the governorship. If he was not elected governor, GT could not appoint Adams to his senate seat. And if Teague was voted out of office, Teague would lose his political power and he could not pressure the senator to resign. Senator Nelms did everything in his power to encourage the voters that GT was not to be trusted, and therefore he was not good political timber for the Governor's chair.

The race for governor became very competitive.

Bob Barnes concentrated his efforts on the voters in the I-4 corridor. The candidate traveled to every event he could find in order to shake hands. He was even seen campaigning at the rest stops along the interstate route. He worked the editorial boards of the Daytona Beach News Journal, the Orlando Sentinel, the Lakeland Ledger, the Tampa Tribune and the St. Petersburg

Times. In the end, every one of the newspapers endorsed him and adopted his mantra that it was time for a change in Tallahassee.

Bob Barnes did not have the money to spend on a private pollster, but the national party was polling for the next election cycle and they included questions in the polls that were relevant to the governor's race. What was interesting was that Bob's recognition factor was higher than Teague's. Teague was well known in South Florida, but he was little known in the rest of the state. GT had never run in a statewide election.

The party smelled an upset.

Chapter 39
Political Issue

Faircloth was more chauffeur than investigator during the last days of the election. Teague's pollster must have told Gregg Teague that the race was close. GT's campaign strategy included an attempt to disqualify Bob as a candidate through a lawsuit. Teague increased pressure through the courts in one line of his attacks against Bob Barnes. Teague was alleging in court and in his political ads that Bob Barnes was not eligible to be Governor because he was not a resident of the state of Florida but instead he was a resident of Alexandria, Virginia.

This issue was relevant. The Florida Constitution required the Governor to be a resident of the state of Florida.

Teague's attorney had prevailed upon the judge who was assigned the case to hold the final hearing in the case on the last two days before the election. This would cause Bob two problems. First, the judge might rule Bob was ineligible to run for office. Second, even if he was determined to be eligible, Bob would be sitting around the courthouse in Tallahassee rather than campaigning during the last days of the race.

It was true that Tom and his wife owned a house in Alexandria that they purchased. The family lived there while Bob performed his duties as Secretary of the Department of the Interior across the river from Alexandria in Washington, DC.

But it was also true that Bob and his wife and the two children were domiciled and took their personal mail and voted from the Homestead in Holly Hill, Florida. Teague's attorney subpoenaed

Bob to court to testify in Tallahassee during the last days of the campaign. Through the use of the subpoena, GT's attorney forced Bob Barnes to sit around the courthouse in Tallahassee for a full day. Bob took the witness stand and testified that the Homestead had been his residence address for 50 years.

Bob missed numerous political engagements, but he was able to salvage the time by granting interviews to the TV stations about the court proceedings and Bob's belief that the courtroom was the best place to determine the issue. Bob figured he got as much good out of the TV appearances as he would have on the trail. After he testified, Bob flew out for a final blitz of the state before the vote the next day.

* * *

Although Tom did not believe the judge in Tallahassee should or would accept the argument that Bob was not a resident of Florida, this was politics and there was no telling how the court would rule. The judge was a Democrat, and he had been appointed by Teague's friend, Governor Adams.

Tom was concerned about the outcome until the attorneys completed their closing arguments and the judge gave an oral ruling stating he considered Tom's argument to be the most persuasive. He ruled Bob was a resident of the state of Florida and eligible to run for the governorship.

During the trial, Tom entered evidence into the record showing that almost every one of the federal officeholders from Florida who worked in Washington representing the state of Florida, and the members of the US Senate and the US House owned homes in and around the Washington, DC area. Simply owning a home could not be the basis to establish residency. If it did, office holders would have to rent. That would be discriminatory and unconstitutional.

The judge ruled that since Bob testified his residence was in Holly Hill, Florida for the past 50 years the burden of proof swung to GT. Gregg Teague had failed to prove Bob Barnes was not a resident of Florida simply by showing Barnes owned a house outside the state of Florida. The court's final written ruling came on Election Day.

* * *

Following the court's ruling for Bob Barnes and against Greg Teague, Faircloth collected all of Tom's papers and loaded the car while Tom asked the attorney for Mr. Teague who Tom should send his bill for attorney fees to, in as much as Teague had lost the suit.

Tom and the attorney were two old bulls. They almost came to blows, but Faircloth was able to pull Tom away and into the elevator and out to the car.

* * *

Faircloth had to drive his boss from Tallahassee to Orlando to the celebratory party where they would wait for the election results, which would be announced sometime after 7 p.m. Faircloth intended to follow US 19 to Wildwood and then catch the Florida Turnpike to Orlando. They would make the festivities by 10 p.m. or so, if there were no tie ups on the roads to Orlando.

When they got to the city of Chiefland, Tom said he needed an aspirin. Faircloth had kept the aspirin bottle handy during the three day hearing in Tallahassee and he had the bottle on hand in his top pocket when Tom requested the pill.

Unfortunately, the pill did not help and Tom said he needed to lie down. Tom did not want to go to a hospital, he wanted to forge ahead. He wanted to be on time to hear Bob's acceptance speech.

Tom was convinced that Teague was in trouble and he was going to lose the election. The reason Tom had that belief was the effort that was being made by Teague's attorney to convince the judge that Bob was not eligible to hold office because he was not a resident of Florida. The court proceeding had become an act of desperation on Teague's part.

* * *

When Tom arrived in the town of Wildwood, Faircloth pulled over at a McDonald's to check on Tom, but he could not rouse him. There was no hospital in Wildwood, so he sped back north to Ocala and to the first hospital he could find. Tom was taken from the car on a stretcher and into the ER. Faircloth was told to have a seat, and he watched television in the waiting room while Tom was examined.

It was 8:30 pm. All the channels had the election results. Faircloth watched until 10 p.m. when they announced Bob Barnes had won in a landslide.

Teague conceded at 11 p.m., congratulated Bob Barnes and said he would cooperate with the new governor. Unfortunately for Bob Barnes, Teague had run his 18-year-old son for his house seat. GT's son won the election and since GT controlled his son, he still controlled his old seat as a house member from Ft. Lauderdale. Bob would have to deal with GT during the regular session. GT would still operate through his shill.

Bob's acceptance speech was short. He said he had not prepared a long address as he felt he had little chance in winning. Bob's remarks were received with laughter.

* * *

Faircloth wondered if Tom had heard the news about the election. No one had come to tell him about Tom's condition. He went back to the nurse's station and made inquiry. A doctor said Tom was still in treatment. He was stable, but he remained unconscious.

Faircloth called the office. Alphonse was still there with Coleen, working on the purchase of forest land in Madagascar. Faircloth told Alphonse where he was and asked him to contact Darlene.

Alphonse told Faircloth that Darlene was in Orlando at Bob's headquarters.

"I know," said Faircloth. Faircloth knew that to be a fact because he had seen Darlene on television when the reporter showed a picture of the ballroom where the Republicans were meeting, waiting for the election results.

At midnight, Darlene received Faircloth's message. She called and Faircloth told her what he knew about Tom's condition. Darlene said she would have someone drive her to Ocala as soon as she could. She was three hours away.

At 4 a.m. Darlene arrived at the hospital. She spoke to the doctor. Tom had had a stroke and he was in a coma.

* * *

Darlene took a room in the Hilton in Ocala after she had waited two days in Tom's hospital room for Tom to awaken. There were many visitors who took the time to personally offer her assistance and condolences. She got no rest.

After she was at the Hilton for three days she realized the hotel would not work. She needed to move Tom home to St. Petersburg. The doctor in Ocala insisted Tom be taken to a hospital. He needed around-the-clock care.

Faircloth made arrangements for an ambulance to take Tom to Mound Park Hospital. Faircloth followed the ambulance in his car and Darlene and Jenny followed him in their vehicle. The group proceeded slowly down US 19 so they could stay together.

It took hours to arrive back in St. Petersburg. It seemed like every traffic light was red.

Chapter 40
LTNOC (Pronounced: Lit-Knock)

Long Term Non-Orthopedic Care (LTNOC) is a reality that is unreal. It is zombie land on earth, imagined, conceived and created, but unimaginable. It is a place where the unconscious are conscious, where the unrecognizable is recognized, where the living are perched on the edge of life and death. Admittance to the LTNOC ward can be for a term that is short or long, but always indeterminable.

Tom had pushed too hard. He treated his transient ischemic attacks (TIAs) as though they were a condition like a headache that could be treated with an aspirin under the tongue. He did not consider that the condition would not reverse and he could suffer a stroke—a full-fledged blowout of a blood vessel in the brain.

At first Tom was treated conservatively at the hospital in Ocala.

But Darlene wanted him home. He was transported to Mound Park Hospital in St. Petersburg. There at Mound Park the treatment became more aggressive. He was taken to surgery. The thinking was that there was blockage of the carotid artery. The blockage needed to be removed. During surgery, the vein was stripped and a new procedure involving the placement of a stent was attempted. During the stenting process the clot of plaque was removed. Hope was that no plaque would escape from the stent and cause a new blockage in the brain.

But afterward, something was wrong. The surgery did not go as planned and Tom could not talk and could not move. He could only blink his eyelids and then only randomly, without any design that could be used as a method of communication.

Tom's doctor's orders recommended LTNOC. It was an acronym that was used in place of the words. The term LTNOC was not a happy ending. It was care without care. It was lack of hope. It was the best argument there was for euthanasia.

Darlene had asked to see the facility before she would consent to LTNOC for her husband. She would not sign the form unless LTNOC was shown to her and explained to her and she could see patients experiencing the regime. When she saw it, she felt it was so awful, understanding that the patient could possibly be aware of his surroundings and know that there were others in this ward of beds who were making human verbal noise. Darlene realized that it was possible Tom could know where he was and the utter hopelessness of his predicament. Worse, it was loud. The patients were attempting to communicate, perhaps, but without speaking coherently. The patients were not blind and the patients were not deaf. They could see and hear, but the care givers did not know what the unconscious patients knew or when they knew it, or the emotions they felt, or if they felt pain.

This was insurance-subsidized care provided by the lowest bidder.

Darlene could not bring herself to sign the permission to treat form for LTNOC.

Darlene brought Tom home and hired someone to help her and they put him at the window and positioned him to be able to see the water if he could see and they put on the radio so he could listen to the music and the commercials if he could hear. His eyes were always open except to blink, but only randomly.

* * *

"I thought it would happen in a plane."

Darlene was surprised to hear Tom speak. Could she be dreaming? He had not said a word in her presence. It had been weeks. He was under the care of Hospice. The doctors had recently prescribed strong opioid and anxiety medication. Tom's breathing was labored and shallow, and he spoke quietly with a raspy voice.

"What did you say?"

"My death," said Tom. "I thought it would happen in a plane ... that I would be expelled into the air high in the sky and I would extend my arms and legs and sail like a bird to the earth. I have that dream of being a fish out of water before I fly in a plane. Do you remember?"

"You are at home in your leather recliner." Darlene fluffed the pillow. "Are you comfortable?"

It was 4 a.m. Darlene had been told Tom might have lucid intervals when he might speak. He was a mass of tubes for input and output. The nurses came daily and left at midnight. Darlene slept on the couch in the living room with Tom from midnight until the nurse returned at 8 a.m.

Tom could be seen sometimes watching the ships in the bay, their wakes tracing through the green sea, coursing to the banana docks in Tampa. The wakes of the large ships left traces in the calm bay, skaters pirouetting on the smooth ice of a rink ... or maybe swans.

"I don't feel anything really. Have I been sleeping, Darlene?"

"Yes."

"For a long time?"

"Yes. Do you want anything?"

"Ice, if it is handy."

* * *

Tom lasted almost two weeks.

* * *

Bea Barnes and James and Marla Reynolds rode together to Tom's celebration of life ceremony in St. Petersburg in the Senator's old Packard. Since Reynolds and Marla had been operating Plantation #7, Reynolds had kept the Packard in good condition. Unfortunately, it had no air conditioning.

The celebration occurred a week after Tom's burial, which was a private affair. Tom was buried next to Senator Barnes and Frank Barnes in a plot at the Plantation house in north Ormond Beach, Florida. Marla intended to allow the back yard at her house to become a cemetery, and offered spaces for plots to Tom and Darlene, herself and Reynolds, and Bea and their children. At first, Reynolds said he thought having a graveyard out in the back yard would give him the willies. But then, he thought he too would be there soon. He would probably be the next to follow Tom.

Tom's public ceremony would be held on January 1, 2000 (1-1-2000) the start of the new millennium. There were many dignitaries expected and Governor Bob Barnes would give the eulogy. The three friends were driving over to the service a day earlier on December 31, 1999 and would drive back on January 1, 2000, if the world did not come to an end on that date.

There was a new technology scare connected to the New Year: 1-1-2000.

Whether true or not, there was a fear that all computers, and therefore all machines together with the systems that the computers controlled, would crash at midnight on 1-1-2000. Worse, all the computer hardware manufacturers were using the new millennium date as a sales tool. They issued press releases arguing that computers would freeze up when the time changed to the new millennium and every machine that relied on a computer to function would no longer operate. Reynolds thought it was a great marketing ploy and he had invested heavily in infrastructure manufacturers supplying the computer age. This turned out to be a great play. (Unfortunately, he also invested in Internet retail sales companies. These companies were all overvalued and ultimately Reynold's lost his shirt on his investment in those companies.)

Reynold's said no one knew what would happen to all the modern machines when the clock struck midnight and the computer was left to discern what the date was. Would the computer roll over to the year 2000 and continue to function or not? It seemed like everything was controlled by a computer. Even automobiles had their black box that the vehicle's systems relied on to operate efficiently. The old Packard did not rely on a computer, so the three friends drove together in the old reliable car to St. Petersburg and left the new Lincoln, which was controlled by its black box, in the garage.

If you didn't want to take a chance that a system controlled by a computer would fail, you had to buy new hardware. Of course, nothing untoward happened when the clock struck midnight on January 1, 2000.

It was in fact just another fraud perpetrated on the American consumer.

* * *

None of the three spoke about Tom's death or the way he died as they rode across the state on I-4 to the ceremony, or back to the east coast. The trio knew that it had taken a while for Tom to succumb, but he was comfortable and he died sitting in his favorite chair.

The three had kept in touch during Tom's final illness. They had to find a new attorney, and they spent hours on the phone with Karen, coordinating the transfer of their files to a firm in Ormond Beach on the east coast. Karen was keen to explain how Tom was feeling as she dealt with his old clients. Karen had been Tom's most loyal employee. She was his eyes and ears for 30 years.

Chapter 41
The Eulogy

The old Catholic Church on Fifth Avenue South in St. Petersburg, Florida was called St. Mary's.

The restroom next to the entrance to the iconic Pier was designed in the identical architectural style as the church and was called "Little St. Mary's". It was a "little me."

Little St. Mary's was notorious as a meeting spot for same sex encounters, dalliances and trysts. The Catholic Church tried to win the approval of City Council to have the bathroom facility demolished because of the association between the church and the banõs. The vote was close. A large minority of the council members thought destruction of the small, well-constructed and maintained bath house next to Spa Beach was a waste. However, the wishes of the church were honored after the church agreed to pay the costs of the destruction of Little St. Mary's, and the construction of the new bath house. The restroom would be constructed in a modern style to imitate the Pier, which was designed after an inverted pyramid. The new bath house would be located at the entrance to the Pier on Spa Beach.

It would be very expensive. The Catholic Church was willing to pay the price because it was so sensitive to the fact that St Mary's Church suffered the bad connotation of the name Little St. Mary's. Of course, the citizens of St. Petersburg were aware of the attempted subterfuge by the Bishop and continued to call the new facility Little St. Mary's even after it was rebuilt.

Bob Barnes, the newly elected governor of the state of Florida, sat at the altar of St. Mary's, next to Bishop Lemon. The governor had been invited by Tom Night's wife Darlene to give the eulogy at the funeral service for Tom Night. The bishop officiated at a funeral Mass for the benefit of the mostly agnostic congregation. The church was filled. You needed a crowd of non-believers before you could fill the church anymore. The Barnes Family and Tom and Darlene had become members of the Catholic Church after the death of Jimmy Barnes and the death of the Senator, Francis Aloysius Barnes and his son, Frank. The church had volunteered a priest to officiate at the funerals of Jimmy and the Senator and Frank Jr. Thereafter the Night and Barnes families began to attend services at the Catholic church.

Bea Barnes had encouraged her husband Frank, her daughter Jenny and her husband, James DeMarco, and their three children, to attend Mass regularly on Sunday. About once a month the service caused the family to gather at the Homestead on Sunday, and have a noon day meal before James and Jenny and their children got in the car for the trip on I- 4 and then on I- 275 back to St. Petersburg. When the family was on the east coast they went to Mass at St. Paul's on US-1 in Daytona Beach, and if they were on the west coast of the state they attended services at St. Mary's.

Bob and his wife, Smiling Waters, were ambivalent to organized religion. Smiling Waters, a Native American who was called by her nickname, Smiley, and their children, did not attend a particular church but rather, they participated at services in the congregations of various religious practices and visited temples, synagogues, churches and at the change of the seasons they attended rituals of the North American Indian tribes that were held outdoors. Bob and his wife and two children had been to St. Mary's in the past when they visited the west coast of the state.

The eulogy would be Bob Barnes last act as a civilian. The day after the speech he would begin serving his term in office as the Governor of the Great State of Florida.

Bob was a little nervous. The church was full and he wanted to do a good job to honor the memory of Tom Night even though Bob and Tom had issues during their acquaintanceship. If Tom's life were weighed on a scale, Bob should have mentioned Tom's love for Marla James, because that love consumed Tom for years. But if he mentioned that love for Marla in the eulogy that would be an embarrassment to Marla's husband James Reynolds and to Tom's wife Darlene. Bob also, to be honest, necessarily would need to mention that he loved Marla and lived with her for about a year.

And if Bob mentioned the relationship between Tom and Marla, Bob should have mentioned Tom's battle with alcoholism. The bottle consumed half of Tom's life and Johnny Walker "Red" destroyed his relationship with Marla.

As he considered topics to hit on, Bob decided the speech would contain no mention of Marla and no mention of alcohol.

What about Family? Tom had no children, and his mother and father and brother died when he was a teen. Tom was raised by two aunts who were English professors at Stetson University. The aunts had been buried years back and Tom's only family was his wife Darlene. Darlene had been a loyal wife who had an abiding love of her husband.

Bob would mention Darlene.

Because Tom became the ward of his two aunts, he had the opportunity to attend the university free of charge during the Great Depression. Children of professors were eligible to attend the college as a perk to benefit the child's parents or wards.

Tom attended the law school. He and Frank became friends at Stetson and Tom met the rest of the Barnes family, Frank's wife, Bea and their child, Jimmy, and he helped with the adoption of Bob, Albert and Jenny into the clan. Tom also became acquainted with Frank's father, the Senator, through their relationship in college.

The Senator purchased 40,000 acres of land during the recession and Frank used his training as a forester at Stetson to husband his father's acreage and, using Tom's legal skills, the trio grew the 40,000 acres to 500,000 acres and a logistics company that milled and transported finished timber to the northeast to build homes for the soldiers that returned from World War II.

Bob would mention the beginning of the business called CCC Corporation.

The Barnes family businesses were legendary, and the rise and fall of the timber company and the rebirth of the company as Barnes Creamery, and Barnes Lime Rock in Florida and the mines in Belize, was the subject of courses taught in business schools at Duke University and Harvard. Those relationships and accomplishments should also be mentioned but the bankruptcies, and claw-back actions would necessarily need to be ignored if Tom could be viewed with empathy.

The glue that held Tom's life together was the practice of his profession. He was a business lawyer foremost. He was involved in transactional law that allowed his clients to build great companies from nothing. At the same time, he defended scurrilous, murderous individuals. Because he represented murderers, he was cursed in the newspapers and by the general population and by the victims of his clients, particularly by the families of the children who were destroyed by Mark Luke John Person, the child killer.

Bob could not mention the good work in the business arena and ignore the criminal clients.

Bob somehow needed to refer to Tom's life experiences in total or not at all.

Bob realized as he sat next to Bishop Lemon that there was little he could say that would speak about Tom's profession except to say that he was loyal to his clients.

In the end, the speech was probably the worst speech Bob had given and it was not reflective of the memory of Tom Night. But Darlene was pleased and very grateful for the fact that Bob excluded so many facts in his recitation of the remembrance of the life of Thomas Night. Bob generalized that Tom had a love of mankind and that he fought for the principles enunciated in the Constitution of the United States of America.

DeMarco's comment to Jenny was: "The speech was all B.S."

Chapter 42
Firm Meeting

Tom's celebration of life had been two weeks ago.

The firm meeting of Night, Adams, Street, Alesse, DeMarco and Barnes, PA, was held at the law office building on Beach Drive in St. Petersburg. It was attended by Darlene, Alphonse, James and Jenny. The question for discussion was whether the firm would continue, and in what form and at what location. The building had been owned by Tom, individually, and it was an asset in his estate. The building would have to be disposed of in some manner.

"Well personally, I do not think I will have any time to devote to my old civil practice," said Alphonse. "The Frasier Foundation takes all my time."

"I understand the foundation is expanding and is purchasing a large portion of the island of Madagascar. Correct?" asked Jenny.

"Yes, Coleen wants to try to save what is left of the forest for the lemurs."

"That would be good," said DeMarco in understatement. "I don't expect you will be taking calls from your old will clients if you are in Madagascar." DeMarco commented to Jenny that the trees on Madagascar had been burnt to manufacture charcoal.

Everyone laughed but no one knew why the fact that the people of Madagascar traded their trees for charcoal would be funny. Perhaps the partners were pleased that Alphonse had become the CEO of The Frasier Foundation. He still denied that he and Coleen were more than just friends, however, Alphonse had moved into a suite of rooms at Coleen's mansion on Razor Clam

Boulevard. Coleen insisted Bosco continue to act as a chauffeur, which meant he needed a passenger. Alphonse enjoyed riding in the Silver Cloud Rolls Royce. Under Alphonse's guidance the mansion ran like a Swiss clock. Mary made dinner, and Mike did what he did, which was to annoy everyone.

The Frasier Foundation had purchased 500,000 acres of wetlands in north Florida, and it had entered into an agreement for a preservation easement to restrict development of the Mayan Mountains in Belize to protect the jaguar. The easement was made in coordination with the Belizean government. Alphonse had been able to negotiate a price for the acreage that was very low. Alphonse had been able to collect large chunks of land in Florida, Belize, and now in Madagascar, and the foundation still had 2.8 billion dollars in the bank.

Alphonse became adept at management of the foundation's lands after their purchase. Essentially, he left the land alone and let nature take its course. He allowed natives who were squatting on the property to remain there so long as they followed the rules and acknowledged they did not own the land or any other right in the land they squatted on. No one could fault this approach. In fact, other individuals, groups and foundations wanted to invest in The Frasier Foundation and share in its approach to saving the planet.

"So Jenny ... your plans?" asked Darlene.

"Bob Barnes has asked me to be the governor's Chief Counsel. That would be a fulltime job and I would have to move to Tallahassee. I guess we would have to sell the house in Old Northeast. I will miss the house the most."

Alphonse turned to James DeMarco. "So will you stay behind here in St. Petersburg?"

"I will go with Jenny, if she will have me," replied James. "I was thinking I will take care of the kids for a while as we see how successful Governor Barnes is. He may be out of office in two years, or this could be a stepping stone to the next level, either in the Cabinet of the next President or he could be on a national ticket as Vice President or perhaps President of the United States. Maybe he would run for the US Senate. In any event, there are a multitude of options available to us."

Darlene asked, "You have taken care of Jenny and Bob ... what happens to Albert?"

"Albert loves Belize. He will run the lime rock mine in Big Creek until he dies. Bea will visit him when the weather is good in the Caribbean. We think he will be satisfied there."

"So that leaves you, Darlene. What are your plans?" asked Jenny.

"I was thinking that if the firm was to close, and it seems that is logical, that I could donate Tom's building to the Office of Public Counsel. My thought is that the staff here, Karen and Faircloth and the secretaries and clerks, could be hired by the government agency and they could work for the office, handling indigent criminal cases."

"Have you talked to the head of the agency?"

"Yes. They need an office building close to the courthouse here in St. Petersburg. They are renting now and it's very expensive downtown, so they would welcome Tom's building. They said they would put a plaque in the lobby that states that Tom donated the building. They are trying to work out offers of employment for the staff. I think it will work. The staff would be enrolled in the state pension plan. Tom had always worried that the firm did not have a pension plan for the employees."

"Then we are set," said Jenny. "Everyone has a place to go. At least they do for now."

The attorneys had met in the library. The centerpiece of the room was the conference table that had been hand crafted in Belize. The tabletop was made of a large single slab of mahogany. They all admired the table.

"Are you going to leave the table?" Jenny was hoping Darlene would give her the table.

"No, I will take it home to the condo," said Darlene.

Chapter 43
Marla and Reynolds

James Reynolds found he was not a hands-on manager. Marla was much more adept at dealing with the employees in the Plantation House, the fruit tree orchard, the jelly processing factory, and the sales office for Plantation #7.

Marla was content to run the business.

James Reynolds was more contemplative and he began to write historical tracts, concentrating on the history of Volusia and Flagler and St. John's Counties. The writing below was his first published piece.

Sovereign Homicide

To European explorers, La Florida was first thought to be an island. When discovered in 1513, Ponce De Leon could not comprehend the size of his find. Ultimately, La Florida included all of the lands that are now the Carolinas, Georgia, Alabama, Florida and Mississippi.

Ponce de Leon and his crew, on three ships, first landed somewhere between what is now Melbourne Beach and Ponte Vedra Beach, Florida. The explorer made a number of trips to Florida. He was killed in Florida, after being struck by a poisoned arrow hurled at him in battle by a native, during his voyage in 1520.

Ponce de Leon claimed all of the lands of Florida for the King of Spain, but he did not establish a permanent settlement in Florida to stake and hold this claim.

Forty years went by. The Spanish landed on Florida shores many times but they were expelled by the natives.

In 1562 the French landed at a bluff on a large river (presently called the St. Johns River) at what is now Jacksonville. The settlers called the river the River May. The French, led by explorer Jean Ribault, did not stay on the bluff but sailed north and founded a colony in what is now South Carolina. They built a fort called Charles Fort. Ribault left 27 men at the fort and he returned to Europe to England, where he was arrested. The settlers at Charles Fort suffered from hunger, Indian attacks, and mutiny while Ribault was in prison, and the settlement failed.

In 1564 Jean Ribault was released from prison and he sailed back to Florida with hundreds of soldiers and colonists to establish a colony for Protestants. He chose a site for a settlement at the mouth of the River May and it was named Fort Caroline. The settlement remained viable. After a year, Ribault returned to France and enlisted 800 new settlers and five ships to populate the new fort for France. He arrived with the new settlers and his army at Fort Caroline in August 1565.

The Spanish king became aware of the French fort on lands Ponce de Leon had claimed for Spain more than 50 years before. The king appointed Don Pedro Mendez to establish a colony in Florida and rout the French from Fort Caroline. Spanish warships and crew landed in St. Augustine in September 1565.

The French learned the Spanish had landed and they intended to drive the Spanish from Florida. After leaving a contingent of women, children and guards at Fort Caroline, Ribault set sail to destroy the Spanish. There was a skirmish at sea between the French and the Spanish that was interrupted by a violent storm that destroyed the French fleet.

The Spanish were able to land at St. Augustine during the storm and they were safe. Mendez ordered his men to march from St. Augustine, which was south of the French fort, through the storm to Fort Caroline. The Spanish made a surprise attack and 200 Frenchmen and 50 women and children surrendered. Mendez had the men executed if they did not renounce their Protestant beliefs. All of the men, called Lutherans, were slaughtered. The women and children were taken to St. Augustine.

Jean Ribault and more hundreds of his men had escaped from their ships that were sunk near what is now Daytona Beach. They tried to march north but were impeded by a large inlet north of the Tomoka River Basin. They were captured in two groups of over a hundred men each by the Spanish troops who were searching for them. These Frenchmen faced the same fate as their brothers at Fort Caroline. They were killed if they did not accept Catholicism. It was reported that all the men were slain by the Spanish.

Mendez' report to the king of Spain noted that Ribault was beheaded and his head was quartered and displayed at the four corners of Fort Caroline, which the Spanish renamed San Mateo. Even the court of the Spanish king was dismayed by Mendez' savagery toward Ribault and his men.

The location of the slaughter of Ribault and his men was called Matanzas Inlet. The word Matanzas means massacre.

These conflicts were said to be the first international conflicts in the New World between European sovereign states.

It could also be said that Don Pedro Mendez was homicidal, employing the orders of his king as an excuse to murder Protestants, who he hated.

In 1568, the French attacked the Spanish fort at San Mateo and captured all the Spanish soldiers at the fort. The French then murdered all the Spanish soldiers in retaliation for the deaths of Jean Ribault and his men.

/s/ James Reynolds

* * *

Reynolds expanded his idea to include the wars between the Spanish, French, English and Americans in Florida into a book called "Blood in the Sand." The book included a history of the Indian wars and deportations of the Native Americans to the

West, and was so inclusive as to have a chapter concerning the U-boat versus destroyer battles fought off the Coast of Volusia County in the Atlantic Ocean during WW II.

Once the book was published, Reynolds had to market it, and he spoke at writer's conferences. Reynolds began to turn out a couple of books a year. All of the books were highly successful.

Chapter 44
The Homestead

After Frank Barnes had his heart attack, his doctor had prescribed a new drug called a "statin". The pill was truly amazing. Not only had Frank not had a recurrence, his heart had healed and no scar was visible on the EKG from the first attack. The drug probably gave Frank decades of life.

Bea had high blood pressure which was controlled by medication that she took religiously. It seemed like everyone who had a doctor had a prescription.

The pair was active in the operation of the small dairy on Flomish Street and Frank rose early to oversee the milking operations.

The Homestead was a lot of trouble. The pair could have traveled. They had the money. But if they got in a motor home they would miss the visits of their grandchildren, four girls and two boys. The girls were not interested in dresses; they were athletic and wanted to play hard. Frank got a couple of rowboats and introduced the children to the Halifax River. They fished for snook, red fish, drum, and sheepshead, and netted mullet and harvested clams and oysters.

The river basin was within the confines of Tomoka State Park and Frank allowed the kids to explore the land and discover what was left of Old Florida. There were still many birds, particularly herons ... grey, night, green, black and white, and snowy egrets. There were raptors—bald eagles, ospreys, falcons, hawks. And every season there were small birds that passed through. There were wild turkey and doves and quail to hunt. There were still many white tail deer, and a few black bear, but no panthers.

Frank taught the children about the forest—the big trees, the pines and the cypress, the hickory and the bay and the oaks. He explained how the oak eventually stole the light from the understory trees (tupelo, persimmon, water maple and dogwood) and bushes and sedges, and smothered everything under the oaks dense leaves.

Bea Barnes let the female grandchildren learn to cook and clean, but she did not push the experience to the extreme. She also led by example, and enrolled in classes at the Junior College to learn to operate a computer. Bea did not appear to play favorites, but it was obvious she had come to love Robert and wanted him to succeed in life.

Robert was interested in the flint mine near the spring and pond on the 800 acre Homestead. The rock had been mined to produce points. Robert tried to identify the tribe that mined the flints and manufactured the hard rock into arrowheads, blades and knives. The tribe was lost ... extinct. Logic would say they were Tomoka Indians because the whites recited a legend involving a Chief called "Tamokie" who violated Indian law by drinking from a sacred spring in order to become invincible. However, Tamokie was killed by a warrior princess named Oleeta, who shot Tamokie with an arrow. This was legend. The Indians who had inhabited the area were not Tomoka Indians according to the experts, they were Timucua Indians.

Robert's research showed that there was a Timucua village in the area named Nocoroco. Robert believed the Timucua tribe was located closest to the mine and would have the best need for the points mined from the spring on the Homestead. However, the Timucua could not be asked, because the tribe had left no written history, and there were no members left to repeat the oral history of the tribe. The Timucua had been a highly successful Native American people until their lands were invaded by the whites.

Some experts say these people numbered 200,000 individuals in 1492 and they inhabited Northeast and North Central Florida and South Georgia. They shared a language with at least ten dialects, and Catholic missionaries produced a grammar and a catechism of the language. Their existence was verified by the French, who studied and drew images of them when these Europeans landed and constructed Fort Caroline in 1564 on the River May near what is now Jacksonville. The Timucua's may have been the first natives to see Ponce de Leon in 1513, and it is believed they made contact with Hernando de Soto in battle in 1539. Ultimately, all of the Timucua succumbed to European diseases and war by the time the United States acquired Florida in 1821. At that time the last five members of the Timucua tribe were deported to Cuba.

The fact that the tribe was lost made an impression on Robert. The lesson was that without adapting to change he also could be the last of his tribe. Robert did not know his natural father or Indian ways. His mother Smiling Waters' only explanation for his father, Yellow Dog, being the person he was, was that his father was a lost Indian boy. Robert's mother said he could do better.

Robert decided that he could do better. He would go to law school.

Bea provided a bequest in her will so Robert could attend.

Chapter 45
Fort Lauderdale

Bob Barnes called his sister Jenny at 4 a.m. He needed an attorney to represent him. Governor Barnes was allegedly in Contempt of Court. The charging paperwork had been served on the Secretary of State the preceding afternoon.

Bob Barnes had only been in office since the swearing in ceremony the day before. Bob was unaware of the notice of the contempt hearing. The Attorney General (a Democrat) had failed to notify the governor (a Republican) of the hearing in Circuit Court in Ft. Lauderdale. Luckily, a clerk in the office of the Secretary of State (a Republican) passed the notice on to Bob's aide. (a Republican)

Jenny was the only attorney he knew who he could contact in an emergency and fly with him to court so they would be on time at the courthouse in Ft. Lauderdale at 8 a.m.

The hearing concerned the failure of the state to provide emergency care for abused infants. The Department of Children's Services (DCS) had failed to respond to complaints that caregivers had failed to properly care for children, and in the worst cases the children were victims of infanticide, or were severely and permanently injured by their wards.

From the pleadings in the court file, Bob learned that 13 infants had been killed or injured by caregivers appointed by DCS, and this occurred after the department had been given notice of the dangerous propensities of the parent or caregiver who subsequently committed the assault. The court had made findings that the assaults had in fact occurred and the failure of the department to remove the children from the custody of their caregiver was negligent and inexcusable.

The allegations stated that the court had ordered the DCS to take corrective action, however, the department failed to comply with the court's order. Finally, the court stated the governor of the state was ultimately responsible since the department was under his control. If the department failed to comply with the order of the court and provide care for the children in its control, then the governor was personally responsible and the court intended to impose sanctions on the governor, including incarceration.

The allegations of the petition for order of contempt got Bob's attention. Before he called his sister, Bob had contacted the assistant Attorney General (AG) in Ft. Lauderdale. The AG told the governor not to worry about the hearing. In fact, the AG advised the governor that he did not have to appear. The AG claimed the judge did not have the power to hold the governor in contempt. Bob thought that advice was ludicrous.

"What happens if I don't show up and the judge holds me in contempt?"

"If he holds you in contempt, we will appeal."

"What if we lose the appeal?"

"Trust me, we won't lose the appeal."

Bob ignored the AG's advice and told the AG he would meet him in court. Bob had no intention of ignoring a court order. As soon as he hung up the receiver, he called Jenny Barnes.

* * *

Bob was flown to Albert Whitted Airport in St. Petersburg from Tallahassee in a small state-owned airplane. They picked up Jenny at 6 a.m. and landed in Fort Lauderdale in time for court at 8 a.m.

Bob tried to understand the logic of the AG, and he was smart enough to realize the AG would so inflame the court that Bob would be jailed, at least for a short period of time. The courtroom was packed with journalists waiting for the ax to fall on the new governor. Bob advised the AG that Jenny Barnes would speak on his behalf. Bob asked Jenny to carefully explain to the court how serious the Governor's Office felt about the situation and that he was horrified to learn the facts leading to the death and injury of the 13 infants, but he had just learned these facts.

"Please grant the governor the time to review the matter and he will appear before you again next week with his response to the problem," said Jenny.

The judge reset the hearing but warned Bob that this was the Governor's office's last chance to comply with the court's findings and resolve the problem.

* * *

The regional headquarters for the Florida Department of Children's Services (DCS) was located in Ft. Lauderdale. Bob wanted to start work on the problem while he was in town. The governor did not have to go far from the courthouse to find the state office building. The structure was modern, recently built. Bob thought it seemed the money could be better spent on children rather than on building materials.

The regional director of DCS saw Bob as soon as he entered the anteroom for the director's suite of rooms.

Bob suggested the director of DCS explain the case histories of the thirteen infants who had been killed by a parent or caregiver.

Bob was impressed. The director was aware of the facts of each case, and his office had proposed a plan to remedy each of the triggers or stressors on the caregivers for the events leading to the deaths and to prevent a recurrence. Three of the children had been left with a partner who was not a natural parent. In all three cases, the baby was ill and colicky and crying incessantly. The caregiver shook the child until the baby was quiet, and dead.

The director argued that the department could not be expected to anticipate the action leading to the death. The department was unaware the legal custodian would put the child in the care of a friend who would commit the killing.

Bob thought perhaps DCS could provide a service where the custodian could call DCS if the child was ill and the mother was unable to care for the child in an emergency. "Could the state of Florida hire babysitters?" Bob asked.

The director commented that there was not enough money in the state to correct the problems involving the neglect of children. As soon as the agency put a program in place to correct a discovered deficiency another problem arose.

Bob shared his feeling that with some problems you had to just keep pushing against the tide of cases until eventually the tide turned. And while you pushed, the agency needed to keep good records so that the social service providers could show the efforts they were using trying to prevent future deaths. Bob recognized there would be more deaths, hopefully there would be fewer.

"We will need more social workers. Which means we will need more money," said the director.

"This is Greg Teague's old district. GT's son was elected to his house seat. Have you talked to him about a special appropriation?"

"Yes, but it's not an issue with panache. Dealing with smelly diapers and screaming kids."

"I will invite Representative Teague to request an emergency appropriation to try to prevent future deaths. You will have to get the paperwork to the judge that shows we are trying to do something about the problem. We start with the three shaken baby syndrome deaths and go from there. "

"I will do my part," said the director.

"I want you to have each one of the social workers identify each of the children in their care who are at risk for injury or death from neglect and then have them explain in simple terms why the child is at risk, and then propose a solution for the problem. Then I want the agency to make some efforts so the proposed solution is implemented. I also want the children to have advocates. They need guardians. Someone who represents them and can speak up if it doesn't look like your office is doing its job."

"I understand. I think that is a good idea."

"Can we implement these changes in a month so the judge does not throw me in jail?" asked Bob.

"We will have to."

Bob looked at the director. "Do you have anything else I can help you with?"

"I sent my resignation. Will you be accepting my resignation?"

"Do you want to resign?" asked Bob.

"No. I think we can do some good for the children in state care if we work together."

"Then I will not accept your resignation."

* * *

Jenny had waited in the reception room for her brother to have his discussion with the director. She had advised that the quickest way to show he was taking action was to fire the director, and she was surprised to learn that the director was not dispatched and instead the director and Bob spoke to the press together and agreed changes needed to be made.

The reporters asked Bob why he didn't fire the director.

Bob explained that dismissing the director would only put more stress on the office, and he hoped the director would take Bob's suggestions and run with them and prove he was an adept administrator. Bob also told the press Jenny was to help. She had the responsibility to establish the guardian ad litem program so the children who were wards of the state had a voice in the system.

Jenny was excited to help. She decided her husband, DeMarco, would be back at work sooner than he thought. DeMarco would take Jenny's place and be the Governor's Chief Counsel.

Chapter 46
One Hundred Days

The Governor was flown back to Tallahassee the night after court in Palm Beach. The pilot dropped Jenny at Albert Whitted Airport in St. Petersburg, where she was met by her husband James and her three children.

Bob was tired and he hopped in the co-pilot's seat of the two engine Rockwell prop jet. It was the newest plane in the state's fleet. There were three other passengers who hopped on for the flight back to the state capital from South Florida. Bob had suggested to the pilot that the plane should fly full so as to not waste the use of the plane on only one passenger. The governor controlled the final destination of the plane, but if there was an empty seat available, they should try to fill it.

This was another small way Bob tried to make changes. During pre-inauguration meetings with aides and staff, he invited the members of the executive department to bring him ideas of ways to save time, energy, man power and money for the state.

Bob also read a book about Lincoln's presidency. He was impressed that Lincoln personally saw his citizens and listened to their complaints and their pleas. Most of the visitors arrived unannounced, without an appointment, and the president would see them. They just had to stand in line and wait to be heard. When Lincoln first took office he spent almost all of the time he was present in the White House seeing visitors. Finally his staff was able to prevail upon him to limit the number of hours in the day that he would see fellow Americans and acknowledge their complaints and pleas for redress.

Bob Barnes thought taking a few hours a day to visit with Floridians would be a good political exercise. He hired young college students from Florida State and Florida A&M Universities who were well-versed in the issues of the day, and Bob would listen to citizen complaints and then decide if the governor could solve the problem, and if so, a student was assigned to research the issue and bring the report back to the governor. A copy of the report, written by the student, was mailed to the citizen. The report was condensed to less than 50 words and read by the governor and he made notes to the report, and a plan of action, if action was to be taken, was developed from there.

The Democrats said the Governor was acting like a Chief solving individual problems and not statewide issues.

* * *

Over a six month period Bob said he found the issues of concern to the people through these meetings with citizens. Some legislation was needed. Outdated statutes should have been amended or should be repealed. Old laws criminalizing the action of consenting adults in the privacy of their home were brought to the attention of the legislature. The governor suggested these acts be decriminalized, particularly since the US Supreme Court had already held the laws to be unconstitutional because they violated the right of privacy owed to American citizens as interpreted by the US Constitution.

Florida's Constitution specifically stated the citizens of Florida had a right of privacy. The action by the governor suggesting these laws be stricken invited a raft of proposed laws to decriminalize many acts that could be accomplished in the privacy of one's home, such as the use of recreational drugs. There was no difficulty finding a legislator to sponsor suggested legislation, but most of these citizen-initiated bills died before they came to a vote. When Bob Barnes was criticized in editorials for the limited success in the enactment of these bills, the governor simply shrugged his shoulders and said if the people were sufficiently upset with the Congress for failing to pass the legislation, they should vote against the legislator. If they were upset with his suggestion that these bills be enacted, the voters could vote for his opponent.

Governor Barnes' party did not command a majority of the members of either house of the legislature, and the House of Representatives and the Senate were forever passing legislation that was onerous and more expensive than the state could afford. Bob Barnes used his veto pen and struck those laws. He had exercised his right to veto legislation more often in his first 100 days in office than other governors who had served two terms (eight years).

The Democrats in Tallahassee mocked the Governor at every turn, and if they knew he was to give a speech that was open to the public they sent a pair of actors in chicken outfits who would follow the governor and when he gave his speech, the chickens began their routine harassing the governor with calls of "bac, bac, bac." The actors were effective and exasperating.

The citizens of the state knew the Democrats had sicked the chickens on the governor because the Tampa Times had interviewed one of the actors when his chicken mask was removed. The actor revealed he was paid by the Democrats.

The Times also included a question in their monthly poll asking if the citizens of the state thought the chickens were a fair exercise of political speech. Fifty percent of respondents thought the Democrats were not being fair to the governor, and when asked to comment they said the chickens interrupted the governor, and the reader was unable to understand what the governor was proposing. They could not hear the speech. They thought the Democrats were not only unfair to the governor; the chickens were unfair to the voters.

But only half of the voters agreed. The voters were split 50/50. Bob ignored the division.

* * *

Casimir V. Pulaski had been laid off by the Department of Motor Vehicles (DMV) for the State of Florida six years ago. He did not consider his discharge to be warranted and he had fought the action by his supervisor for the last five years. First, he petitioned for a hearing before an examiner with the DMV, and when he lost he filed an appeal in Circuit Court. When he lost there he appealed to the First District Court of Appeals, and after he lost there he asked the Florida Supreme Court to review the action taken at each level below.

When the litigation began, Mr. Pulaski had been married to Julie Pulaski for seventeen years. They had three children living at the home which the couple owned in Tallahassee, Florida. The couple had $100,000 in the bank and he owned a pension with the State.

When the Florida Supreme Court ruled against him he had no wife, no kids, no savings and no house or pension. Worse, he was living at home with his parents and he was under a doctor's care for mental strain. His doctor said he was unable to work and he applied for Social Security Disability. Naturally, the benefit was promptly denied.

Pulaski was at his wit's end.

His father read an article in the newspaper about the fact that Governor Barnes was holding court, so to speak, and that he would listen to any State citizen who had a complaint about any State action. All the citizen needed was to do was appear at the executive offices in the State Capital with his driver's license to prove he was a citizen of Florida and the governor would see him in the time available.

The following Wednesday, Pulaski appeared in his suit and tie and lined up behind twenty or so individuals. Some had thick files explaining their complaint. The governor would take the file and give it to one of the students from Florida State or Florida A&M who volunteered to help the governor review the grievances. The student would get a current phone number or contact information, review the file and write a report. If there was an avenue available to right a wrong the student would suggest the action and the governor would act if he could, and if he couldn't he would explain why in short succinct language.

Pulaski did not bring a file although he had a file cabinet full of court records and documents. When it was Casimir's turn he spoke simply and from the heart. His story was as follows:

"Six years ago I was a driver's examiner for the State of Florida giving driving tests to individuals whose licenses were suspended by the State. On the day in question, I rode with an 84-year-old woman. Because of her age, the court ordered a re-exam. The woman was not competent to drive, in my opinion. She could not parallel park or drive backward in a straight line or perform a three point turn. When we returned to the office I explained that I had failed her. Her attorney was with her and began to argue with me, and questioned my findings. He had the woman examined by an off-duty Highway Patrol officer, who said she was a good driver and that I must have acted unprofessionally when I gave the exam. The judge gave her license back to her and recommended that a hearing be held on my fitness to act as an examiner. The judge questioned whether my testimony should be believed in court on the issue of a citizen's ability to safely drive an automobile. There was a hearing at DMV and I was fired by the department. Before my hearing, the old lady was in an auto accident and she was killed. The accident was her fault. I was never able to call the lady as a witness in my case because she was deceased. DMV ruled that the judge had found I was unprofessional in the driver's license reinstatement case and that was "the law of the case," and the judge's finding that I was unprofessional was used against me in my case. I have been fighting this for six years and I have lost on every level.

"Can you help me?"

"I'll see what we can do," said the governor.

The student had made notes of Pulaski's statement. "I'll get on it."

This was just the type case Bob Barnes wanted his office to solve.

* * *

After the first 100 days in office Bob Barnes' poll numbers were good. He had high positive numbers. The poll numbers were helped by the fact that the Governor kept his door open to citizens every day he was in his office.

It was interesting that Bob began to hear multiple complaints or comments about the same parochial issues. Most of these comments concerned the environment. In particular, hikers, fishermen, hunters, ranchers, tree farmers and outdoorsmen reported almost constant flood conditions in a swath of land running through the north of the state from north of Crystal River to the Northeast through Mayo and then the National Guard Reservation by Camp Blanding to the Headwaters of the Tomoka Basin and the St. Johns River Basin and to the point of discharge of the St. Johns River at Jacksonville/Mayport harbor.

The citizens were reporting a new river cutting the state in half, although the river was very shallow and more like a sheet of water in most places. Bob reported the phenomenon to the head of the Department of Environmental Regulation (DER). The agency said it was aware of the complaints and that the Commissioner of Agriculture was involved.

Bob thought he had done his job by making his report to the DER, but he decided to take his stepson on a camping trip and see what they could find.

The pair took a map that highlighted the rivers of the state. There was a small river called the Waccassassa that ran through the Goethe State Forest, and they hiked along the bank of the river until they found the area where the sheeting was occurring. It was evident the flow of the water was in a northeast direction. They followed the water. The young Bob pointed out that the grasses and shrubs that were touched by the water were dying and turning brown. Perhaps it was an indication that the sheet of water was permanent or perhaps there was something in the water that was killing the plants.

They took a sample of the water.

The pair made it as far as Mayo following the new river, then called Smiley, and she and the baby came to pick them up. They were both exhausted and fell asleep as soon as they were in the vehicle. Bob managed to stay awake long enough to say they had a good time .

* * *

The sample of water the governor retrieved showed the water had a high saline content, which was probably what was causing the plants and grasses impacted by the sheet of water to die.

It was another interesting problem. Bob noted the information in his daily journal.

Bob Barnes loved this job.

The date was 9/10/2001.

* * *

The next morning Bob was up at 5:00am and he was on the road by 5:30. He intended to head back to Mayo and complete his inspection of what he now referred to as the River of Dead Grasses. He turned west at the intersection on the Interstate at Gainesville. He intended to drive to US 19 and then South to Waccassassa.

In an area near Crook's swamp his FM radio reception was bad and he had to contend with static for about 10 miles. He only half understood what the announcer on NPR (National Public Radio) was reporting.

There was breaking news from NYC. A commercial passenger jet had flown into a tower of the World Trade Center. The first report was that it was an accident. Bob felt that was hardly likely even though an expert called on air by PBS (Public Broadcasting System) to give background information to the listeners cited the fact that a plane flew into the Empire State Building in the past.

The expert stated, "This was not the first time, There is too much air traffic over the city."

Then the announcer reported a second strike of an airliner into the other twin tower.

What the Hell, thought Bob.

Bob tried the cell phone. No good. (But it rarely worked when he was in the woods...no coverage.)

Bob pulled over at a 7/11 to a pay phone to call the office. There were three phones. All three phones were out. (No dial tone)

Bob caught SR 100 and drove east. He was 25 minutes from Plantation # 7. Bob thought Marla's business phones would work. She had a phone bank to solicit sales of jams and jellies.

Now there was a report on the radio that the Pentagon had been hit by another commercial passenger airplane. With no confirmation of the source, PBS relied on a citizen's tip that the Pentagon was in flames. Next the announcer was reporting rumor. There was rumor being reported that other passenger planes had fallen from the sky. There was verification that one crashed in Pennsylvania.

The announcer ventured his opinion that America was under attack.

The US Government remained silent on these issues but could not hide the fact that the White House was being evacuated. The President was going underground according to his press corp. Bob remembered the President was in Florida? "I was going to be with him today but I begged out," Bob mumbled to himself.

* * *

Bob pulled up at Plantation # 7. He found Marla at the boat dock.

The tour boat that visited the plantation daily was pulling off heading back to Daytona.

Everyone in the packing plant was working and they were oblivious to the disaster in New York.

Marla was speaking to a guide at the plant. Bob tried to get Marla's attention. "I need your phone."

"It's not working. None of the phones are working. The workers are here. They can't sell product without a phone."

Bob explained what he knew about Washington D.C.

Marla could not comprehend what he said. Instead she insisted: "This is America. A sneak attack? That cannot be."

"I need to get to a phone that works. I'm heading to City Hall in Ormond."

"Wait a minute. Look at this first." Marla took him around the house to the four grave sites in the back yard. "Look at this."

Bob was looking at the newest stone monument. It was on Tom Night's grave. Marla's husband James saw Bob and Marla and he joined them.

Tom's grave stone had been erected recently. On the stone was carved the epithet: DEAD MEN WALKING.

James said: "What was Tom saying with that carved on his headstone?"

"They got it wrong said Marla: It should say : DEAD MAN WALKING, not DEAD MEN WALKING."

"Tom was a crackpot." said James.

"I think maybe the stone mason got it right. The stone should say: Men, not Man," said Bob without an explanation. "I've got to go. I need to find a phone that works."

End of Book 5.

Acknowledgements

Thank you to Cynthia Petelle; Anthony Falcone; John Rehg; Andrea Asiala; Rebecca Frank; Diane Huszai.

Sources: The Internet is a rich source of facts to fuel an imagination. The writer acknowledges that he has used the resource the same as a writer previously used an encyclopedia.

The writer primarily used Wikipedia and read the following titles:

Timucua; Illegal Drug Trade; Narvaez Expedition; Weeden Island Culture; Chattahoochee River; Ellen Call Long; King's Road; Creek War; Wounded Knee Creek; Patrick Tonym; Diego de Rebellolo; Desoto Map; Bojinka Plot; Sint Maarten: Dawes Act; Cobell v. Sulgar; USCENTCOM; T. McVeigh; ANFO; Tempe, Arizona; GIS; Mandamus; Veracruz; Moon Pool; Tarahumara People; Delirium Tremors; Mesoamerican Ballgame; Palenque; Corpus Delecti; Section 90.502; Frank Ragano; O'Connor v Donaldson; Electric Chair; Ft. Caroline; Jean Ribault; Pedro Menendez; Ft. Matanzas; Carotid Artery Stenosis; Antigua, Guatemala; Apraxia; Polygonal Rifling; Piper PA-11; Daytona Beach Killer; Danny Rolling; Gerald John Schaeffer; Dissociative Identity Disorder Serial Killer; Chloroform; Payne's Prairie; Lucha Libre; Siege of Vicksburg; Telex; Boeing 707; List of Recessions in US; Daytona Beach and Racecourse; Munchausen Syndrome by Proxy; Bulow Plantation Ruins; Schizophrenia; Phenothiazine; Castillo de San Marcos; Emory University Hospital; Lockheed L-188 Electra; Coquina; Harry T. Moore; Land Rover; Belize; Military of Belize; Aero Commander 500; Zacapa; Montague River Valley; Spar (aeronautics); Blue Hole; Plantation Pine; Belizean Pine Forests; Cocoa

Bean; Copra; Naval Stores Industry; Mountain Pine Ridge; Francisco Hernandez.

The writer also used the NY Times Newspaper and read the following:

A dilemma for humanity; Effort to switch cultivation; Flaws in forensic science; North Korea's young leader

Orlando Sentinel: Judge David McCain

Yahoo News; Drug killings

Mother Jones; Light triggers

New York Post: Belize/ Death Trap

Titles of various other books, articles, reports; Ohio State University Origins- Latin American Drug Trafficking; Fla-Then and Now- Tocobaga Indians; Gizmodo- Humans in Fla nearly 15,000 years ago, G. Dvorsky; Word Press- Timucua Indians in Volusia; US Dept. of Int.- Native American Indians; HISTORY-Persian Gulf War; University Presses of Florida- 18th Century Florida; State Budget Development Process- State of Florida; Creel, Mexico- Lonely Planet; Info Please-Sierra Madre; Ultra legends- Tarahumara; Cultural Survival-Tarahumara; U. of Okla.-Palenque; Monday-Belize Economic Citizenship Investment Program; Nat. Geo.-Birds; Arbor House, NY, Rabinowitz- Jaguar; Augustine.com- The Matanzas; firearmsid.com- Bullet Ident-ification; blackrocklodge.com; webmd.com- Pectin; legal diction-ary-mutual combat; Ruger-Mark lll Standard Rim fire Pistol; Athena Review- The Grijalva Expedition; Hurricanes-Princeton Press; The Aero Commander-S.J. Wift; Douglas C-47, DC-3; Belize Blue Hole Cave; Ecoearth.org-Montagu Valley.